SHATIU is also accepting nominations for achievement awards in translation from and into the following languages:

Language Pair	Prize
Translation from Arabic into Pashto	(100,000 USD)
Translation from Pashto into Arabic	(100,000 USD)
Translation from Arabic into Bengali	(100,000 USD)
Translation from Bengali into Arabic	(100,000 USD)
Translation from Arabic into Swedish	(100,000 USD)
Translation from Swedish into Arabic	(100,000 USD)
Translation from Arabic into Korean	(100,000 USD)
Translation from Korean into Arabic	(100,000 USD)
Translation from Arabic into Hausa	(100,000 USD)
Translation from Hausa into Arabic	(100,000 USD)

Deadline for submissions is 30/6/2020

Please visit our website

www.hta.qa/en

for information about the Award, rules of submission and nomination forms.

  HamadTAward   Phone: (+974) 66570349   Email: info@hta.qa

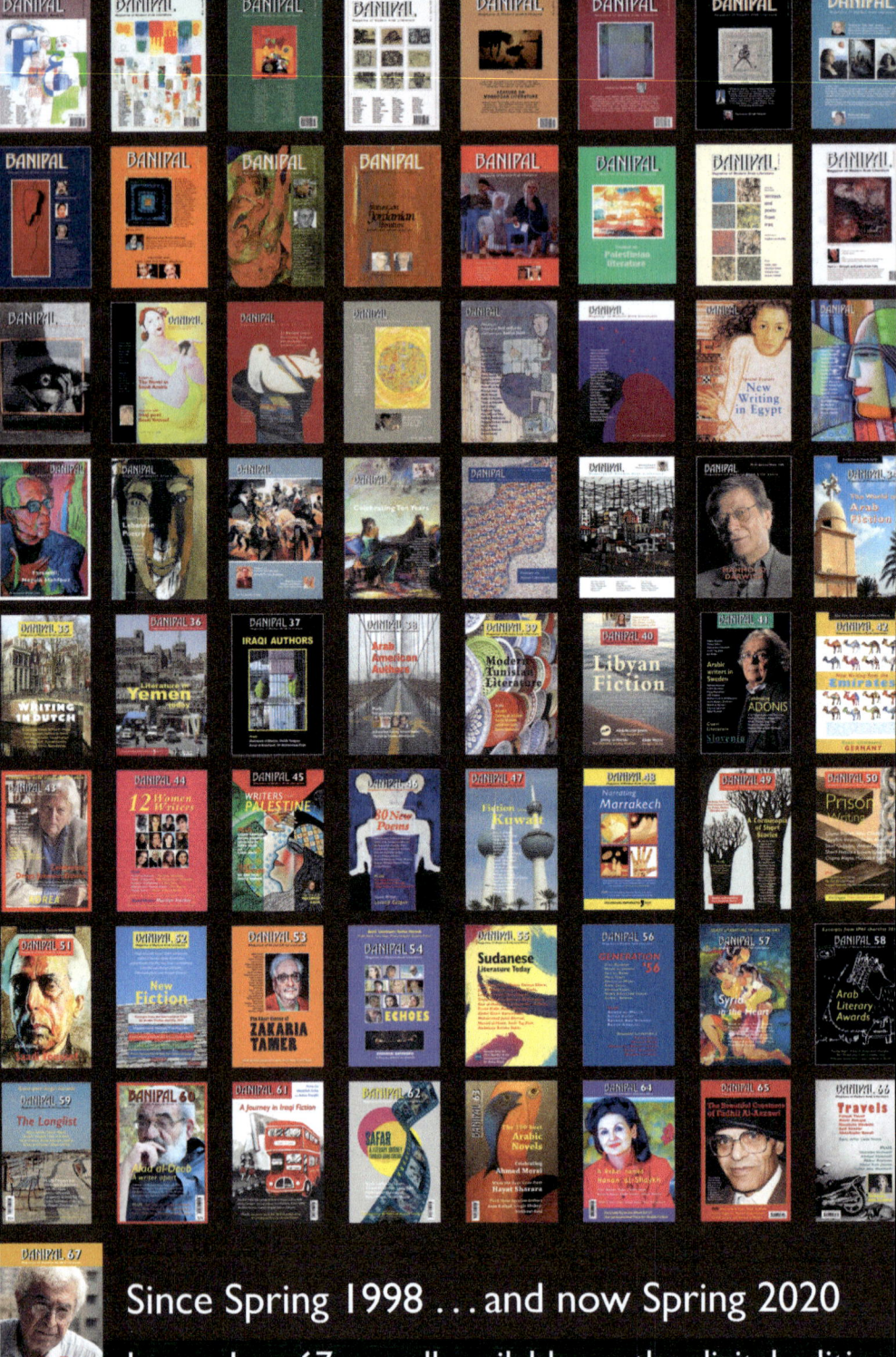

I have the same command of Arabic as I do of my Kurdish language, perhaps even more. During my attempts to start writing down this novel, Arabic drew me powerfully into its vast realm, but I blocked it. I resisted its great seduction, fearful that I might drown in the pleasures of its infinite depths. The Arabic language was a stunningly beautiful woman, seducing me, tempting me, and bewitching me with her allure whenever I was gripped by anguish and sensed the inability of my language to express the fire burning between my ribs. I loved my Kurdish language, I had excavated the strata of its mountains, I had plunged into the depths of its sea, but it was keeping me from my infatuation with Arabic and from falling into her snares. I fended her off and suppressed my passion in the furnace of my heart.

Then recently I was faced with a terrible dilemma. I found myself in the force field of two different languages. One is the language of my mother and father, my siblings, and my friends from childhood playgrounds and school desks. The language of the first girl I fell in love with. The language of my heart – my broken heart – and my dreams, nightmares, rantings and ravings, novels, and poems, half of which I burnt one profligate night. The other is the language of my first books, my first day at school, the language of my God in heaven, my faith, and my Qur'an. The Qur'an whose cover my mother would wave in the face of any member of the family who'd come down with something, so the holy characters would waft the scent of healing. The language, too, of my country's police, secret service, and strict teachers; the language of the books which filled the library of my grandfather, uncles, and father, the sheikh. Those were the first paper beings in the world I set eyes on.

I had an adventurous idea to write my new novel in Arabic. I certainly desired her, and she desired me, but I soon discounted the idea after I thought, "My four earlier novels in Kurdish have brought me praise and a sizeable readership. I shouldn't betray them. It's a big risk for a novelist who respects his fans and his literary history." Then the idea of writing in Arabic came back again more insistently and more seductively, when I thought, "What am I going to do with my store of this captivating language? The vigorous rival wife to my first language! What shall I do with the accumulated myriads of sentences and expressions that have percolated into the depths of my imagination like subterranean water waiting to burst forth as a sacred spring. Wouldn't it also be a betrayal, and a betrayal of those who speak and read Arabic, if I bottled up that wellspring of feeling in the profound depths of memory?"

JAN DOST

Syrian Kurdish writer
Translated by Raphael Cohen

From the introduction to his novel *Dam 'ala al-Mi'dhana*
(Blood on the Minerat), written in Arabic, published in Cairo, 2013

DIGITAL BANIPAL

Complete archive of issues for institutions and individuals

Free trial issue

Banipal's digital edition offers readers all over the world the chance to flip open the magazine on their computers, iPads, iPhones or Android smartphones, wherever they are, check out the current issue, search through the back issues and sync as desired.

A year's digital subscription comes with full access to the full digital archive, back to Banipal No 1, February 1998 – for individuals and for institutions (based on FTE). Print and digital subscriptions are still separate for the moment.

Download the free iTunes App or get it on an Android smartphone.

Preview the digital archive, preview the current issue or check out the Free Trial issue: *Banipal 53 – The Short Stories of Zakaria Tamer*

For more information, go to:
www.banipal.co.uk/subscribe/digital/

Subscribe Directly to Digital Banipal
Individual: exacteditions.com/banipal
Libraries: institutions.exacteditions.com/banipal

International Prize for Arabic Fiction

Excerpts from the 2020 Shortlist – page 164

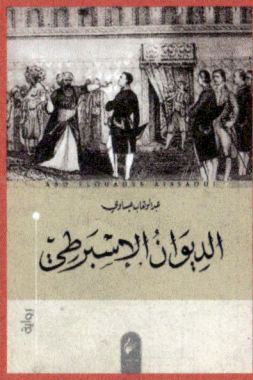

The Spartan Court
by Abdelouahab Aissaoui

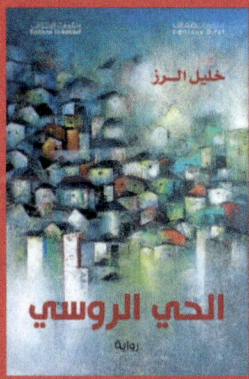

The Russian Quarter
by Khalil Alrez

The King of India
by Jabbour Douaihy

Firewood of Sarajevo by
by Said Khatibi

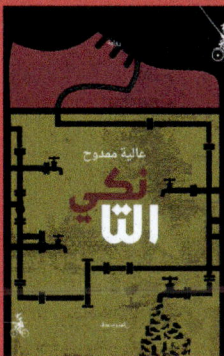

The Tank
by Alia Mamdouh

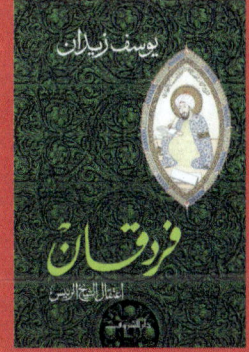

Fardeqan – the Detention of the Great Sheikh
by Youssef Ziedan

JUDGING PANEL: Muhsin Al-Musawi (Chair), Pierre Abi Saab, Reem Magued, Amin Zaoui and Viktoria Zarytovskaya

Sheikh Hamad Award for Translation and International Understanding (SHATIU) is accepting nominations for the year 2020 in the following categories:

1. Translation from Arabic into English   (200,000 USD)
2. Translation from English into Arabic   (200,000 USD)
3. Translation from Arabic into Persian   (200,000 USD)
4. Translation from Persian into Arabic   (200,000 USD)
5. Achievement Award   (200,000 USD)

BANIPAL
Magazine of Modern Arab Literature

PUBLISHER: Margaret Obank

EDITOR: Samuel Shimon

CONTRIBUTING EDITORS
Fadhil al-Azzawi, Peter Clark, Raphael Cohen, Bassam Frangieh, Camilo Gómez-Rivas, William M Hutchins, Adil Babikir, Imad Khachan, Khaled Mattawa, Clare Roberts, Mariam al-Saedi, Anton Shammas, Paul Starkey

CONSULTING EDITORS
Etel Adnan, Roger Allen, Isabella Camera d'Afflitto, Humphrey Davies, Hartmut Fähndrich, Ibrahim Farghali, Naomi Shihab Nye, Nancy Roberts, Susannah Tarbush

EDITORIAL ASSISTANTS: Rosie Maxton, Hannah Somerville, Annamaria Basile and Stephanie Petit

COVER PHOTOGRAPH: © Khéridine Mabrouk

LAYOUT: Banipal Publishing

WEBSITE: www.banipal.co.uk

EDITOR: editor@banipal.co.uk

PUBLISHER: margaret@banipal.co.uk

INQUIRIES: info@banipal.co.uk

SUBSCRIPTIONS: subscribe@banipal.co.uk

ADDRESS: 1 Gough Square, London EC4A 3DE

PRINTED BY Printforce, Biggleswade SG18 8TQ, UK

Photographs not accredited have been donated, photographers unknown.

This issue: **BANIPAL 67 – Elias Khoury, The Novelist**
This selection © Banipal Publishing.
All rights reserved.
This issue is ISBN 978-1-913043-06-3.
RRP £10, €12, US$15

No reproduction or copy, in whole or in part, in the print or the digital edition, may be made without the written permission of the publisher.

BANIPAL, ISSN 1461-5363, is published three times a year by Banipal Publishing, 1 Gough Square, London EC4A 3DE

Banipal magazine, founded in 1998, takes its name from Ashurbanipal (668–627 BC), the last great king of Assyria and patron of the arts, whose outstanding achievement was to assemble in his capital Nineveh, Mesopotamia, from all over his empire, the first systematically organised library in the ancient Middle East. The thousands of clay tablets of Sumerian, Babylonian and Assyrian writings included the famous Mesopotamian epics of the Creation, the Flood, and Gilgamesh, many folk tales, fables, proverbs, prayers and omen texts.
Source: Encyclopaedia Britannica

Supported using public funding by
ARTS COUNCIL ENGLAND

www.banipal.co.uk

Amjad Nasser

Mosab Abu Toha

Muhsin al-Musawi

Huda Fakhreddine

Wadih Saadeh

1	Jan Dost: *Writing in Kurdish and Arabic*
10	EDITORIAL
12	Fakhri Saleh: AMJAD NASSER (1955–2019) *When the Arabic Prose Poem Met World Literature*
20	Muhammad Khudayyir: Literary Influences: *The Baghdad Tattoo,* translated by William M. Hutchins
30	**ARGANA INTERNATIONAL POETRY PRIZE WINNERS**
31	Wadih Saadeh: *Selected Poems*, translated by Huda J. Fakhreddine
38	Hawad : *A Poem*, translated by Jake Syersak
43	Huda Fakhreddine: *A Poem*
44	Mosab Abu Toha: *Three Poems*
47	Mohamed Arbi: *Six Poems*, translated by Huda Fakhreddine
50	Muhsin al-Musawi: Kamoun's Corner, a chapter from the novel *Takhatur (Telepathy)*, translated by Mbarek Sryfi and Roger Allen
66	Abdo Wazen: *Interview with Muhsin al-Musawi*
70	**SPECIAL FEATURE – ELIAS KHOURY**
72	Bibliography of novels of Elias Khoury
73	Elias Khoury: *Stella Maris*, excerpts from the novel, translated by Humphrey Davies
91	Maia Tabet: *Discovering Elias Khoury*
95	Maher Jarrar: *Language and Textual Strategies: A Reading of Elias Khoury's Novels*

104	Abdo Wazen: *Elias Khoury and the Lebanese Civil War*
108	Saif al-Rahbi: *Testament of the Lebanese Civil War*
111	Aida Fahmawi Watad: *Elias Khoury as the moral intellectual in the* Children of the Ghetto *trilogy*
117	Yehouda Shenhav-Shahrabani: *The Hebrew-Speaking Universe of Khoury's Palestinian Novels*
125	Raef Zreik: *Writing and Guilt: Thoughts on Elias Khoury's Project*
130	Fakhri Saleh: *Narratives of the Nakba and Holocaust or when Palestinian Adam tries to disguise himself as a Jew*
136	Suneela Mubayi: *A Mentor for the Ages*
140	Chip Rossetti reviews *The Kingdom of Strangers* by Elias Khoury
149	Stephanie Petit reviews two novel by Elias Khoury *City Gates* and *White Masks*
150	Paula Haydar: *On Translating Elias Khoury Full Circle*
155	Elias Khoury: *On the Interrelations of the Circle*, a chapter from the novel, translated by Paula Haydar

INTERNATIONAL PRIZE FOR ARABIC FICTION

164	The six novels shortlisted for the 2020 prize
166	Abdelouahab Aissaoui: Excerpt from *The Spartan Court*, translated by Raphael Cohen
172	Jabbour Douaihy: Excerpt from *The King of India*, translated by Paula Haydar
179	Alia Mamdouh: Excerpt from *The Tank*, translated by Nancy Roberts
185	Said Khatibi: Chapter from *Firewood of Sarajevo*, translated by Paul Starkey
192	Khalil Alrez: Excerpts from *The Russian Quarter*, translated by Sophia Vasalou
199	Youssef Ziedan: Excerpt from *Fardeqan – The Detention of the Great Sheikh*, translated by Jonathan Wright

BOOK REVIEWS

206	Susannah Tarbush: *Daughter of the Tigris* by Muhsin Al-Ramli
212	Barbara Haus Schwepcke: *1001 Buch – Die Literaturen des Orients* by Stefan Weidner

BOOKS IN BRIEF

215	Fiction
220	Teen & Young Adult Fiction
221	Memoir, Non-Fiction
222	**CONTRIBUTORS**

Muhammad Khudayyir

Maia Tabet

Aida Fahmawi Watad

Fakhri Saleh

Paula Haydar

EDITORIAL

This issue of *Banipal* has coincided with the pandemic of coronavirus that has led to thousands of deaths, and to lockdowns and quarantines in most countries of the world. We are endeavouring with our distributors to bring you both print and digital editions. We hope you receive your copy safely, either print or digital, but do check out all options on our website if necessary and be in touch.

The main focus of *Banipal* 67 is the celebrated Lebanese and international author Elias Khoury, who is an essayist, editor, teacher, playwright and short story writer, but above all a novelist. Elias Khoury published his first novel *'An 'ilaqat al-da'ira* (On the Interrelations of the Circle) in 1975, and in 2019 his latest novel *Najmat al-Bahr (Stella Maris)*, which is the second part of his trilogy *Children of the Ghetto*, the first being *My Name is Adam*. During these 45 years of his literary career he has published 14 novels, of which 10 have been translated into English. Followers of Khoury's career will notice that he published two novels in one year, 1981, *Little Mountain* and *White Masks*. But then he stopped writing fiction until 1989 and the publication of *The Journey of Little Ghandi*. During that period, Khoury published four books of literary criticism, essays and political articles. One of these was *Zaman al-Ihtilal* (1985, Time of Occupation), a series of articles on the Israeli occupation of Lebanon after the 1982 Invasion. These articles were to attract the attention of a Lebanese reader, who would translate some of them for her friends; later they would lead her to discover and translate Khoury's first novel into English. The full story is in Maia Tabet's article below.

Along with Naguib Mahfouz, Elias Khoury is certainly the most translated Arab author, in English and in other languages (many of the works of Naguib Mahfouz were translated only after he became Nobel Laureate for Literature in 1988). In Arabic, Khoury's books have been constantly reprinted.

The feature, "Elias Khoury, The Novelist", opens with three excerpts from his latest novel *Stella Maris,* the second part of the trilogy, translated by the inimitable Humphrey Davies. It is followed by essays, articles on the corpus of novels, and reviews. The excerpts from *Stella Maris* pinpoint the endless contradiction that Adam lives, so he must "divide Adam into two halves, one for presence and one for absence", and though victims are enveloped in silence and "stripped of language" in the face of humanity's barbarity, the essence of civilisation is that language is "the only tool the dead can use to speak".

Maher Jarrar examines how readers enter the world of Elias Khoury's novels, drawn in by the first-person narrator, becoming "live witnesses" impelled to respond to the questions the author asks. His innovative and "experimental language" and "textual strategies" make him a "luminary" of world literature. Khoury's early works, written during the Lebanese Civil War, pioneer a new and "second beginning" for the Lebanese novel, writes Abdo Wazen, re-visiting Little Gandhi's and Beirut's lost memories in *The Journey of Little Gandhi*. Saif Al-Rahbi also looks through the lens of the civil war, remarking on the shattering of language in *City Gates* and *White Masks*' "harsh indictment of the civil war period". Aida Fahmawi Watad takes on Elias Khoury's moral questions in *Children of the Ghetto* – who writes history, who writes literature, and how can someone who is absent write his story? Yehouda Shenhav-Shahrabani explores the literary space-time continuum that he discovered on translating five of Khoury's novels into Hebrew, while Raef Zreik discusses the author's "suspicion of language and words" in his novels, the role of silence, and the "image of anti-writing". Fakhri Saleh wonders whether the two novels of the trilogy may be "a kind of re-writing or meditation" through intertextuality to what has been previously written on the Palestinian cause. Suneela Mubayi relates how Elias Khoury became her mentor while studying for her PhD at NYU, and how she had the chance to visit the tomb of Ahmed Faris al-Shidyaq with both Elias Khoury and his translator Humphrey Davies. Chip Rossetti and Stephanie Petit review afresh *The Kingdom of Strangers*, *City Gates* and *White Masks*.

Our feature on Elias Khoury ends with the opening chapter of his as-yet-untranslated first novel, *On the Interrelations of the Circle*, translated by Paula Haydar, who has already translated three of Khoury's early novels.

Other features in *Banipal 67* are poems by two winners of the Moroccan Argana International Poetry Prize, Wadih Saadeh and Hawad. It also features more poems, by three young poets: Huda Fakhreddine (Lebanon), Mosab Abu Toha (Palestine) and Mohamed Arbi (Tunisia). Plus works by two well-known Iraqi writers: Muhammad Khudayyir writes "The Baghdad Tattoo", about the influence on him of Iraqi pioneer short story writer Abdel Malik Nouri; Muhsin al-Musawi gives us a long chapter from his new novel *Takhatur* (Telepathy) which reveals the uncanny world of parapsychology and the fantastic; following it is an extract from an interview about the novel.

Every Spring issue of *Banipal* we introduce excerpts from six shortlisted novels of the International Prize for Arabic Fiction. This year the 2020 prize will be awarded online on 14 April.

The issue opens with an examination by critic Fakhri Saleh of the poetic vision of sorely missed poet and writer Amjad Nasser, who tragically died last year, a poetic vision which harnesses "the creative power of narrative with the special features of the prose poem".

And our Page One spotlight is given over to Jan Dost, who writes about the dilemma of the force field exerted by his two languages, Kurdish and Arabic.

Keep safe and well and far from coronavirus.

Margaret Obank

FAKHRI SALEH

Amjad Nasser: When the Arabic Prose Poem Met World Literature

The poetry of Amjad Nasser (1955–2019) embodies the transformations undergone by Arabic poetry over the course of more than half a century. At a time when traditional conceptions of poetry and poetics were being upended, Amjad deftly navigated the ensuing changes in style and form, as well as the issues that compelled these changes. While his poetry retains a deep-rooted lyricism, his overall poetic vision remained fundamentally antagonistic to lyrical modes of expression. Through his verse, Amjad strove to quash the sentimentality and tragic self-righteousness that dominated Arabic poetry in the second half of the twentieth century.

Amjad's experiments would put the traditional Arabic poem to the test, and subvert longstanding assumptions about the nature of poetry itself. The "poeticism" of poetry, he maintained, lay not somewhere outside the text but within the inner structure of poetry itself. He would blur the boundaries between prose and verse, enhancing poetry with the spirit of prose while nourishing his prose with the spirit of poetry. He remained keenly aware that any attempt to straitjacket poetry into a single mould would result in hackneyed images, limited horizons, and old images that failed to stir audiences.

In his first collection, *Praise for Another Café* (Beirut, 1970), Nasser gives pride of place to the free-verse poem. The form of his poetry evinces, nonetheless, a certain instability and restlessness, as Nasser is writing under the influence of the great Saadi Youssef, who desired to rid Arabic poetry of its excessive metaphors and of figurative language generally.

Amjad Nasser, Café Slavia, Prague. Photo by Samuel Shimon

The collection oscillates between free verse and prose poetry, not just between the poems but within the individual poems themselves. The poems appear split, like the two faces of Janus, each looking in a different direction.

Although Nasser's captivation with free verse in his early poetry is clear, his attempts betray other lingering influences. The poem that opens *Praise for Another Café*, for example, echoes Adonis's translation of Saint-John Perse's poem "Étroits Sont Les Vaisseaux" (Narrow are the Vessels). The result is a rather inelegant composition. The following poems in the collection, by contrast, are very finely crafted, presaging his later achievements.

The heart was stubborn,
a boy with reckless hair
stumbling through night's dilapidated branches.
The city had not yet become
a losing bet.

Nasser's attachment to the prose poem would also lead him to be influenced by the new wave of poetry produced in the 1970s, as well as Saadi Youssef's translation of the Greek poet Yiannis Ritsos. Along with other poets, he would abandon the high moralism that characterized Arabic poetry in the 1960s and 1970s, and would come to focus instead on the finer details of everyday life. He turned to the desert for inspiration, channeling the lived experiences of the Bedouin people through a new ritualistic idiom. Yet he eschewed the romanticism that so easily accrues here, and produced instead the image of a Bedouin lost in the concrete jungle.

Where will these feet take us
when they're only made of ten toes?
They are our feet's hoarse bells
climbing the concrete steps
with a mixture of vine fibre,
fear,
and a little blood.
No way to deny them, these feet,
low-bound lumps
swimming in prairies of cement.

Nasser pursued a vision of poetry free from the excessive lyricism that characterizes much of Arabic poetry. We can also observe this in his collection *Since Gilead, Climbing the Mountain* (Beirut, 1981), where the prose poem reigns supreme. The influence of Saadi Youssef's translations – i.e., the poetry of Constantine Cavafy, Vasko Popa, García Lorca, Yiannis Ritsos, among others – is less evident here. Instead, we find other connections to Arabic and world poetry, such as the verses he excerpts from the work of Ounsi el-Hajj and Rainer Maria Rilke (as translated by Fu'ad Rifqa).

In *Since Gilead*, Nasser settles on a uniquely hybrid style of poetry, combining the conciseness of the haiku with the spirit of the epic, together with something of the pastoral hymn and short narrative. The narrative element in particular will prove to be a recurring feature of his other collections. Thematically, too, the collection presages his later works: the Bedouin who arrives in the concrete jungle, remembrance as form of relief from the bitter present, alienation from the world that closes in on the poet, and eroticism as a temporary relief from this very alienation.

In "Shoes", one of the poems in *Since Gilead*, the poet deploys the shoe as an expression of the subject's alienation in modern cities. The shoe is woven together from both cruelty and tenderness. While implacably firm, it offers itself as a prop for traversing a world constructed from fish bones.

Shoes irritate us, and as we don't go crazy
from all the leather and plastic that
slip from our feet,
we invent shapes and colors for them.
We chatter about their elegance
in cafes
and in friends' homes.
Shoes torment us
and we grieve, because we are in these cities
built of fish bones
where we cannot live
without shoes.

In *Shepherds of Solitude* (Amman, 1986), we witness a dramatic shift in the poet's concern with the everyday, as he turns to uncover the hidden links between sundry events and phenomena. Most remarkable in these poems is the centrality of objects, as the human subject fades into the background. It is a poetry of heightened sensations, striving to reveal the meaning of existence in a world beset by stifling solitude. Nasser scrutinizes the relations between the self and the world, between things and phenomena, and attempts to crack their impenetrable code.

The poet's focus on objects and his desire to unearth hidden connections does not wholly remove the human subject from the scene, however. The subject emerges, rather, as blurred image at the depths of the poem: a retrieval from a distant past, a first-person voice submerged within itself as interlocutor and interrogator.

In *Shepherds of Solitude* the poet begins with a question that contains its answer, echoing the contradiction between an original innocence and its subsequent loss:

Who will describe his transformation,
and outline with a Bedouin dagger
the parameters of his wisdom?
Who will write about a boy flung by the forces
onto solid concrete
where no dream grows
that is not crowned with defeat?

Amjad Nasser's brilliance shines forth most spectacularly in his portrayal of the move from desert life to the concrete jungle. He is able to craft a language of stark contrasts and diverse resonances, invoking at once Qur'anic lexicon and the idiom of modern poetry. In their simplicity and power of allusion, the poet's imagery bespeaks an innocence that is almost primeval. In addition, the collection abounds with the poet's casual reflections on everyday occurrences and oddities.

It will be too much for us,
as it was for those before us, and we'll
strike one palm against another
till loneliness falls from the hanger
into the drawer.

In his next collection, *The Strangers Arrive* (London, 1990), Nasser ruminates on the same themes that dominated *Shepherds*: the individual's alienation, and his inability to adapt to new places. As an expression of the poet's own dislocation, some of the poems in *Strangers* do not exceed two lines, while others unfold as extended narrations. In the latter, the poet alternates between a collective voice and second-person address, as if to console the solitary stranger in a strange land.

The collection's titular poem is composed of a series of recollections, submitted as offerings at some fantastical shrine. Or perhaps the message is one of irreverence, an ironic take on a familiar scene.

The strangers came from other shores and huddled
in forts that stood high above the postal roads.
He thought of boys who ambushed mailmen in alleyways
and forced them to confess the strange sources of their stamps.

He thought of public notaries and scribes
who sat on wooden platforms, sending their minions
to the markets to catch farmers and nomads who had lost
their way to the circles of justice and relief

Nasser achieves his poetic vision by fusing structure with significance, and meaning with form. His commitment to the prose poem, with its diverse palette of expressive forms, and his abandonment of free verse, despite its potential, would prove to be felicitous; indeed he foresaw the former as representing the future of Arabic poetry. In his collection *Joy to All Who See* (London, 1994), Nasser employs a mixture of poetry and prose with unevenly spaced lines and many blank spaces. The result is a stridently erotic text that pants and pulsates with sundry themes.

Eroticism is deeply ingrained in the poet's previous collections. But in *Joy to All Who See*, and a few poems in *Life Like a Broken Narrative* (Beirut, 2004), we witness the body given over to the utmost expressions of arousal, passion, and desire. Here, ambiguity and figurative speech – which Amjad had long eschewed – return to dominate the text, in order to keep the poet from descending into open pornography.

FAKHRI SALEH ON AMJAD NASSER

The scent reminds of gifts no one gave,
of beds in rooms drenched in mid-morning light,
of clothes wilting on clothes lines,
of sunrays that break on shoulders,
of the dust of ruins falling on fists,
of breaths trying to find new paths to the highest air,
of the water of bones
spilled on lace.
of loam,
of rams aroused by the scent of urine
of space explorers taken by the moon's expressions
of the colour of amber,
and lilac
sodden with rain fallen on mud roods,
of wheat stored in stables.

In *Ascent of Breath* (Beirut, 1997), we witness a turn towards history as a means of dealing with the traumas of the present. Here the poet combines the creative power of narrative with the special features of the prose poem, which he distributes across the pages as a boisterous jumble of words and blank spaces. One is able to feel the fall of Abu Abdallah al-Saghir, together with his Granada, as a true and total catastrophe in all of its reverberations.

O my lightness,
the stranger arrived
with a yesterday or a tomorrow,
the stranger has arrived
on his
last
breath.

Ascent of Breath is a large metaphor for endings, whatever they may be: the end of an empire, the end of a people, the end of a tempestuous romance in its last breath, such as that suffered by Abu Abdallah al-Saghir. The book mixes together the poetics of Rimbaud, Lautréamont, Walt Whitman, Muhammad al-Maghut, and Ounsi el-Hajj; it opens new imaginative horizons and offers the reader multiple ways in.

Life Like a Broken Narrative represents another sharp turn in Amjad Nasser's poetic oeuvre. The texts assembled in this collection limit themselves to description, narrative, and storytelling, with no pretences of figure or metaphor. Still, one discerns a nod towards traditional poetics that surely derives from the poet's interest in not wholly erasing the difference between poetry and prose.

From Seville to the Salihiya of Damascus, I delved into the scents of their kitchens and the voices of their insistent salesmen until I was guided to you. The sky, master, may be one with clouds raining here, and clouds withholding their rain there; or filled with angels engaged in acts of mercy that never reach their targets; or birds with bloated gizzards pursued by the pellets of chasing guns, and other birds still with the straw of their first homes in their beaks stitching winters to summers.

One might deem to call this type of writing the 'block poem', as it borrows that shape from regular prose. In any case, *Life like a Broken Narrative* succeeds in returning the prose poem to its proper path, reconnecting it to its Euro-American sources. Here is the true prose poem, the poem that subverted the poetics of old in countless languages, the poem that follows the smallest clue, contemplates the ordinary moment, and finds its inspiration in everyday things.

Note: Translations of poetry lines in the article are by Khaled Mattawa

Amjad Nasser's first collection of poetry in English translation by Khaled Mattawa, *Shepherd of Solitude, Selected Poems*, was published by Banipal Books in 2009.

Literary Influences

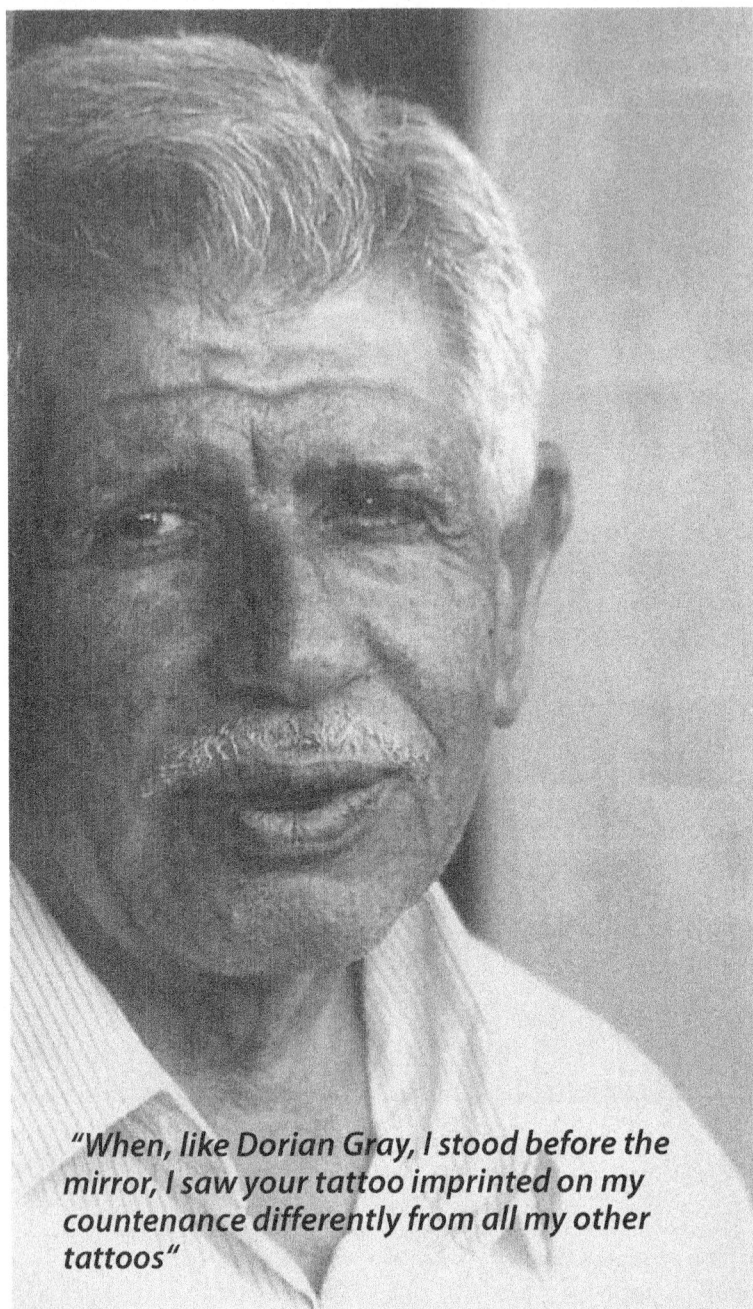

"When, like Dorian Gray, I stood before the mirror, I saw your tattoo imprinted on my countenance differently from all my other tattoos"

MUHAMMAD KHUDAYYIR

The Baghdad Tattoo
A letter to Abdel Malik Nouri

TRANSLATED BY WILLIAM M HUTCHINS

First Epistle

Sir: the only method I have found to address your short ghost, which casts a long shadow on the fissured wall of narrative fiction, is through these short epistles, which are insignia extracted from their original setting and placards covering the ancient wall of our storytelling. You are the maestro of this method of free association with the scattered voices and continuous chatter that you spread through it and by means of the tattoos you sketch on dissolving bodies. You departed from our physical world in 1998. I never saw you in person and never sat with you, but your original creativity and your tattoo reached my body faster than the edge of the chisel that Edgar Allan Poe continued to direct toward my face, which was ransacked by literary influences. I acknowledge that your spectre stretches higher than those of Borges, Pasternak, Salinger, Kundera, Robbe-Grillet, and the other ghosts waiting behind the door. I allow your ghost to speak with its aristocratic heart while I address you – as if I were one of your characters speaking to another with the consciousness of the speaker who addresses the character itself. This is your style of recognition; I acknowledge your influence on me as if it were the influence of some other writer. I recognize your influence at the end, after paternal bonds have dissolved and texts have pranced forward with their own strength. This confessional monologue halted abruptly, and the heart of the oration returned to its headquarters in the Baghdad stable.

MUHAMMAD KHUDAYYIR

Second Epistle

Allow me to say that a genuine influence should be invisible. The source of this influence may be a ghost, a totem, or an intellectual star in the great galaxy of influence, a total fusion, an asynchronous equilibrium, or a tattoo. When, like Dorian Gray, I stood before the mirror, I saw your tattoo imprinted on my countenance differently from all my other tattoos – the black flower, stallion, and cobra. Your tattoo stands out among all those that preceded or succeeded it. I was mangled and ransacked by your tattoo. You who are invisible left a prominent mark on the ribs of my narrative. It is an aristocratic emblem that leaves its form whenever it wishes and mixes with the emblems of mangled stable residents like me.

Third Epistle

I say that the precondition for influence is for the discourse to rise from the bottom to the top – from the stable, where we who were mangled by your tattoo dwell, to the palace you inhabit alone. But you reversed this direction when you addressed your characters in their colloquial dialects. You descended to their stable. Then your texts were a discourse that reflected your disguised self and turned influence's pyramid upside down. You used your aristocratic emblem to pass through the barriers of prohibition and proscription, the regions of strife and tension, and then landed in our world, where you drank from our cup and punctured us with your tattoo.

Fourth Epistle

The condition for influence is for the sources of this influence to change and follow each other consecutively, for the marks of the tattoo to become more numerous, for the countenance reflected in the mirror to splinter, and for its image to dissolve. But I try to isolate your tattoo, considering it to be an original tattoo that does not change. Successive experiences may tear it apart with their hooves and teeth, but then it emerges again and shines with an enigmatic mystery. Your tattoo settled beside the Indian tattoo that

LITERARY INFLUENCES

Abdel Malik Nouri (1921-1998)

Tagore pressed deep into my dissolving narrative flesh – a cobra that never stops dancing and transmigrating. I attempt to separate out these two tattoos as original, transmigrating influences among the other transitory influences, some of which trample others underfoot till any trace of the former one vanishes. Your emblem was an intersection for the discourses of experimentation and innovation that disturbed the calm of the stable as well as a departure from the texts of the 1920s, the foundational period after the British occupation of Iraq in 1914, and from those of the boom period after World War II. We transited through the documentary report and the political slogan in the discourse of the original revolutionary elites and their successors. Then we left the stable to experiment with stream of consciousness writing. The revolt against the monarchy spat us out – with the texts of Nizar Abbas, Muhammad Ruznamji, and Yahya Jawad – on night's desolate shores. There, in the midst of the subsequent chaos, we met the experimentation of the French nouvelle vague authors and pulled their bridles into our stable. We guided ourselves by your emblem. You were our guide in that transformation from the structure with the fissured wall and the disappointment of the revolutionary dispersal and for our entry to the experimentation of the new, emigrant texts. Your large paternal palace crumbled, the emblems were obliterated, one by one, and your beloved, diminutive ghost stopped visiting our stable. The first wave of emigration occurred then, coinciding with the coup of February 1963, when a new tattoo appeared on our bodies.

MUHAMMAD KHUDAYYIR

Fifth Epistle

An influence, by definition, provokes anxiety and instability. I marvel at the transfer of your experimental angst, which settled as a youthful spirit at the outset of our experimentation and suffering. Anxiety over influence was an unruly storm that travelled from the capital's stable to the distant limits of the republic. I realized then that this fractiousness was part of a cloud moving like heavenly horses and covering all areas of Iraq. This cloud occupied schools, cinemas, theatres, and coffeehouses, and not even a newborn could escape its influence. The Revolution of July 14, 1958, filled the clothes of boys and girls with crimson Mayakovsky clouds, and his poems transmitted to us the contagious Bolshevik insanity. I absorbed my share of this cloud and took it to the countryside, where I allowed it to graze with my sheep – my placid pupils. My anxiety subsided, and I began to pasture it far removed from the communal parade, which you had anticipated with your story "Nashid al-Ard" (1954, Hymn of the Earth) before the Revolution. Years after that July cloud dispersed, I poured the thoughts of your story "Al-Rajul al-Saghir" (The Small Man) into my story "Nafidha 'ala al-Saha" (Window overlooking the Square). This was the first intertextual emblem of the influence of your civilian tattoo on my anxious discourse – after nature in the rural regions had affected my mangled countenance.

Sixth Epistle

The government stable in Bab al-Muʿazzam was a symbol of royal Baghdad, which was a city of horses, of carts and swanky carriages, horse races, and coachmen whom our authors adored. You were fond of horses, and your father, Abd al-Latif Nuri, who was Minister of Defence in the government of Bakr Sidqi in 1936, may have given you a stallion so you could learn to ride. You became friends with your father's grooms in the military barracks. After the revolution you were photographed on horseback during diplomatic postings to Indonesia and Japan as a representative of the leader Abd al-Karim Qasim, in 1962. Conditions changed, but hooves in stables remained firmly etched in your imagination. The scene of three huge horses – in your story "al-Rajul al-Saghir" – rounds out my memory. They whinny and clatter by before disappearing into the dark. Little Abbas loses his way to his sister Mas'uda's house when horses appear suddenly before him on a dark, narrow alley. They terrify him as their racing forms follow each other past him in rapid succession. He plasters himself against the wall of a house. Then he spots a horse with only one, frightening eye. It snorts in his face several times before vanishing into the gloom. I imitated little Abbas' disorientation in more than one now-lost short story but never dared appropriate the scene of horses racing down the alley. I estimate that half the stories in my first collection *Al-Mamlaka al-Sawda'* (1972, The Black Kingdom) originated in Baghdad's stables.

Seventh Epistle

How did your influence reach our abode in the nation's southernmost city, where there were no massive buildings or stables? Instead, there were dense groves of palm trees and vast expanses of lakes. Meanwhile, the Revolution's sun continued to roast the backs of our rural folks with its flame. From 1964 to 1968, we were banished to the farthest limits of the ill-fated republic. Stream of consciousness writing infiltrated our formation, which was tattooed with the fundamental emblems. At the time, I taught in the countryside – I remember that Kafka was a rural physician – and placed on the shelf in my room, which adjoined the primary school, a copy of your first short story collection *Hymn of the Earth*. The oil lantern (*fanus*) cast its quivering light on pages of your book, which were stained with the blood that mosquitoes sucked from me night after night as I read.

Eighth Epistle

Weekend fun for us meant boarding the train at the Ur Station in Nasiriyah and disembarking at Baghdad's western station, where the conical dome of Zumurrud Khatun's mausoleum greeted the traveller. We used to walk down the sidewalk from the train station to the Museum before heading to al-Saraya Alley to look for copies of old books that ghosts from the Baghdad stable had consigned for sale. What fun! What an impact the books' jackets, titles, pictures, and marginal notes made on us! These immediately became our lodgings, excursions, and vistas. The way visitors from the south disappeared among abayas, shoes with heels, short haircuts, and long dresses was a famous topic for Baghdad's authors. I was one of those outsiders who gazed through the front window of the Brazil Coffeehouse on al-Rashid Street at Baghdad's elite, who assembled there to monitor the sidewalk, which was teeming with wandering folks. I would try to stand exactly where your stories were set and direct my piercing gaze at the stable's residents through the coffeehouse window. I didn't hope to catch a glimpse of you or to sit facing you, because I had a deep-seated conviction that you were one of the stable's invisible ghosts, if only to increase your influence as a presence in roof dreams among the elite of the Brazilian Café.

Ninth Epistle

Breaking into the circle of the pioneers of the Brazilian Café was alien to my nature, and joining the capital's literary cliques of the younger generation wasn't something my travelling cloud desired. To rise above the top of the stable of ghosts, I ascended with my cloud over the roofs of the hotels lining al-Rashid Street, accompanied by your singular characters. After touring the city nonstop, even on a sweltering summer day, Baghdad's perfumed cloud, which was saturated with the perspiration of tender skins in the evening, would lift me to the roof of a hotel where sleep was doled out to beds lined up in no apparent order. The roof's surface was splashed and sprinkled with water, and the hotel continued to receive patrons all night long. They would climb to the roof terrace whenever they chose and stretch out in their underwear on whichever bed they fancied. I expected to find your famous character Sattar ibn Salih Jarbaza in the next bed and to listen with pricked ears to him narrate his search for his imprisoned son. I would dream about the solid walls of prisons, stables, and houses that shelter men without women and women without men – like the young newspaper vendor al-Jurdhi and his girlfriend who worked in a coffeehouse. We could empathize with the humiliation, deprivation, and misery

Coffeehouse in Baghdad

of these two characters in your story "al-'Amila wa-l-Jardhi wa-Rabi'" (The Waitress, al-Jurdhi, and Spring). The expansive night from which prolonged sighs rose with a Baghdad maqam reached its acme and apex on the rooftops. I wonder about the many women in your short stories. I wanted to absorb their influence to apply to the bodies of my southern women, who were covered in black. I don't believe the rumours about your rowdiness and sexual abstinence. Your stable has provided me stories about countless women. They suffered inconsolable heartbreak when their worthless menfolk abandoned them to lethal solitude. Perhaps your friend Fuad al-Takarli was luckier than I have been when – in "Al-Wajh al-Akhar" (The Other Face) he added a blind woman to the list of women of Baghdad. Your friend al-Takarli linked us to you when he dispatched your mysterious, phantom influence through his peerless women. With this observation I wish to draw attention to the intertextuality of his story "Basqa fi Wajh al-Hayat" (1948, Spitting in Life's Face) and your story "Jiyaf Mu'attara" (Perfumed Cadavers), which was written the same year. That was a grand time for influences.

MUHAMMAD KHUDAYYIR

Tenth Epistle

It is almost three a.m., houses have lost electric power again, and mosquitoes are commencing a crazed assault after slipping through the window screens. My rural notebook contains a text dated to a night in 1962. I was in a village near the city of Suq al-Shuyukh in al-Nasiriyah Province. That was the night the school term ended, and I was preparing to leave the lodgings attached to the school and return to my family's house in Basra. The notebook records details of a raid by mosquitoes from the lakes against my white mosquito netting on that last, farewell night. They sucked enough blood from me to make me a cupper of texts. Your stories were the target of my early morning foray. I mixed the languid blood of the rural villagers and the still blood of the stable with my own irascible blood that was seeking an urban influence that would draw me to the centre of the great transactions in the capital of fashions, songs, murals, and films as well as to the elites associated with the coffeehouses, newspapers, and art exhibits. My rural notebook contained poems, descriptions of harvest scenes, and drawings of pupils' faces. I cast it aside and turned to you. You were a new, radical influence on me and turned me toward sucking the stream of consciousness from the heads of the mangled characters with all the appetite of the mosquitoes that continued to prey on me and feast on my blood.

Eleventh Epistle

Dawn – now night's words are erased by the day. What I found empowering about the mosquitoes' strategy was suggested by what the critic Hatim al-Saqr called "the seeing cane". Blind men, deprived of the tattoo's influence, may seek to find their way with more than sensation and physical evidence. Ships stranded on the shore are evidence of the sea's expanse, and the length of the trip. The narrative sea is too vast for a tattoo, lighthouse without a flame, or an abandoned stable to encompass. Forgive me, Mr. Abd al-Malik. You do not care for this type of narration. You knew your goal very well. It lay within your reach, but you refused to grasp it. You renounced every initiative that did not bring you closer to Dostoyevsky and Joyce. These two authors were very far removed from your tattoo. You do not like for anyone to remind you of this tragedy. Let us circle back to the start of our discourse.

Twelfth Epistle

Between the Baghdad tattoo and the Indian tattoo lay years when I stumbled and lost my way. The curse of the journey to your texts would pursue me like a cloud of crazed mosquitoes. I waited for this cloud to disperse before I fell into the garden of relinquishment. Then I landed in the garden of tattoos. This was my destiny and my first countenance, which dissolved under the influence of your original tattoo. I have tried to separate myself from your image, to leave your stable, and to reach my destination, which is now a tattoo atop a tattoo and a bone atop a bone in a cemetery of dissolving texts. My breathing is irregular on account of this separation and transformation. I will narrate what is left of my discourse – my destination or yours.

Thirteenth Epistle

My anxiety has calmed down, your influence has grown more remote, and your tattoo has faded. After my countenance dissolved, I became transparent. The tattoos have quickly become a cloud of intertextuality, the memory of which showers diverse dreams on roofs raised above the history of the ancient stable. This is the destination, but I will not consider it reached until my cloud of intertextuality sends its rain to a different locale. Memory may fixate on a pitch-black tattoo of a group of women at a wake, but it may also move on to another memory. Your tattoo shows clearly whenever I read a short story that exudes its unique influence as strongly as your short stories. Quickly the tattoo moves away, because the effect of new stories multiplies in more than one form or manner. No influence is stronger than your Baghdad influence, but it is futile to imprison it in a building that travels through the history of the ancient stable. This is the destination. Allow me to return the heart of the discourse to its place.

Basra, May 2012

Two winners of the Argana International Poetry Award

Here we present poems from two winners of the major Moroccan literary prize, the Argana International Poetry Award – Tuareg poet **Mahmoudan Hawad** in 2017 and Lebanese poet **Wadih Saadeh** in 2018.

The prize was awarded to Hawad for "this innovative poet's four decades of dedication to make a lyrical and intellectual space for the nomadic life. He has journeyed ceaseless and tirelessly through language in search of a meaning fortified by inner knowledge of the self and outer knowledge of the world."

Regarding the Lebanese poet Wadih Saadeh, the judges said that "he was awarded the prize in recognition of his unique poetic contribution over fifty years, the aesthetic values of which have contributed to a new departure for the Arabic prose poem towards universal horizons celebrating the personal, the human, and the existential".

The Prize was first awarded by the House of Poetry in Morocco in October 2002, during the 3rd Casablanca International Poetry Festival, an annual festival that was held from 1998 to 2003. The prize awards a poet whose originality is recognised internationally and is named after the argana tree that is unique to south-west Morocco. It was hoped it would be an annual prize when the first award was made to Chinese poet Bei-Dao at the festival, whose participants included Adrian Mitchell from the UK, Jordanian poet Amjad Nasser, Marie-Claire Bancquart from France, and many others, as reported in Banipal no15/16 (2003).

However, the next award was made in 2004 to the Moroccan Mohamed Serghini, then in 2008 to Palestinian poet Mahmoud Darwish, after which it became an annual event on Morocco's poetry calendar, awarded to Iraqi Saadi Youssef in 2009, and to Moroccan poet Tahar Ben Jelloun in 2010. Banipal's publisher Margaret Obank was invited to be chair of judges for the 2011 prize, which was awarded to the American poet Marilyn Hacker. That year marked the award ceremony taking place for the first time during the Casablanca Book Fair, a move that broadened the audience and gave the prize greater prominence among book-lovers.

The Award has been presented there since then, in 2012 going to Antonio Gamoneda from Spain, in 2013 to Yves Bonnefoy (France), in 2014 to Nuno Júdice (Portugal), in 2015 to Volker Braun (Germany), in 2016 to Morocco's own Mohammed Bentalha, in 2017 to Tuareg poet Mahmoudan Hawad, and in 2018 to Wadih Saadeh (Lebanon). In 2019 the winner was Serbian American poet Charles Simic, with the Award ceremony postponed at least until the end of this year owing to his necessary convalescence after surgery.

WADIH SAADEH

Selected Poems

TRANSLATED BY HUDA FAKHREDDINE

1

In this village
the evening poppies are forgotten
shivering behind the doors.
In this village which wakes
to drink the rain,
the glass of the world broke in my hand.

2

These waters
open in the body the channels of night.
These waters and these boats

are the pennies of the blind
who left themselves out on the sidewalks,
and forgot
to lift up the net of life.

12

There is a project for a poem,
a bank
on which I spread the dry fish in my head.
Go away,
You, O dark woman at my door. You, O ships.
Go on!
My dreams are enough for me to shut this door
and sleep.
My waters are enough
to drown me.

13

There must be another path
to the forest.
The cord stretched between my eyes and the trees
is about to snap.
You are my forest, O words,
You are the tree, dead in my mouth.
Along the way are streams and flowers,
stones for the tired,
a sun for the day and a moon for the night,
but no consoling bird on your alphabet.
There must be another way.
Voices are cages.

From the collection *Evening has No Brothers* (1981)

THE DAILY WORK

Hey you!
Come.
We will do nothing today.
The sun is boring and the rain monotonous,
and I have no patience, not even for my hat.

Hey you!
Don't say you're in a rush
and surely on point like a bullet.
You'll lose nothing if you cancel the whole trip.
You can give up on God
and talk to me.
Do you have to learn all the words
only to say
goodbye to friends?
Help me out a little.
Let me lie on this sidewalk
and block passage to that spot over there.
Just help me out a little
so that the air may pass through.

THE EROTIC LAKE

I fell from the sky
and although this movement isn't musical,
I will spend the night outside
with new stars,
perhaps.
I, Wadih,
sit on the sidewalk like a crab
waiting for my friends.
I crossed
God's erotic lake
and lay down.

WADIH SAADEH

AN INVITATION TO DANCE

I want a dog to come out of this poem.
I will lure it with a bone, with a dancing nipple.
I will tempt it with a soft letter, an O curled like the tail of a bitch
    ready to mate,
with pictures of the most voluptuous bitches in history.
A dog or any other diversion, until the end of the poem,
what else can I do?
Drag God by the collar and invite him to dance?
Tailor undergarments for ambassadors' wives?
Build a factory to support the national economy
or print secret documents in service of the government?
Or should I divorce my wife?
Listen! Can a man divorce his wife if he wrote a poem and dog
    came out of it?
I want a dog to come out then.
For in a previous poem the world came out.
I convinced it to return to the sanitorium.
It promised me it would go but it didn't.
I used all the marine words but no fish bit.
What good is paper?
Just let the dog out.

THE TIRED

The tired sit in the square
listening to breezes pass,
breezes which probably used to be peddlers or loiterers
but have now lost their feet.

The tired have a square.
Its paving stones, with time, have acquired human traits
and every time someone departs,
they weep.
The faces of the tired in the square soften day after day
and their hair sways

in the night air and the tender light.
When they look at each other
their eyes soften too
until they think themselves glass
and they break.

> From *A Man in Used Air, Sits and Thinks about Animals* (1983)

I THINK THE FAN IS TURNING, ALLEN GINSBERG

Listen, Allen,
I'm on the sidewalk, my tobacco has run out.
I open my eyes and close them,
and sometimes I remember that night when we wiped saliva from
    the mouths of the dead
then descended the ladder together
and walked along the shore.

The fan is turning now.
I like to think that the air is a gentle swallow while I lean on the
    corner watching my knee go numb.
The fan is now turning in my head, Allen,
and my mouth which resembles a newsstand
is silent.
Inside it are some teeth, dead like animals.
It happened that
I discovered patience under a tree
one day,
and I spoke of the soul in a simple carriage,
as we passed along the river.

The smoke, Allen,
the smoke and beautiful beats!
On the other side of the beach,
the sand stands alone.
Sometimes the fish throw it a rock
to sit on.

WADIH SAADEH

Is this a fitting scene?
In my hand is a murdered day
and I want to bury it silently.

> From *The Seat of a Passenger who Left the Bus* (1987)

MY MOTHER

She gave the last drop of water in her pail to the basil
and slept next to it.
The moon passed, the sun came,
and she slept on.
Those who used to hear her calling them in the mornings
to a cup of coffee,
didn't hear her voice.
They called to her from their balconies. They called to her in the
    fields.
They didn't hear her voice.
When they came,
a drop of water was still oozing from her hand,
creeping towards the basil.

> From *Because of Cloud Most Likely* (1992)

JACK KEROUAC!

Many errors in the signs and the names along the way, Jack Kerouac.
The arrows pointing to places
lead to other places
and the signs that say "springs"
are deserts.

What happened, Jack, that I now see the field as a whale about to
    swallow me
and the butterfly a wall?

Was the swallow that fell dead in front of me
passing through, tracing the way
or erasing the passage?

Jack, O Jack, take down the signs on the road.
Cancel the springs, the forests, and the places,
and point me to the path with no signs and no names.
I just want to pass through.

From *Who Took the Gaze I Left at the Doorstep* (2011)

CLOUDS

There are clouds in his eyes.
So he stares at the ground
hoping for rain.

HOW?

How will the swimmer make it
if the sea is drowning?

NO

Don't knock on the door.
Leave.
Whoever's on the other side of the door is knocking too.
Nobody opens the door.

From *Tell the Passerby to Come Back, He Left his Shadow here* (2012)

ARGANA INTERNATIONAL POETRY AWARD

HAWAD

A POEM

TRANSLATED BY JAKE SYERSAK
FROM THE FRENCH TRANSLATION
OF HÉLÈNE CLAUDOT-HAWAD

XIX

Not one cloud over Tanezrouft,
Ténéré and Tafassisset,
Télé and the Tin Marsoy valley,
not one cloud
except for the mist of gunpowder.
The splatters of dried blood and the sterile sky
grinding down the shadows of yesteryear,
Tuareg, nomadic shadows
in motion toward purgatory,
bald sky, fossil sky,
and the rainfall of shells and rockets
bombarding the chimeras of the wind.

Ekhay!
Chaos, exile of the vital Tuareg breath,
shadow of the entryway life and death,
world between two thresholds,
this year too, the resistance will be a long one
to endure for our backsides and bullish
haunches covered in bedsores.
And our backs will squeal as well, backsides in motion
dispersing across sands pebbles steps horizons
and water points without name.

Hawad

By the outstretched arm and clenched fist,
offered to the peaks, vaults of the sky,
and by the left arm
drawing the rifle and the quill,
I cry out, salute and affirm
to all the comrades of lost causes,
who wish to accompany us
but aren't prepared
to fix their gaze upon that evil
wearing their entrails as a belt:
"It's useless to follow us this year,
if your hope is confined to filling your gut.
Go back and squat down
beside the anthill,
unless the appetite of the garrisons
has left nothing there as well,
nothing to graze its granaries."

Ley ley ley and touf!
Deliver us the path!
Steer your way clear of our march!
In the hollows of our way, there is room only
for the hooves of the heifers

and the rebellious young bulls,
unfettered from their mother's milk
and chains and shackles
and other pointless affirmations of weakness,
captivity, throat tied to the knee,
yes, the young bulls and the heifers of the Maquis
who long ago trampled over
the enclosures and the crook of their masters!

Where are the women and men,
cheetahs and lions of the ferocious struggle
willing to take a barrage of machine-gun fire
bound to chisel away my shoulder blades or diaphragm
while extracting from my body
my intestines, serpents swarming about every day
for a ladle's worth to swallow
obtained from the backs of their brothers,
just as long as it isn't their own,
bellies tunnels and quarries
wind cavities feeling out and imploring
for yet another spoonful to devour
to satiate their hunger.

Over the corpses, my armaments,
skeletons of my people,
the bald sky, without a tear, belches
a sulfuric rain,
smoke-colored dust and fiery exhalation
the burning resistance fighters' breath,
I smell the decades
of untold suffering,
march of the resistance,
vibrating and marching *en vrille*,
so long to endure.

But there's nothing to worry about
nor any time for a regretful dance along the path.
To us there remains neither orientation nor space,
hiccup, truce to whoever offers up our chests,

outside the fatal flashing, thunder followed by the lightning,
which the gunfire of the enemy spills
in order to welcome our eyes.

But what enemy fire might crush our pupils,
for a long a time rockets, spears, pitchforks
of our nomadic shoulders outside our bodies
holding up the horizons
which our dream still waves around
like crude straps
cut from the virility of the rapist,
rapist of wombs from which we leapt
with feet joined, well poised to cast off
the tears and the distances.
Our eyes already hollowed-out, abysses,
abysses marching every day,
tying the enemy's gaze
into the bottomless and edgeless view
of the battle which marches on its knees,
by the shoulders or by the hinges,
roaring for revenge,
pebble in the sling of the song.

In the animalistic grunt of the marching,
wandering in quest of our lost dreams,
through our songs which soothe
the progression of the Tamazight language
"to have shoulders" means strength
"to bear pain between our shoulder blades", resistance,
"to entrust the kidneys with our burden", endurance,
and we, we are the passersby
of this twilight which shall have no aurora
unless we are to wrest it
with approval from the horizon
and with our spines
rotisserie it,
like prey.

HAWAD

We, the swimmers of the twilight without shore,
have gathered these three packsaddles
of the march,
needle howling and transpiercing
the rosary of wounds,
abscesses, gunshots, encampments and roads,
progressions of the pain and joy
of carrying the resistance's
meteorite-stone over our backsides.
Is revolution not the march *en vrille* itself,
movements and actions which are unsatisfied
with labor's turning over the earth from below
into what stifles from above?
Otherwise it would be a simple coup d'état,
theft of authority which won't deviate
from its old adages:
"Push me that I might push myself."
The march in spiral,
is infinitely revolutionary
the cerebral muscles
seeking to constrict
the other hemisphere, the other stratum,
in order to scrape them like a silt,
weave and twist them
like a woven rope,
march, serpentinely, cramp,
not slippery with anguish,
this is what the revolution is,
not a shovelful of earth from below
which even before seeing the daylight
already broods over the throat of that preceding
with its cold hen-like posterior.

Selected by the poet from his collection
Le coude grinçant de l'anarchie,
translated into French by Hélène Claudot-Hawad
from the original Tamazight and
published by Editions Paris-Méditerranée, Paris, France, 1998.
ISBN: 978-2-84272-050-6. 131 pages.

HUDA FAKHREDDINE

A Poem

In our West Philadelphia neighbourhood, there is a cemetery. It is fenced in by a stone wall and has an iron gate that stays open all the time. Some days, a little after sunrise, I tie the laces on my running shoes and set out for the cemetery. Speeding along roads still shrouded in darkness, I go through the iron gate to run on dirt paths that wind their way between the graves. I am not the only one here. Like me, other people come here to run between those graves. After all, a cemetery is like any other green space: trees, grass, and soil that breathes.

I run faster, unsure if I'm chasing something or escaping from it. On both sides gravestones rush past me: fathers, sons, mothers, grandchildren, friends . . . Words, numbers, and complete lives, all falling between the cracks.

The sun rises higher. Running still faster, I exit through the cemetery entrance toward the city, still stirring from sleep. I return home, the clamour of the dead trailing behind me.

From *A Small Time under a Different Sun* (2019)

MOSAB ABU TOHA

Three poems

THE SAFEST PLACE IN GAZA

I will start from scratch:

With every earthquake,
with every arrogant bomb that falls,
with every blind rocket that flies,
my computer dies.

Having gone haywire,
my mouth feels sandy and dry,
my belly squeaks.
The fridge still empty,
my dreams flattened,
my head aches.

Flying rockets and falling bombs
light up the sky –
a deserted sky,
save for warplanes and drones.

With every explosion, our door bangs
the lights flicker for a second –
and then
die.

I panic.
I don't want to close my eyes;
My family might think I've died
of fear or a heart attack.

With the tea kettle whistling,
I try to hide with my wife, my kids
all petrified,
only to realize again:
no house in Gaza
can withstand a bomb attack.

So where to hide?

The safest place in Gaza
Is – the grave

BLOCKADE

Sleeping,
I discover my own theory
of existence.

I write my new poem.
A new Kubla Khan.
I get up and look
at myself in the mirror.
It tells me that I still exist.

On my face,
I see a new poem,
written in a foreign alphabet.
I smash the mirror.

MOSAB ABU TOHA

The pieces falling down
create a word that probably
could become the title of my final piece:
"Loss" —
a word that describes perfectly
my current Palestinian reality.

LIKE A CLOUD, WE TRAVEL

Wiped out by every wind over Gaza,
we are scattered on this earth,
footsteps in the desert.

We do not, or cannot, know
when and how to return
to the homes
our ancestors loved
for centuries.

Like clouds,
we try to give shade and rain:
the best we can.

As deep down, we do not know
whether we even belong
to where we happen to exist.

Like clouds,
we might visit our homes
without knowing that they still are
ours.

Invaders have changed much
of our landscape,
much of our lives.

MOHAMED ARBI

Six Poems

TRANSLATED BY
HUDA FAKHREDDINE

WRITING

I write like one making a hole in a wall
for the light to come through.
My dark thoughts are my hammer
and fingers of flesh and blood are the nail.
I write
like a prisoner digging his escape with a spoon,
thinking of the same light
beyond endless walls,
beyond fences that rise
every day
to block
his life.

ANOTHER BIOGRAPHY

Gushing like a river,
striking like lightning,
trembling like a tree trunk,
sharp like an axe,
loud like desolation,
discreet like a well,
exposed like disease,

simple like a meadow,
obscure like a forest,
beaming like a garden,
sad like a poet's funeral,
nobody stands out but I,
master of my self and its servant,
its hero, the author if its glory,
and its haunting shame.

I have no direction or destination.
I am all this crowdedness,
running like a madman
to avoid being covered
with flies.

A WISH

I want to write about some joy,
no matter how small.
I will sit it at my table
and order it a glass of strawberry juice.
I will speak to it of my happiness when alone,
when no new illusion knocks on my door.
Filled with excitement,
I will pat its frail back
and stare at its blushed cheeks
until my eyes well up.

POETRY
to the poet Omar Ziyada

Random gunshots in a street
is approximately what poetry is.
That's what you told me, as we descended to Ténès city
where we first met,
two strangers on an Algerian bus
speaking of poetry and its many sins,

of marble in Bassam Hajjar's eyes,
of the gaze Wadih Saadeh left at the door,
of Sargon Boulus's boat,
and of Ounsi el-Hajj's messenger with her hair long until the springs.

To the last drop of blood in our veins,
poetry remains our path on the never-ending slopes.
How many homes did we inhabit between Nablus and Tunis?
How many embraces did we leave behind in Algiers?
How many bullets did we shoot, O Poet,
as we held words like one holding down the trigger.

FRAGILITY

I am more fragile than an egg about to crack,
more miserable than a poet sitting alone
in the Oscar bar
without beloved or friends.
My city is dejected,
my days all alike,
and my life, which I don't think
will last too long,
is a lie too.

POETS

Poets are wretched too.
Don't you know
how a fleeting glance
can mess up their lives?
How a harsh word
can make them disappear forever
without reproach
without a trace?

> From the poet's collection *Heena kunti hatahaddadhina 'an al-hub*
> When you were talking about love (2019)

MUHSIN AL-MUSAWI

Kamoun's Corner

A CHAPTER FROM THE NOVEL *TELEPATHY*

TRANSLATED BY MBAREK SRYFI & ROGER ALLEN

It could have just been coincidence that brought him here today. For him, such a place was not uncommon. He had been before to places like 'Telepathy' – a café-restaurant turned into a gateway, elegantly furnished with carpets and pillows made of soft wool and dyed dark red, black, and dark green. The shiny, thick wooden tables and chairs did not hide the colourful blend of black and pomegranate that saturated the room, like embers glowing in a fireplace.

From my dark corner in the restaurant, I watched as he surveyed the place. The vivacious lady who accompanied him didn't seem much impressed. He was of medium height and had large eyes, his hair still fighting against a sneaking onset of grey. I found his combination of frizzy hair and black eyes fascinating, perhaps because his symmetrical facial features otherwise seemed so familiar amongst the people of this ancient city. Yet I was more drawn to the young woman. She was wearing a bright pink, two-piece suit with a knee-length skirt. Her light brown face was tinged with blondish tones, making her black eyes submerge into the light of the lantern under which they had deliberately chosen to seat themselves. Her shoulder-length hair matched her complexion, and her sharp nose and lips – which might in another woman have seemed 'refined' – appeared rather unremarkable. She was slightly taller than him, and her slender figure seemed to endow him with a vigour and vitality that were otherwise absent.

As he came in, he glanced in my direction, but I don't think he could make me out me from the furniture and dark surroundings. She paid me no attention. I felt a bit envious when I noticed the way another customer had selected a different corner-spot as a lookout for people coming and going. This man was alone. His blue suit made his face seem sharp and fair. He looked dapper – apparently it was 'smarten up' day. Everything matched: the blond hair, the green eyes, the pale complexion, the pressed white shirt, the blue tie. Like the woman, he also didn't notice me. Or maybe he did not want me to think he did. Or could it be that my ebony complexion, gleaming under the lantern, made me seem like part of the place?

Fortunately, my sense of hearing was still sharp and could catch whispers from afar. This allowed me to pick up the names of new customers coming into Telepathy, which I co-own as partner and manager with my associate Jaafar, who looks after supplies, staff and finances. However, I am the one who chose the name, which admittedly sounded strange at first. When I first suggested it, Jaafar threw me a confused look. "People are attracted to radiant names, tourist city names, sexy double-entendre names," he said, "but 'Telepathy'? Really? That's all your talented mind can come up with?"

Jaafar was obliquely referring to the candidate certificate that I hold from the Moscow Institute of Oriental Studies, where I studied in the so-called 'Krachkovsky School', named after Ignaty Krachkovsky, a scholar with an encyclopedic knowledge of geography and literature. Jaafar rarely mentions – obliquely or otherwise – my PhD in Communications from Moscow State University, or my various publications on parapsychology. I have always regretted that he – I mean Krachkovsky – died in 1951, at least a decade before I arrived. But I don't regret attending Vasiliev's courses on telepathy at the University of Moscow. I never tired of those courses.

Leonid Vasiliev was a passionate believer in telepathy. He passed away in 1966, but not before taking care of me like his own son for five years. You'd think I would have followed in his footsteps, but my love for the practical rather than the academic brought me to Jaafar and running this café.

I heard the blond man answer his phone: "Yes, Saad speaking." Now I had a name! His girlfriend had arrived too. She was tall, dark-skinned and gracefully slender. Jaafar is continually in awe of my auditory talents; it makes him overlook my weaknesses in other departments. I overheard the other girl, who was with the dark-skinned man, address him as "Shawqi", while he teasingly called her "Fawz" – whispering it as though it were a lyric from a famous song by the esteemed poet 'Abbas Ibn al-Ahnaf whom, incidentally, the late Krachkovsky quoted rather often.

At that moment the waiter, Jabr, came over to me. "Do you want something to drink, Uncle Kamoun?" he asked.

"No thanks, I'm alright."

He was smiling because I always use classical Arabic with him. Then, I don't know how exactly it happened, but a bird managed to slip inside the place, fluttered around the lamps, and landed near the table at which the blond Saad and his slender girlfriend were sitting. I hadn't picked up her actual name yet. But I soon learned it.

"I wonder, Dalia," Saad commented, "why the bird landed by us."

She laughed. Her deep red lips parted, revealing a glittering set of teeth. That made me happy, perhaps because, despite her radiant teeth, I was still the reigning shiny teeth champion of Telepathy.

Vasiliev never insisted on the necessity of detailed knowledge exchange between sender and receiver. However, he would stress the importance of keen concentration while awake or lucidity when dreaming. Remaining focused is not a difficulty: no one entering or leaving Telepathy ever notices or greets me. I have experienced much pleasure from being in this state, for it allows me to read other minds and psyches. My mind frequently sees other realms, which open up before me like novels where the real and the imaginary are seamlessly intertwined.

Early in the day I usually make arrangements for the waiting staff and chefs and let them know about Telepathy's special dish of the day. Every day, a small neon screen announces the specials, and the people come flocking in. The café continues to be a popular spot, with a steady flow of both dedicated regulars and the usual newcomers. Today I see faces I have never seen before. That's why I advised the waiter to leave me alone, uninterrupted, until told otherwise.

"As you wish, Uncle Kamoun." Jabr left to tend to the customers. He was tall with a dark complexion. His sharp features made me think he had spent some previous life in the desert, with its simoom winds. At the same time, he has the agility, kindness and cheery disposition of a city dweller. This is what makes me perceive in Jabr a bizarre series of disconnects – something that doesn't happen by chance. I have never asked him about it before. Hiring staff is Jaafar's realm. I have nothing to do with that. If I dared to ask, and Jaafar found out, he would say: "You're so nosey! You keep poking your nose into things that don't concern you." However, as I had pointed out to him before: "The name of this place is Telepathy. Now you can see why I chose such a name: it has brought us customers!"

"But it's a winning location, right?"

"True. All these schools and bookshops that have sprung up from the ruins of what used to be have undoubtedly played a role. But then, look at Jenvas's cafés. You don't see discerning customers going there, do you?"

Jaafar may have been convinced by what I had said, or he may have been reluctantly abstaining from responding. That is because he is like me: he hates carrying on an empty conversation – which, oddly, is exactly how Telepathy came about.

This morning Jaafar surprised me, showing up unusually early: the rare occasions he does come to Telepathy to see me are nearly always late in the evening. He was cheerful, humming a part of 'Afifa Iskandar's song *Filfil wa bahar* (Pepper and Spices) that he had memorized. He was holding a map that he proceeded to spread out in front of me.

On it I saw an urban plan, clearly the work of an expert engineer and architect. Everything was crafted with the utmost diligence and accuracy. The lateral plans for the big marketplaces were visibly extravagant. But what really caught my attention was the map's projection of this new urban entity: the ancient city forcibly removed, replaced by a newly manufactured, ready-made specimen, just as the interested parties had imagined it and instructed the architect and engineer to make it happen. Streets and buildings, similar on one side and radically different on the other. Along the streets, evergreen trees were carefully lined up.

Jaafar was visibly cheerful. "Now we can plan a road map for Telepathy."

"Do you mean a plan for its development or for actually getting to it?"

"No. This map means we'll be on the outskirts of the growing city. Anyone can get to Telepathy if they so desire."

"What if we get thousands of customers?"

"I don't think so. Telepathy is a niche market."

At that moment, with the map of the alternative city in front of me, I felt someone infiltrate my mind. It happened as I had resolved to wrap up my conversation with my wife, Natalia Vasiliev. She felt it too and hung up. That immediately shut off any remarks I might have kept in reserve for responding to Jaafar. He noticed the anxious expression on my face.

"What's wrong?"

"Just a nagging doubt . . . I wonder, should we trust the 'durability' of these alternative cities? What if they're just a fleeting moment in time, based on something ancient and potentially productive, that some day manages to retrieve its existence from memory to reality?"

Jaafar did not seem interested. "Life is changing, Kamoun," he said. "This is the era of vertical buildings. Social relations are being severed. Tenants may run into people in the lift, but within a matter of seconds they can leave them. This is a new world, and we have to accept it. It's a world of strangers."

I reluctantly agreed. "But," I replied, "such things only serve the inevitable overcrowding and the appetites of major capitalists and neoliberals in social communications, satellites, and consumption. Everything is polluted by the desire for profit."

"What does that have to do with this map?"

"The map necessitates the birth of the city-state: a gigantic distortion, formed only from coercion, not desire. The buildings will cry out as the memories seep from them . . ."

I said this to Hajj Hamadi, but he laughed at me. "Money's the master," he bellowed. "Memory dies, and then there is a race to grab some space where money can multiply. Listen son, forests aren't only made of trees and plants. It's a cement forest, whether we like or not."

So then, the map is a fact, one that is to be imposed on us all, and on Telepathy. I don't know why at this particular moment the voice of the Iraqi singer Kadim Al-Sahir filled my ears:

I leave you to God's wrath, you heart breaker . . . I wish I had never met you, why did you come into my life . . . I've wasted my life on you. . .

I laughed. When I told Jaafar what was going on in my mind, he laughed too. "I have to mention this song to Hajj Hamadi!" he told me, by way of support.

I was glad that Jaafar was leaving the subject of the new cement city. "But what will he say?" I asked.

"He doesn't have time to listen to songs. He'll definitely start scolding me: 'The world is not a pair of pyjamas,' he'll say. 'It's a trap for miserable people.' The Hajj isn't who he used to be."

"What'll happen when he listens to the song?"

"Nothing. Except he'll probably try to interpret it, or else repeat it in some affected manner, for Hajj speaks formally like he learns. 'I shall place you in the hands of God,' he'll say, 'you who have hurt me. Ah, I wish I had never set eyes on you, who sent you to me? Oh, how I regret the misery that I have suffered with you!'"

I laughed. "Meaning, in Hajj's classical Arabic rendering, the song loses both its value and its spice."

"True. When confronted with emotion and stimulation, Hajj's use of this Arabic is an astute choice. Everything will be as the grammarians want it to be, not the way poets and singers try to spin it . . ."

We both immediately started singing Kadim Al-Sahir's song:

I leave you to God's wrath, you heart breaker . . . I wish I had never met you, why did you come into my life . . . I've wasted my life on you . . .

The customers heard the singing emanate from the distant dark corner. A cheerful round of applause mingled with the two voices in search of the tenderness and affection in Kadim al-Sahir's voice.

At the end of his class, the Russian scientist, Konstantin Kotkov, used to assert that "those who have this knowledge abstain from obstinacy, because their minds are busy with more important things." That may well apply to me, but does it apply to Jaafar too? I did not actually ask that question, for it is in itself a sign of obstinacy. Right then, I should have been worrying about my own situation.

I overheard Shawqi whispering to Fawz: "Why is that blond man looking at us? Don't look now. Wait a minute, then look."

"I noticed that too – do you think he likes me?" she asked with a flirtatious grin.

I almost laughed when I observed Shawqi straighten up and throw a jealous glare.

"Screw him. Am I not good enough for you?"

She laughed out loud: "You're acting like a rooster! What's wrong with you? I'm just teasing!"

Saad, the blond man, was staring at Shawqi. There were many tables between the blond man's corner and Shawqi's, but his stare was steadily gaining attention. Shawqi, the dark-skinned man, could not hide his discomfort. He kept puffing and staring at the corner where the blond Saad and beautiful Dalia were sitting. The scene calmed down. Nothing suspicious here so far: just looks, which were being shamelessly exchanged. When it was Shawqi's turn to look at the blond man, the latter waved and smiled amiably, the kind of smile that allowed me to see his teeth from afar. They were perfectly straight teeth. No dents, no stains. He looked as though he had been groomed by a sculptor; one who had dressed him in an elegant suit and given him a reassuring pat on the shoulder. The sculpture ordered Jabr to bring him the very best food and drink, the only thing missing a bouquet of flowers. But the flowers weren't necessary: he was inhaling Dalia's Christian Dior perfume, which even I could smell from a distance. I heard myself whispering, "Lucky . . ."

Shawqi, the dark-skinned man, seemed perturbed. He did not

know what to do: the blond man a few tables away was waving at him. But for the quiet and orderly etiquette at Telepathy, he would have let out a joyful shout to express his delight. Now he needed to return his greeting and get Fawz to smile and give him a nod; then he would have achieved his goal and could relax in the face of such persistence. Waving back, he forced himself to smile at Saad (albeit with some resistance from his lips, which twisted themselves to the right). He didn't appear to recognize him. Now they both busied themselves with chattering and whispering. I sensed, however, that Shawqi was a bit anxious. He kept scratching his head, as though trying to stir his memory to retrieve all the names of the blond men he knew.

The list was not long; something I could deduce from the way he was shaking his head: *I wonder who this blond man is?* When he could not remember the face and name, he turned toward Saad the blond, but was startled to see him smiling and waving back, as if they were life-long friends. Fawz noticed this bewilderment and put her right hand over his left on the table. It was a tender, comforting moment, something he sorely needed. He stuttered, anxious to say something and confess to her that he didn't recall this person.

I could tell he was embarrassed by the desperate way he was looking at Fawz. For her part, she did not look surprised by what she was witnessing, as though she were used to such situations. But he was in another world. I heard some thoughts passing through his mind and memory: *Maybe I saw him at the airport during my last trip. No, that couldn't be. Was he with me at university? There were few blond people. He wasn't one of them. What if he were a friend of 'Abd al-Bari, 'Abd al-Samih, Hamid, or Raisan? Or Naji?*

In fact, Fawz *was* closely following what was going on, worried that their weekly rendezvous would be marred by this apparent memory test. "Let it go," she whispered. "Let's call Jabr and order now. Either we'll remember, or else the man will remind you."

The suggestion soothed him: at this point, it was exactly what he needed and desired.

Jabr came to their table, full of good cheer as always with the customers. He had to bend down to speak quietly to the two of them: "Today's special is chilli fry, but with extra sliced potatoes, onions, and minced beef. Yes, and dried lemon. We also have various grills. Drinks are in the menu."

"Does the chill fry have more potatoes or more onion?" Fawz asked.

"It's got just the right amount of both, with small chunks of meat, dried lime and extra curry powder."

She nodded, while Shawqi the dark-skinned ordered dolma. Fawz looked surprised. "You don't even like dolma," she said, staring at him. "What's going on? Are you angry?"

He shook his head, as though he himself didn't fully understand this strange choice. He was searching his memory and didn't want to get distracted by food. The dolma dish was brought in; it was just a pretext so as not to disappoint Jabr the waiter, who had so courteously and respectfully introduced himself to them both. Shawqi's mind was preoccupied, but the last thing he wanted was to reveal this to Fawz, whom he had promised an especially wonderful day, free from any anxiety or worries. "Let's make it one of our happiest memories," he had told her earlier.

Yet it was unnerving to watch this blond man who appeared to be a smiling robot, programmed to wave whenever he looked in his direction. But so be it. Why not go over to him, shake his hand, introduce Fawz to him, ask him to remind him of his name, and then be done with it?

Fawz could read what was going through his mind, and indeed found it to be a sensible solution. Sure: let's get it over with. However, at that very moment, Jabr appeared with their order. Aromas of chill fry and dolma wafted through the air, and the drinking glasses seemed to dance beneath the lantern's rays, shimmering with burgundy and golden hues. The beam of my telepathy was now infiltrating the mind of Shawqi, the dark-skinned one; it writhed and churned like a desert storm.

Rest in peace, Dr. Leonid Vasiliev. It was his books, *Mysterious Phenomena of the Human Psyche* (1959) and *Experiments in Mental Suggestion* (1962), that drew me to this side specialty. That is why I enrolled in his courses in the mid-sixties. I've followed him closely ever since. His side specialty became mine, an essential part of who I was before I became a co-owner of Telepathy. His research concluded that both long- and short-distance telepathic communications are possible.

You might wonder how the Soviet-era parapsychologist and physiologist Leonid Leonidovich Vasiliev (1891-1966) got involved in parapsychology. Well, there's a nasty rumour that, in the 1950s, the Soviet government got wind of evidence that the first American nuclear submarine, *Nautilus* (SSN 571), was successfully communicating with the CIA via telepathy. So they recruited Dr. Vasiliev to run a telepathy laboratory at the University of Leningrad. Other than the fact that the *Nautilus* was indeed a real submarine, these are all Cold War fabrications.

If it were not for Vasiliev, I would not have been who I was and would never have become who I am. Rest in peace, Vasiliev. You did not believe in the afterlife but, whenever you see me moving my lips at the sight of food, you must be smiling: "There are many types of belief, and I respect yours." This is what he told me once while his daughter Natalia was testing his knowledge of biology, the science in which she so excelled.

This same mentality now opened up before me. Shawqi the dark-skinned was tossing and turning through his own mental pages while knife and fork crisscrossed between his left and right hands, slashing their way through the dolma. Poor stuffed onion-head, whose innards were being chopped and strewn beneath the erratic swoops of the cutlery! Up until now, only the tomato was left intact. He hadn't eaten a bite. Fawz reached across with fork and spoon to feed him some chill fry. She managed to reach his mouth; it opened reluctantly under the insistent gaze of her wide, bluish-black eyes.

I stopped my telepathic exercises when his mind had finally pinned things down: *This blond man is the one I saw at the crossroads, at the Gorki Café between Lenin Street and Red Square. I think he works at the military section of the embassy. Yes. I think it's him. But that blond man was acting ridiculously; he was not proficient in Russian. He would stutter a couple of words to order a "cup of coffee". I helped him then with his order. I even paid, despite my own miserable financial status. He thanked me, stuttering as he did. I don't know what his profession is. I assumed he was a relative of some rich person who was sent to Moscow for respite. As I followed the blond man that day, he behaved very stupidly. I had infiltrated his mind. There was nothing more to him than a desire to sleep with a blond woman who frequented Gorki Café. His mind was possessed by this lust. Nothing else could dislodge it. Poor, foolish man!*

The thoughts of Shawqi, the dark-skinned man, stopped me in my tracks – could his mind read others as well? Was he in Moscow? When? I never saw him at Gorki Café from the years 1965-1979. He wasn't there. Did he come later, when I decided to leave after Vasiliev's health had worsened? Was it after Vasiliev had passed away, and I had finished my own studies at the University of Moscow, and later Leningrad? This meandering exchange between our two minds may have been amusing and entertaining, but it was difficult too. I didn't know who he had studied with. I would need to find out more some other day, perhaps somewhere far away from here.

I returned to Shawqi the dark-skinned and his mind. Fawz was trying to entice him to eat and drink . . . maybe he would forget his worries. But now, another idea carried him away. His memory had been shaken by this whirlpool of reminiscing!

Wasn't this blond man Issam al-Asali? The tall blond man with blue eyes, the one who tried to make his voice sound gruff and devoid of any human resonance when he interrogated me in the intelligence building? That was when he telephoned me after I had returned the previous night, ordering my presence there. I didn't see a reason for that. "Why don't we meet at the Hyatt Hotel, in Café Mandarin?" I had asked.

"I'll expect you in the hall of the intelligence building at eight a.m.," he had retorted angrily, before hanging up.

Animal! That night he had robbed me of any sleep. I waited for eight o'clock in agony. I didn't want my eyes to betray me in front of this odious person. How else could I describe this repugnant behaviour? I informed my neighbour, Abu Isma'il. I also told a friend of mine. Couldn't be too cautious. I could easily vanish there, and no one would ever know. I resolved to pretend I had stayed up late checking some experimental samples that I needed for a research paper I was currently working on. I couldn't tell the truth to whoever asked me about this fatigue. What good would it do me? Acquaintances and friends would give me the cold shoulder, thinking badly of me. Today, lying was the way to go.

I went to the meeting hall. The tall blond man reached out to shake my hand, while a short man in a grey suit remained seated and mumbled an unintelligible greeting in reply to the exaggerated one that I had proffered in an attempt to simulate a cheery, relaxed demeanour.

The conversation began with my research. Neither of them paid any attention to what I was saying. They kept looking at what was in the middle of the small table between the comfortable pomegranate-coloured 'seats'. I thought the ashtray was chic. It was made of crystal-clear glass, without any cigarette-ash residue. I stopped talking. The tall one surprised me by asking a question about my trips and travel. "Have you shared your research with anyone else? I mean, did you meet anyone in Moscow?"

"Of course I did. I visited the Academy of Biology and Mental Research. I was selected by my government to do that. What I'm researching will benefit my country as well."

They smiled dryly. "But, did you associate with anyone?" the same man asked. "I mean, on a personal level?" He reached out his hand, as if to create a friendly atmosphere. "Did you sleep with a blonde woman, for example?"

"What's wrong with that?" I stammered. "I knew Katalina from before. She's an expert scientist and very young."

They laughed in a perplexingly light-hearted manner and thanked me for my cooperation. Suddenly, the short one surprised me with a sharp question: "Can you invite her to visit you here?"

I felt my bafflement manifest itself in my facial features. "She's a scientist," I repeated. "She attends conferences and scientific panels."

"We're scientists too," said the tall one, "and we can organize a conference that Katalina can attend."

"As soon as a conference is organized," I replied, "I'll invite her."

With that, the meeting ended. I took my leave, the dryness in my mouth almost paralyzing my tongue. I rushed to the closest café, which may well have been attached to the intelligence services, given its proximity to the building. I was right. The waiter brought me cold water, then fried eggs, cheese, and green salad, as if prepared especially for me. Everything looked planned. You leave here only to fall in there. I had to outsmart them. How could I warn Katalina not to come when she received an invitation in my name?

I thought of Jalil, who graduated from the same university in the humanities. He had told me a few weeks ago that he was getting ready for a week's travel to attend a conference. He assured me that the university had pulled all the necessary strings for that purpose. He knew Katalina. We used to meet in either her apartment or mine. Jalil loved vodka so much that we had nicknamed him 'Vodka Jalil'. We used to spend beautiful evenings there. His Russian wife, Eliona, was a poet. While he studied, she decided to stay in Moscow, provided that he visit her from time to time. As he sipped vodka, the usual entertainment involved poetic exchanges in Russian.

"Let me be a poet for once," I told myself, "despite my bad poetical knowledge and poor lexicon. Let my letter to Katalina be a poem oozing emotion, even though I am not as literary or well-versed as Jalil:

She nodded from afar
Let's get closer
She nodded from afar
Let's remain farther

apart.
She misread me
And she threw away
my paper with sadness . . .
Closeness is remoteness
And the promise is yet too far to foresee."

I was translating from Russian, as though I were at one of the gatherings with Katalina, Jalil, and Eliona. Let me add that the words were from Yevtushenko's poetry. Katalina, who knew Yevtushenko's poetry so well, would discover the lie. I put all that in a letter steeped in emotion and memories and overflowing with hope and anticipation. I exaggerated; everything was amplified. Katalina would be suspicious. She would realize the dilemma. What if the letter fell into the hands of Issam al-Asali, for example? He would only read it as the idiot person he is, someone who knows nothing but exaggeration. He and his shallow mind would surely be inclined to interpret it as true, passionate emotion.

Fawz took advantage of the situation. While Shawqi's mind was wandering its way around this problem she fed him, like a mother trying to distract a mischievous child.

Now, I definitely do not believe he was one of Vasiliev's students. He couldn't possibly even have studied with any of Vasiliev's students. Vasiliev used to train his students more in 'cessation' than prolonged stay in the overflow. His famous motto was: "Be a puzzle and a mystery, for you are gaps which are hard to close." But no. He can't be one of the first generation of students who practised telepathy with Vasiliev. He was my teacher and my friend. How he had wished Natalia could accompany me as my wife on this journey! After many happy years together, Natalia had wanted that too. But I had a contract with the government, so I had to leave. I had to do my duty, or else my sponsor would be in trouble.

I did not have the money to pay for the sponsorship. We agreed on visits until I had completed my state contract: five years of work. It was definitely possible to take visits in turns. For those who don't realize just how difficult our situation really was: at that time, it was forbidden to marry foreign women. And this was yet another ordeal – how could I possibly bring a Russian woman back with me? Life had become complicated both here and there. I began saving some money to help my new family there. Vasiliev was a friend and so was his wife, Dominica. As for Natalia, she was a soul mate.

Was Shawqi now trying to penetrate my mind? He could. At least this would have been something to prevent his mind from floundering in its search for this blond man's identity, whose name I overheard when he answered his phone, and when he spoke with his companion, Dalia. Even Jabr the waiter informed me: "Uncle Kamoun, his girlfriend calls him 'Saad'."

Was I to be mean and infiltrate his mind? Yes, I thought so. Should the restaurant have to be disrupted by this enigmatic blond man, who kept waving at Shawqi with such warmth and conviviality? The restaurant should exude a relaxed and cheerful atmosphere. For sadness and worries, arak is the solution. Poor Fawz, who came with him today in the hope of spending a merry old evening together. I got through to him then: *Forget about the blond man. Pay attention to Fawz, or else she will compare you to the blond man and get bored. It'll be a double loss!*

He shook his head, as though being pestered by an insistent fly. He gazed long and hard into Fawz's eyes. In his gaze I could see a different

Takhatur *(Telepathy), Dar al-Markaz al-Thaqafi al-Arabi, Casablanca/Beirut, 2019*

worry, the kind that is permeated by burning desire, affection and lust. She put her hand on his. Their eyes exchanged a silent whisper as arousal glazed over them. I could see their hands pressing each other, as though trying to squeeze out the pendulating ecstasy and desire that filled their bodies. They ordered two glasses of Cabernet Sauvignon, and three additional tapas: dried fruit, fava beans with garlic, and a yoghurt and cucumber salad. The only thing missing was the arak. But they didn't order that.

Now I administered a fresh dose of infiltration. In our initial exams,

Vasiliev would tell us: "This should be done at intermittent intervals, so you can access the feelings at a measured pace." Of course, Vasiliev didn't mean the kind of thing that I was doing now. But that was a different story: now I was in Telepathy restaurant, and I wanted to succeed. Otherwise Jaafar would turn up all scowling and devoid of his usual jolliness when he came later to check the takings for the day.

Monday was the toughest day of the week: not many people were inclined to go out then. The new customers were a welcome addition. There was no need to infiltrate the mind of Saad the blond: he was deep in his emotions. Now he and Dalia were each on their fourth glass. They had had more than eight mezze. Saad didn't need any more. If we had more customers like them, Mondays would be more profitable than the weekend – even Thursday and Saturday nights! Telepathy would be doing extremely well. But today was no normal day.

Shawqi the dark-skinned and Fawz called Jabr to their table. He walked over to them, tall and swaying like a branch from left to right. He seemed cheerful and happy. They ordered two glasses of *Zahlawi* arak. Mixing that with the wine would do them in – they'd be totally drunk. Perhaps they're used to that. Jabr was pleased with this new order. He brought them a small bottle and told them it was better than two separate glasses. They thanked him warmly. I think Shawqi was about to stand up to give Jabr a satisfied kiss on the cheek. Feeling shy and uneasy, the latter's expression turned darker as he lowered his head for Shawqi. Fawz was about to follow suit, when someone called out from my table: "Behave yourself! Sit down, what's the matter with you?"

She remained seated, albeit reluctantly. Jabr poured two glasses and added water; the colour looked like flat, stirred milk. They each took a big sip, gulping down about third of their cup. It was all too fast, and certainly not fitting for discerning drinkers. Drowning in their intoxication, Fawz reached for his lips, as though trying to compensate for the missed opportunity with Jabr. They locked together in a lengthy, frenzied kiss that pulled their faces and chests even closer. They passionately embraced. The contagion reached Saad the blond. Pulling the tall, dark-skinned Dalia toward him, he too tried to kiss her.

We don't normally tolerate this kind of excessive behaviour. Jabr looked at me from far away. I waved back at him, insinuating that today was not like other days. Let them be, but within reason. He understood this attitude from my gesture, something that he had got used to over time. I hadn't raised a warning hand. Anything else was fine and permissible. Overcome by her desire, Fawz slowly withdrew to the restroom. Shawqi's hand fondled between his thighs and he kept looking around apprehensively, as though fearing the watchman. He didn't relax until she returned and gave him a quick peck on the cheek. This was the compensation for the kiss that she had not been lucky enough to give Jabr the waiter.

That I remembered Bekhterev at this moment was not as random as it seemed. Shawqi's obvious discomfort had led me in that direction. Bekhterev, the famous neurologist and chairperson of the Brain Institute at the University of Leningrad (Petrograd), asserted – as I was told by his granddaughter, Natalia Bekhtereva, who replaced him as the director of the institute – that such discomfort does not permit a clear reading. The secret behind my enchantment with his scientist granddaughter went well beyond her having inherited her famous grandfather's knowledge of neurology. Vasiliev knew in detail what was going on, and he joined Bekhterev in 1921. It was this knowledge that led me, through Natalia Bekhtereva, to I.F. Tomashimisky and Bekhterev's loyal student Konstantin Platonov, expert in experimental psychology at the University of Kraków. I joined the circle of disciples and graduates who worked in telepathy and experimental psychology and were dedicated to it. I am by no means a specialist. I was merely the amateur who was attracted by these experiments.

Jaafar believes that I was affected by the insanity of reading secrets. "Why don't you join the intelligence services?" he had asked.

I don't know whether or not he was being serious. I had been working in a small consulting circle which included a group of sociologists, psychologists, historians, biologists and astrologers. At that point, I had only told the administration of the Institute of Mental Research about my training with Natalia Bekhtereva, but not about my classes and training with Platonov. I revealed nothing of my specialist studies with Krachkovsky in the humanities and social sciences, not to mention in psychology. Despite that, I was a member of the group of advisers, like some eccentric who had turned up from Moscow and Leningrad. My ideas did not please them. I was the only one coming from there, and they were wary of this background. But the government was strange as well. They used Soviet financial aid and entered into all sorts of agreements with them, but kept a stern eye on their graduates. It didn't take long until I found myself unemployed. Even Krachkovsky, with his abundant work and important services to Arabic and Islamic geography and literature, was considered a marginal figure in academic scholarship. For some time, it was only those who had graduated from England or America who had the privilege of serious acknowledgement.

Interview with Al-Musawi about his novel *Takhatur*

After the publication of the novel *Takhatur* (Telepathy) by Muhsin Al-Musawi, the Iraqi academic, critic, and novelist who resides in the US, an in-depth interview with him by the Lebanese journalist Abdo Wazen was published on the *Independent Arabia* website.

Below are extracts from the interview, which will open up for readers the uncanny world of parapsychology and the fantastic that the author explores in this novel, and which raises existential questions linked to the destiny of human beings, and the ways in which groups interact in precarious times. Published here with permission.

AW: *Your new novel is entitled* Takhatur *(Telepathy), which is also the name of the quirky restaurant in which the novel's events take place. Why did you choose the word 'telepathy' for both the title of the novel and the name of the restaurant?*

MM: The choice of this title arose from serious challenges that are shorthand for places and times. They put a writer in a tight spot regarding connotation – what is implied and what isn't. There are the fourth and fifth learned quantum leaps in computer sciences, the internet, and communication. We are also about to embark on a profound exploration of the world of artificial intelligence. Here, based on that touchstone, there must be a different route to writing from traditional narrative processes. That explains why I came up with *takhatur*, a place that can be the landmark for the present and the future. Historical cities are being systematically abolished and replaced with 'megamall' cities with their glass facades and boxes that morph people into commodities and spectacles, gradually unnerving them and preventing them from taking decisions. These are dangerous transformations. The title *Takhatur* does not reconcile with this transformation, but rather presents it as it is, despite all its charm and magic, and the accuracy of most of what happens and is said. However, it also raises suspicions and questions. This choice acquires truthfulness because of its approximation of the real: its everyday life, taverns and restaurants. It also tricks the reader, who wants to fix the location of a place on the outskirts of Baghdad, Moscow, or other cities. As for my choice of that particular term, telepathy, there is a story behind that. Usually the artist or novelist sits in a spot and finds his/her mind infiltrating another mind – maybe that's just my imagination, but the possibility of intersection or infiltration and interception is still there. Many times you can see someone staring at you or contemplating what you are doing. I remember once when I was sitting in a restaurant that I often go to in New York City and I saw someone sitting in the far corner, staring at me as if he thought he knew me. I understood that people communicate even in moments of ostensible inattention.

AW: The word 'telepathy' conjures up what is termed the 'fantastic' in literature, as analyzed by Propp, Todorov and others. You do not follow this fantastical trend. Instead, you set a limit to what you describe as 'parapsychology', seeking to create your own experience in this field. What about this parapsychological fantastic tendency in your novel? What did you wish to achieve through it?

MM: Todorov developed what Propp and the formalists had done, analyzing narrative principles, morphologies, and poetics of prose. When Todorov came to *The Thousand and One Nights* in his study of the fantastic, he discovered that the presence of the doer (the supernatural, the wonderful, and the uncanny) has a touch of the real. It rarely occurs that jinn or demons materialize, a secret door shakes, or the secret codes of the talisman are decrypted without there also being some sort of human presence. The fantastic is tied to the human. We are now faced with a virtual space to which many have become addicted; we are transformed into consumers, indulgent to the extreme in this use without the slightest reflection on borders and limits. Does this mean that this is the world which the storyteller imagined? Or does this virtual space surpass that imagination?

> Russia, Germany, South and Southeast Asia and Africa, even Latin America, all remained relatively absent from our culture

When *The Thousand and One Nights* and similar Eastern tales appeared in the West, Europe was to witness a drastic change in industry: print, trains, machines and telephonic communications. Our contemporary civilization witnesses something else: it is the leap into the unforeseen – the virtual space. Hence, it is time for an extra dose of the fantastic, one that can combine the sciences of telepathy and psychology. Socialist realism opposed such preoccupations, fearing that it might weaken the hypothesis of a social structure based on class struggle, means and modes of production and surplus value. But scientists have busied themselves with those issues. In accordance with what has been happening in America, they have come up with justifications for their endeavours in parapsychological domains. Parapsychology is a current science: it emanates from the will to fathom the recesses of imagination and justify the presence of the peculiar, the suspect, the sensational and the strange.

AW: There is a Russian presence in the novel, whether in the parapsychologist scientist Vasiliev and the orientalist Krachkovsky, or through Russian poetry by names like Pushkin, Yevtushenko, Anna Akhmatova and Boris Pasternak. What did you seek to achieve by invoking this Russian dimension in your novel? Why Russia? Is it because the narrator studied in Moscow?

MM: Throughout the modern Arab revival (Nahda) and at later times, the Arabic novel has engaged especially with France and England: Taha Hussein, Ibrahim al-Mazini, Yahya Haqqi, Dhu al-Nun Ayyub, Tawfiq al-Hakim, Suhail Idriss and dozens of other famous writers have contributed to the genre. Russia is present in Mikhail Naimy's memoirs, but rarely in poetry; such was the case even during the time of the Soviet Union. Arab intellectuals were fascinated by Europe. That is why they were more interested in European orien-

INTERVIEW WITH MUHSIN AL-MUSAWI

talism and neglected Russian orientalism, which was rich, deep and scholarly. There are many reasons for this: French and English colonialism imposed their two languages on schools in the Arab region, something that led primarily to contact with London and Paris.

The case was different with the members of the Mahjar (émigré) school, and yet the issue remains the same: language is the intellectual's window and path to the Other and, in this case, the road towards London and Paris was the easiest. Russia, Germany, South and Southeast Asia and Africa, even Latin America, all remained relatively absent from our culture. The number of graduates from the USSR was not small, but political realities in the Arab world, the fear of the presence of the 'red' and Cold War restrictions all left that space vacant. With it disappeared achievements in criticism, linguistics, psychology, sociology, and the pure sciences. Hence *Takhatur* blossomed from an aim to fill this vacant space through those sciences and the names of magnificent Russian scientists, orientalists and poets. Yahya Haqqi noted the Realist current among Russian authors, but that particular trend was not pursued, and the field was characterized by severed relationships. It is incredible that names such as Bakhtin and his book, *Dostoevsky's Poetics*, remained unknown until I asked Dr. Jamil Nasif al-Takriti and Dr. Hayat Shararah to translate some of these important works with the Cultural Affairs Publishing House at the Ministry of Culture in Baghdad.

AW: Paralleling the Russian poets we have Abu Nuwas, Ibn al-Mu'tazz, and al-Buhturi . . . how did you come to this strange equation?

MM: Our world today overlaps and intersects; so does the mind. I wonder who among us doesn't experience the ambiguity of denotations and connotations? The world flows through different networks in the process of invading the subdued human mind, not the dominant. Authors find themselves facing limited choices in attending to what is present and what is absent: either to be absorbed in one side or to entertain multiple others. I once attended a reading by the late poet Robert Creeley. He asked me if I had read Henry Corbin's book, *Alone with the Alone: Creative Imagination in the Sufism of Ibn 'Arabi*. At that time I had not read it. I hope that non-Arab intellectuals can interact with Arabic culture as Creeley did.

Translated by Mbarak Sryfi

SPECIAL FEATURE

Elias Khoury, The Novelist

CONTRIBUTORS:
Humphrey Davies, Paula Haydar, Maher Jarrar, Suneela Mubayi Stephanie Petit, Saif al-Rahbi Chip Rossetti, Fakhri Saleh, Yehouda Shenhav-Shahrabani, Maia Tabet, Aida Fahmawi Watad, Abdo Wazen and Raef Zreik

Elias Khoury, who is prominent worldwide as a public intellectual, was born in Beirut in 1948. After studying Sociology and History at the Lebanese University, Beirut, and the University of Paris, he became a journalist and literary critic. He worked as assistant editor and then managing editor of *Shu'oun Filastinia* (Palestinian Affairs). Since 1975 he has published fourteen novels. He also served on the editorial board of the iconic literary magazines *Mawaqif* – with Adonis – and *Al-Karmel* with Mahmoud Darwish. Later he became editor of the cultural pages of *As-Safir* newspaper, and then editor of "Mulhaq", *An-Nahar*'s weekly literary supplement. In addition to his novels, Elias Khoury has published four books of literary criticism, three plays, two screenplays, and a collection of short stories. He has had a distinguished academic career as a visiting professor at both Columbia and New York Universities and at the Lebanese American University, as Global Distinguished Professor of Middle Eastern and Arabic Studies at the University of New York, also teaching at the Lebanese University and the American University of Beirut. His novel *Gate of the Sun* won the Palestine Prize, and its translation was named Best Book of the Year by *Le Monde Diplomatique*, *The Christian Science Monitor*, and *The San Francisco Chronicle*, and a Notable Book by *The New York Times*.

The Novels of Elias Khoury

English titles

(On the Interrelations of the Circle)
not translated into English

1989 *Little Mountain*
translated by Maia Tabet

1993 *City Gates*
translated by Paula Haydar

2010 *White Masks*
translated by Maia Tabet

1994 *The Journey of Little Ghandi*
translated by Paula Haydar

1996 *The Kingdom of Strangers*
translated by Paula Haydar

(Complex of Secrets)
not translated into English

2006 *Gate of the Sun*
translated by Humphrey Davies

(Scent of the Soap)
not translated intoEnglish

2008 *Yalo* – US edition, translated by
Peter Theroux; 2009 UK edition,
translated by Humphrey Davies

2011 *As Though She Were Sleeping*,
UK edn., translated by Humphrey Davis;
2012 US edn., translated by Marilyn Booth

20012 The *Broken Mirrors / Sinalcol*
translated by Humphrey Davies

2018 *Children of the Ghetto — My name is
Adam*, translated by Humphrey Davies

Children of the Ghetto — Stella Maris
not translated yet

Arabic titles

1975 عن علاقات الدائرة،
'An 'ilaqat al-Da'ira

1977 الجبل الصغير،
(al-Jabal al-Saghir)

1981 أبواب المدينة،
Abwab al-Madina)

1981 الوجوه البيضاء،
(al-Wujuh al-Bayda')

1989 رحلة غاندي الصغير،
(Rihlat Ghandi al-Saghir)

1993 مملكة الغرباء،
(Mamlakat al-Ghuraba')

1994 مجمع الأسرار،
Majma' al-Asrar

1998 باب الشمس،
Bab al-Shams

2000 رائحة الصابون،
Ra'ihat al-Saboon

2002 يالو،
Yalu

2007 كأنها نائمة،
ka'annha Na'ima

2012 سينالكول،
Sinalkol

2016 أولاد الغيتو– اسمي آدم،
(Awlad al-Ghito, Ismi Adam)

2018 أولاد الغيتو– نجمة البحر،
Awlad al-Ghito, Najmat al-Bahr

ELIAS KHOURY

THREE EXCERPTS FROM

STELLA MARIS

TRANSLATED BY HUMPHREY DAVIES

Point of Entry: Third Person, or the Absent Conscience

Stella Maris, or the Star of the Sea, is God's balcony looking out over the floating dove that we call Haifa.

On this balcony, at the spot where the hill of the Prophet Elias leads us off into the world of the miraculous, Adam Dannoun, hero and narrator of this story, discovered his many faces, made peace with his names, and wove his history. Here he tasted his first kiss and here he became acquainted with the pleasures, and pains, of love. Here he swore to be faithful to the girl whom he loved and here he taught himself the alphabet of betrayal, so that he could erase the wound to his heart with new wounds.

When memories of God's balcony buffet him as he seeks to draw his image with the ink of words, he sees Haifa falling down to the sea from the towering heights of Carmel and spreading its wings, as though the vast expanse of water had been placed there to welcome it. The dove dives into the water, floats, and becomes a place of refuge for a young boy who has no refuge other than the feeling that the life he is living is no more than shadows of the life of someone who himself was never more than the shadow of a story with no author.

He is seized, now, by a violent yearning for Stella Maris, where he used to sit alone, feeling that he was absent and invisible, longing for the days of absence, and, in so doing, taking refuge in the third,

Najmat al-Bahr (Stella Maris), Dar Al-Adab, Beirut 2019

absent, person, to write that absence.

Here, on Mount Carmel, where history has played fast and loose with the place's own histories, on a flat ledge, the second Adam was born. He would fill his loneliness and alienation with the sea, wash his eyes with the fading of the horizon, and drown in the silence of the sea air as it spread the taste of salt over his face.

Adam, son of Hassan and Manal Dannoun, born in the Lydda ghetto in 1948, decided that his story had begun when he sat on God's balcony, which here they call Stella Maris, to breathe in the air of his freedom with the smell of the sea. He would come to this balcony overlooking the city and sit for endless hours on its stone bench. That bench was where he took refuge from the memory of his mother and from his life, be it in the garage or in the large abandoned apartment in Wadi el-Salib that had been the garage owner's gift to him on his sixteenth birthday. When his girlfriend Rivka had asked him to take her to his house to make love for the first time, he'd told her he was afraid of the ghosts that lived in those deserted houses. He'd said that when he went home, he walked on tiptoe so as not to wake the ghosts of the "absentees" who had been driven out and swallowed up by the sea. He'd said he could hear their voices, which had made their nests in its stones, as they crept about and could see their faces, covered with the darkness of absence, as they roamed around as though bidding the place farewell, or reclaiming it.

Adam Dannoun did not have the right words to tell Rivka that he was afraid of the owners of the house, with whom he had become acquainted, one by one, through their photos that hung on the walls, and that he feared in particular the eyes of the young woman holding her young child in her arms. In the eyes of that young woman, whose name he did not know, he saw the pain that collects in the corners of eyes, the fear that spreads over their whites, and the light that radiates from their pupils.

Adam didn't have the courage to say that he was incapable of betraying that woman in her own home, and a week after he moved into the house, which Mr Gabriel had said was now his, the youth had removed from the walls all the photos of the Haifa family that had lived there. He'd taken all the photos down, put them in one of the rooms, and watched as the places where they had been were replaced by spaces formed of the white ghosts of absence. He lived with the spaces to evade the looks of the owners of the house, which filled his soul with a strange feeling of terror and guilt. The photo of that one young woman, however, refused to let him go, even for an instant, and he'd gone back and hung it in the most prominent place in the house, apologizing to her and giving her the name Shahla, and the photo of Shahla and her young son, whom he would later name Naji, had become his companion in that house filled with the ghosts of the absent.

Had Adam known love in all its aspects, he would have said that Shahla was his first love. How, though, was a youth of sixteen to tell a tale of love that could have formed a chapter in *The Dove's Neck Ring* by Ibn Hazm, the writer from el-Andalus who told tales of forms of love one would never have imagined and, in a tale fit to strike the lover with that despair that is love's highest degree, of how passionate devotion to a picture may transform itself into lust?

The woman in the photo resembled his mother Manal a lot. Time had failed to leave its mark on her youth, which glimmered with sorrow, and she held to her breast her suckling child, who would remain forever young, for the absent never grow old and never die.

Was Shahla, hanging there on the wall of the house's own memory in Wadi el-Salib, truly his first love? Or was she just a picture suspended in the white light of remembrance?

At Stella Maris, Adam Dannoun decided to chase away the memories that had made their nests in his life and begin again, as though born of his own self, and to live alone and put the past in a coffer, to be buried in the earth. Haifa was to be the earth in which his coffer would be buried and he would forget everything. He would bury the story of Lydda and its pain and the tales of the lovers that lived there in the coffer of oblivion, and depart.

ELIAS KHOURY

The question that keeps the writer of these tales awake at night is, how to write of those who are not there? Can the absent write his own story using "I", writing, in such a case, as though remembering? Or should he have resort to a third, absent, person, to write for him?

The game of what Arabic calls "consciences" or "consciousnesses" is amazing and has no equivalent in any other language: the pronouns that stand for persons are called consciences or consciousnesses but the conscience is also the invisible moral compass, and how can a novelist write with an absent conscience? And what can it mean that consciousness should be absent, if it is to tell a tale?

The moment Adam left Manal's house in Haifa, he felt he had chosen absence, which left him with only one option – to divide Adam into two halves, one for presence and one for absence. The first half lives today in New York, meaning that it is absent from the place but present in the text, while the second lives in Haifa, meaning that it is present in a place that has been condemned to absence. And here this "present absentee" (or "absent presentee") wishes to acknowledge before the Israelis their linguistic superiority, in the case of one word at least: the Israeli legislator who coined the term "present absentee" was a genius whose imagination far exceeds that of all the writers of the theatre of the absurd and has turned the name of an entire people into an epitome of absurdity.

The Arab grammarians refer to the third person as the "obscured" person. The writer of this tale finds himself obliged to obscure himself. He will write about Adam as though discovering him. He will forget the child found half-dead on its mother's breast under an olive tree on the long road between Lydda and Naalin and look at his life with new eyes. He will play with absence to the end. He will absent himself in order to write about absent places, but the dazzling spot in Shahla's eyes as they appear drawn in the picture of memory will reveal to him the impossibility of his game, because that woman's absence behind her almond-shaped honey-colored orbs have stirred in his heart a dumb longing for his little mother, whom he has never been able to forget.

On that strange night in the month of December, when clouds veiled the light of the stars in the sky, he made love with Rivka beneath the nets of jealousy that radiated from Shahla's eyes, and discovered that life is simply a deception that we must meet with another of the same kind, if memories of tenderness and fear are not to crush us and transform us into ghosts living among the others who fill the tottering houses of Wadi al-Salib.

The White Dove

Departure
1

Adam Dannoun was fifteen when, on Wednesday, 25 October, 1963, he left his mother's house on the flank of Mount Carmel.

It was two in the morning. Adam picked up his small satchel, walked barefoot and on tiptoe to the door, bent down to put on his shoes, and, straightening up after tying his laces, found Manal in front of him, in her hand a folder that she held out to her son.

He had wanted to leave without saying goodbye, had moved slowly so as not to wake Manal. He would have preferred to do away with the farewell scenarios that he'd knitted together in his imagination and steal quietly out of the house, leaving everything behind him and taking only his school books and a few clothes.

All of a sudden, however, his mother appeared, in her blue nightdress, as though emerging from his dreams. Seeing her before him, he stopped, retreated, and leaned his back against the wall.

She said she'd known he'd leave and had been preparing herself for that moment for the past ten years. That was why she'd hidden away for him this will, the will Hassan Dannoun had left for his only son, whom death had prevented him from seeing.

"This is yours. Take it. It's a will. Your father's will."

The boy extended a trembling hand and took the folder. It was long since Adam had felt the rush of emotion that seized him at that moment. He felt sick and rested his back against the wall, then found himself sliding down and sitting on the ground, the folder in his hands.

"These papers," she whispered, "are your father's will. Even though he left them for me, I'm giving them to you because they aren't rightfully mine. These papers are your father's bequest to you."

"You call these papers a bequest?" Adam said.

"Words are the only thing we have," she whispered.

The darkness surrounding his mother's long blue nightdress transformed the woman into a shadow glowing with a dim light, like a halo, which radiated from every part of her. This halo, which embraced half-shut eyes, trembling lids, and extended hands, was all that Adam could see.

The woman stooped over her son as though she were about to take him in her arms but then pulled back. The youth stretched out his arms to his stooping mother but the woman, whose nightdress blended with the shadows, had disappeared into the blue.

She spoke to him about his dead father's will, her voice emerging from the well of silence and returning to it. He braced his back against the wall to stand, rose a little, then fell back till he was sitting again. The woman stooped over her son a second time and reached out her hand to him. Adam took the hand and gathered his strength. When he was upright, he couldn't think of anything to say. She looked into his eyes and told him to wait until the rain had stopped. Then she turned her back on him, went back to her room, closed the door, and was gone.

When Adam Dannoun remembers that moment of farewell, his knees give way and he sits so as not to fall. The rhythmic tapping of the rain on the windows sweeps through him, along with the sound of blustering winds that rage around him.

The youth had liked to think of his mother as "the collapsing woman". Manal, whose dry breasts had suckled a child who remained thirsty for the rest of its life, was to her son a secret locked in silence and fragmented words. When he thought of her, all he remembered of her voice was disconnected syllables, as though she were talking to herself and permitted to emerge only obscure sounds pointing to unspoken words, or words spoken in such a way that no-one could decipher what they signified. The image of little Manal, as Adam remembered her, was replaced by the image of the woman who had fallen to the ground as she welcomed him home after his return from Nazareth.

His friend Ibrahim had died during the soccer match between Nazareth and Eilaboun, Adam had stayed behind for three days in "the capital of the Galilee", as the inhabitants of Nazareth like to call their city, and Manal had been unable to leave Haifa to be with her son during those difficult days because her husband, Abdallah el-Ashhal, forbade her to do so. And when Adam came home after three days of living with death while the Israelis interrogated him on suspicion of responsibility for that of his friend, Manal had run towards the door with arms outstretched but, before reaching her son, had fallen to the ground. Her body bent backwards as though she was about to sit down and then she landed on her tailbone before falling apart altogether and collapsing onto her back with outstretched arms and quivering face.

As Adam took hold of his mother's hand to stand her up, he had felt the pulse of tenderness in her fingers. The youth remembered the pulse as tender but knows that the description is inexact. It might be better to say that he could feel his mother's vital spirit spreading through her fingers, fingers long and smooth as silk. He stooped over her face, saw the shadows of her closed eyes, and feared she was dead. He believed his mother was dying but he didn't cry out. His heartbeat surged, he began breathing raggedly, he rubbed her eyes with his hands, the woman opened them and began to try to get up, and he printed a kiss on her forehead and helped her to stand. She stood, a shy smile of apology sketching itself on her lips. Then she took him by the hand, led him to the bathroom, placed her finger on her lips to tell him not to speak, gestured to him to take off all his clothes by the door, took the clothes, which reeked of the prison, threw them in the rubbish, and ordered him to take a bath. When he emerged, clean and shining thanks to the water, he found a table on which Manal had set out food – eggs fried with sumac, white cheese, olives, honey, and tea. She sat and watched him as he devoured the food, then told him to sleep.

She didn't ask him anything because she knew he was innocent, and he didn't say anything and didn't reproach her: he was afraid of the effect on her of words recounting the sufferings in gaol of a boy not yet fourteen who had been charged with a crime he didn't commit. Adam felt that when words struck against his mother, they caused wounds, and when, after hearing the shouts and insults of her husband, he'd seen her coming out of the bedroom, he'd felt that his mother's neck was covered in wounds, wounds that were like her eyes. Eyes that shed no tears and a neck covered with wounds that didn't bleed.

Adam had decided to leave. He sensed that his mother didn't want him there as a witness to her humiliations and felt as though the walls of the house were closing in on him, as though there wasn't enough air left in the place. It never occurred to him to ask his mother why shouldn't she come with him, or why shouldn't she take him and flee. He knew his mother had nowhere to go. Going back to her village of Eilaboun was impossible for her as she hadn't merely eloped with the fighter Hassan Dannoun, whose son she had borne, but following the death of her first husband had married again, and to a married man who claimed to have lost his first wife in the darkness of the Nakba. Now Lydda, despite its tribulations, seemed like a lost paradise, one she'd been compelled to leave when the Jews confiscated the house she'd been living in, on the excuse that it was now absentee property and had therefore been transferred to the Jewish National Fund.

A woman without a family, resting her weight on her shadow, which fragmented against the olive and orange trees as she picked her livelihood as a day labourer on confiscated land that had belonged to her husband. Though today, even that ignominy seemed an impossible hope.

Hassan Dannoun's story was drawn on his wife's eyelashes, behind which the woman, who spoke only in whispers, hid her reactions. To understand the signals Manal wanted to send, the boy had to read what her lashes wrote with their movements, rapid or slow.

Adam thought that his mother's life had ended there, hanging from the wires surrounding the Lydda ghetto, wires that had been removed on the ground but that remained entangled in the imagination. Manal had left her village of Eilaboun for the unknown world of her husband in Lydda and had found herself stuck in the ghetto – a young woman, carrying a baby, led by a young man of eighteen who had decided to be the eyes of a woman who knew nothing of the place where she found herself marooned but who had no choice but to stay where she found herself.

Adam remembered the moment when Blind Ma'moun disappeared as an empty, lifeless house. He was seven. He'd come home from school to find the house full of the smell of incense and the woman hiding her face in her hands and sitting in front of the icon of the Holy Virgin holding her suckling child. The woman didn't move when she heard her son's footsteps. "Where's Ma'moun?" he asked. She didn't reply and remained bowed over her hands as though she couldn't see. Then she suddenly got up, clasped the icon to her bosom, and returned it to its hiding place under her mattress. On that day, he realized that Manal had become, like him, an orphan and that he would have to be father and husband to her if he was to save her from her fate. These feelings, which Adam was able to fashion in the course of his re-ordering of his memory, had not yet become clear to him on that cold autumn day when he returned to the house after three days in prison charged with a crime he didn't commit.

Adam Dannoun had been detained in Nazareth on the day of the death of his friend Ibrahim, who was the goalkeeper for Nazareth's football club. Ibrahim, who was seven years older than Adam, had left Lydda with his mother to return to Nazareth, only to die from a ball kicked by Naim Salim, renowned for his unblockable shots. The ball struck him on his chest, his lungs, they say, collapsed, and he died of suffocation. Adam had nothing to do with it. All that happened was that he'd gone to Nazareth as a visitor, and his friend, to honour him as a guest, had given him a Nazareth team outfit to wear while he sat on the players' bench, watching, and then, when he saw his friend writhing on the ground, he'd run to help him and been arrested, while Naim had managed to run away. Adam remembered the story of his friend's death as a missed appointment with sorrow. Detention had made him despise himself, because, instead of feeling sorry and thinking about his friend's fate, he'd feared for himself, and when he was released, his innocence established, he'd felt he could dance for joy, to the point that he'd gone straight back to Haifa without going to his friend's house to offer the condolences that convention demand.

The collapsing woman who met him at the door to the house asked him nothing. She said she'd been sure of his innocence and had left things in the hands of al-Khudr, whom she'd told, "Saint George, you take care of the boy!" She didn't ask him how he'd got back or about the red Chevrolet that had brought him to the door of the house. She behaved as though she knew everything. The question that bothered Adam, and to which he could find no answer, was how did she know that her son was about to arrive? Adam had found the door open and Manal waiting there to welcome him with her fainting fit and that delightful languor that returned in the flutter of an eyelash.

The death of Ibrahim in Nazareth was a turning point in Adam's life. It was the first time he saw death with his own eyes. When Adam recalled the terror of that moment, he'd feel nauseous and be seized by a desire to sleep. The boy born in the Lydda ghetto, who'd lived there a childhood full of stories of disintegrating bodies and the humiliations of a cage, in which people had been placed for whom death was just stories to which he would listen as though they were the fairy tales that accompany a child's growing awareness of its language, found himself for the first time before a real death, and it bore no resemblance to what he'd been told.

He had bent over Ibrahim and told him to get up, but the goalkeeper, his eyes closed and his cheeks quivering spasmodically, didn't answer, as though he could no longer hear. Adam put his arms around him to stand him on his feet, but Ibrahim's body seemed very heavy and difficult to move. The first aid team arrived, ordered Adam to step back, placed the goalkeeper on a stretcher, and took him away. At that moment, the body on the stretcher was no longer Ibrahim's. In place of the features of his friend's face, Adam saw a yellowish mask and understood that he was dead and that death means not only the withdrawal of the soul from the body but the withdrawal as well of the body from the body, leaving the corpse a strange entity bearing no resemblance to its owner.

Adam's first experience with death allowed him to understand how, in Lydda, it had been transformed into stories: at the moment that the soul withdraws from the body, the body becomes anonymous, with no name to protect it from obliteration and dissolution, and at that point, talk of death may become neutral, unemotional, while death itself becomes just a moment of silence between two words and is transformed into a story.

When they took him in for interrogation, Adam was convinced that the person who had died wasn't Ibrahim. His friend had vanished behind a corpse that didn't resemble its owner, and Adam couldn't understand why he hadn't cried: instead of sorrow sweeping over him, the only thing he'd feared had been the interrogators, who'd made fun of his eastern dialect when speaking Hebrew, of his fear, and of the chattering of his teeth, which refused to stop.

After he'd emigrated to New York, where he would die alone consumed by a fire caused by a burning cigarette end, Adam would discover that, through his sudden and absurd death, Ibrahim had reconciled him to the many deaths with which the stories of his childhood were filled, allowing him to look at Lydda and its tragedy as a story drawn on the eyes of its victims.

And then, at one in the morning of Monday, 18 November 1963, which is to say a year after the story of his brief arrest in Nazareth,

Adam had found his mother waiting for him. She had known, without anyone telling her, causing him to wonder in amazement how the woman had come to possess an inner voice that informed her of everything that befell her only son.

Were you to ask Adam to tell you his mother's story, he'd write innumerable pages in white ink, which is how he always saw himself – writing white on white, rather than writing and erasing as writers do; writing a white story limned in silence and confidential whispers, and moving close to what was not said so that he could say without saying.

Adam betrayed his mother only once, when he told Dalia that he would write his story on her body in his white ink. His girlfriend laughed and said he was raving. He was about to reach the ecstasy of ecstasies, when body unites with body, pleasure blends with pleasure, speech is choked off, and the spirit of God beats its numberless wings over the water of love that spurts from the spring of life. At this moment, love becomes the chemistry of the soul, and the man writes on the female body, in his white ink, the story of his crumbling and dissolution into the femineity of the water.

Adam never again mentioned the business of the white ink to Dalia because he felt he was abusing the metaphor, which previously he had used exclusively of Manal, out of all the women of the world.

Manal alone was worthy of the white ink of love, for the little woman with the cracked lips yearned for a love that came only in the form of a mirage. She had wasted her life between three sorrows – her sorrow over her husband Hassan Dannoun, whose wounding before the fall of Lydda had turned her into a nurse for his dying days; her sorrow over Ma'moun, the blind youth who had been her companion during the days of the ghetto as well as a borrowed father for her only son, but who had left the ghetto when her son was seven years old; and her sorrow over her marriage to Abdallah al-Ashhal, the inscrutable man who could never be hers.

Adam had been certain that his departure wouldn't leave a further sorrow on the small woman's heart because she'd wanted him to leave and his decision to do so was merely an echo of her own concealed desire. Today, though, living his life in voluntary exile in New York, he wasn't sure. It would be inaccurate to say that he felt guilty, for Adam believed that there are two words – regret and guilt – that a person must never use, because they trivialize the significance of his choices. The truth is that he felt an overwhelming love for the woman, and even the great story of his love for Dalia could not erase his love for little Manal, which was like an emptiness that slipped in between heart beats.

Adam turned his back and set off very slowly. In his heart of hearts, he expected his mother to call to him and ask him to stay with her. He'd gone over the scenario innumerable times in his mind, each time removing one detail and adding another, saying something and then unsaying it. These moments kept him company at night, when he'd get into bed, close his eyes, and begin the game of permutations, to be cut off abruptly when sleep overcame him.

She would take hold of his hands and shed tears, and he'd roughly push her hands away, saying he was sick of her and her face, drawn into an oval by grief, and that he was going to create his own life, far from the misery of her relationship with that photo of his father-who-had-died-a-martyr which she had to hide in his room so that her husband wouldn't see it.

Another time, he'd imagine himself picking up the photo of his father-who-had-died-a-martyr and departing, and when Manal asked him to leave her the photo, he'd tell her she didn't deserve the man whose memory she'd betrayed with her husband. "But I love him and I'll never stop loving him," she'd say, to which he'd reply, "He is my father, and you have nothing to do with him," placing the photo in his bag and going.

A third time, he'd imagine her wresting the bag from his hand, taking Hassan's photo, and clasping it to her breast. Adam would approach his mother to take the photo from her, stop, hesitate, and then leave.

A fourth time, she'd grab him by the shoulders, look into his eyes, and say she was going with him, and he'd forbid her and say, "Stay with your husband! You deserve him!"

A fifth time, she'd stand and block the doorway to stop him from going out, and he'd look at her and say, "Get away from me, woman!" and his words would make cuts in her neck and Manal would put her hands over the wounds, moaning softly, and step aside, leaving room for him to exit.

A sixth time, she'd ask him, clasping his hands, never to forget that she was his mother and tell him that she'd go on loving him till the day she died, at which he'd look at her and say he had forgotten everything and was going to begin life over again, as though he'd just been born.

And a seventh time, she'd fall to the ground, and he had to bend over his mother and wake her from her fainting fit with his kisses, telling her he was sorry for any pain he'd caused her but he could stay no longer.

Manal talked a lot during Adam's nights. His sleep was full of her voice and he became accustomed to all the permutations of her sorrow, of her fear for her son, and of her anxiety over what might happen to him. When Manal saw her son pick up his satchel to leave, however, she gave the lie to all his expectations, for she didn't fall to the ground and didn't extend her hands seeking help. She just whispered a few words to him and then stood there like a shadow swaying in the darkness, and after she'd helped him get up, she gave him his father's will, left the entryway, and went back to her bedroom, where she quietly closed the door.

Adam found himself alone, so he left without looking back.

Like Walking on Words

Like walking on words: that was how the visit came to be engraved on Adam's memory and his emotions. Streets of words, names that leapt up before one's eyes and then dissolved, a life that had been and a death that would be.

Today, when he wants to write of Warsaw, all he finds before him are streets paved with the words of the elderly guide, whose gasping obscured half of what he said, so that Nadia would then have to ask him to repeat, which he would do, grumbling, his voice emerging through his large nose, which was full of black and red spots that he covered with the handkerchief with which he constantly wiped his face.

Adam walked next to the student group as they tried to imagine the scene, of which nothing remained but a few landmarks that helped the guide draw a map of a place that had lost its map. Everyone felt tired because the imagined failed to transform itself into the actual. They walked with bowed heads on streets fashioned out of words, the names flying around them – Umschlag Platz, Chłodna Street, the Small Ghetto, the Large Ghetto, Próżna Street, Sienna Street, Złota Street; names and more names that the guide tried to point to so that he could draw the features of the ghetto that had once been, though its features melted into the groans rising off the asphalt, the pavements, and the streets, as though those stifled groans were now the sole witness to the calamity.

"We are walking over the Jews' largest graveyard. Here a hundred thousand Jews died of starvation, illness, and epidemics, while the rest were transported on the trains to the extermination camps," the old guide said.

"No! We are not in a graveyard of the Jews!" said Prof. Yacov. "We are in the graveyard of human civilization."

"Never again! It must never again happen!" shrieked Isabella.

They walked to the rhythm of a monotonous voice, into whose folds Nadia's voice insinuated itself to translate disconnected words that flew about in the air before falling to earth.

After the tours of the ghetto were over, Adam told Nadia her translation hadn't been needed because the rhythm of the guide's voice had been enough for them to understand everything: a voice that would come close to choking and then die away as it recounted the history of a place erased. He told her he'd felt he was choking when they arrived at the remains of the wall that had hidden the ghetto from the city, at 55 Sienna Street and 62 Złota Street. The ghetto had been enclosed by a wall three metres high, topped with barbed wire. He said that children had been the first heroes of the ghetto, because they'd taken charge of smuggling in food from the Aryan zone.

He said that children were the bearers of life and therefore the first to die.

He said that life bestowed by a killer appears meaningless amidst debasement, hunger, and epidemics. It derives its meaning from itself and no longer needs words of any kind. Its meaning is present within it and requires no additional meaning.

Did Adam really say these things to Nadia, or is he imagining today that he said them? Or is he saying them only now, when death has matured within him?

It is incumbent on the writer of this text, as he recounts the story of his life, to ask himself why he is revisiting this trip to Warsaw, and why he stammers, loses his skill with words, and finds himself unable to write. Wouldn't it be better for him to ignore it? Isn't it just a recapitulation of the events of the time of the ghetto, in Warsaw? And isn't his account of the trip to Auschwitz just an attempt to say what cannot be said? And what could he say, after all that has been said?

The writer of this text knows that his testimony adds nothing new to "the banality of evil" that transforms itself into a crime. Even God, who "forgives whomever He pleases", has lost his capacity for forgiveness and wrapped himself in the cloak of absence.

The voice of the guide began to fade into nothing, Adam felt he'd lost the capacity to hear, and silence enveloped his ears in a soundless ringing.

The silence became total. Even the footsteps on the ground were inaudible, a ringing emptied of its sound, so that all that remained was its echo, like a heavy white emptiness. This was true soundlessness, thought Adam, as he tried to write about the strange sensation that filled him as he walked on words that he couldn't hear and that he knew, in the bottom of his heart, that none could, since even the one whose job it was to narrate them repeated them and yet was incapable of listening to the meanings that emerged hoarsely from his lips.

In his New York exile, he couldn't keep out of his mind the poem by Rashed Hussein entitled "God Is Now a Refugee, Sir", but at the time he went on that trip he hadn't yet met Rashed Hussein or read his poetry to be able to use it to confront the echoes of deafness that assailed him. Of its own accord, the poem, in which that poet announces God's absence, steals out from within his memory:

> God is now an absentee, Sir,
> So confiscate the very carpet from the mosque.
> Snuff out the wicks of the stars lest they light
> The path of the homeless wanderer.
> Should I squeeze a loaf of your bread,
> You'll see how my blood runs from it over my hand.

Adam was aware he'd made a small adjustment to the first line, since Rashed Hussein had written "God is now a refugee" but instinct led him to substitute "absentee" for "refugee," since God is the prime "present absentee," His absence justifying everything, His presence bestowing holiness on everything. He is the stranger, and the stranger is one who has become estranged from himself, meaning one whose name has become his accusation, his identity, and the epitome of his humiliation.

It isn't about accusing God, as did Albert Camus in *The Plague*. To accuse God is to take the easy way out, because it's meaningless, and the thing that drove the French existentialist to ask God why He permits the death of children is merely an evasion of the real question, since the plague in this case is simply a metaphor concealing a colonialist reality, a reality Algeria suffered at length and that the writer dared not approach.

The Palestinian poet, rather than accusing God, accuses humankind, just as Adorno, faced by the horror, proclaims the death of poetry and the savagery of the metaphor. In either case, we find ourselves before an impossibility: in the first, the stars go out; in the second, the language dies. Humanity's barbarity brings us to utter nakedness, which is to say to being stripped of language.

When Adam wrote about linguistic nakedness, he felt as though he'd closed all doors, for human beings may strip themselves of everything except language. Even the dead reject the idea of linguistic nakedness. Here, we are dealing with the essence of what we call civilisation, for humanity invented the rites of religion and the classics of literature so that language would not die with the death of the individual, for language is transformed into the only tool the dead can use to speak, a speech which acquires a holy stamp even when it has nothing to do with religion.

This is why the silencing of the victim through violence or oppression is meaningless, because the victim proclaims his final protest by abandoning words, and when the slain becomes voiceless, the language of the slayer turns into a meaningless babble.

On the streets of Warsaw, no-one could find it in himself to speak. And when Uri Nebrasky, the representative of the ministry of education who organized the trip, tried to lead the students in a rendition of Hatikvah, Prof. Yakov ran over to him and put his hand on his mouth, whispering, "Shut up! This isn't a place for singing, it's a place for dying," in a voice audible to them all. So Uri shut up, all sound vanished, and the only thing that could still be heard was the rhythm of feet tramping over the ground.

The four days that the group spent in Warsaw seemed endless. Sorrow may be one of humanity's noblest emotions but is also its most monotonous. Even the meetings held each evening to evaluate and extract lessons from the trip and which, according to Prof. Yakov, were "the place where knowledge and grief come together so that we can extract the moral", became impossible. The professor, who wanted to read the tragedy in its universal dimension, as an expression of the savagery of humanity, the impotence of civilization, and its surrender to its death wish, failed to find an adequate echo from either the organizers or the students. On the contrary, Uri Nebrasky insisted on offering an alternative reading of the tragedy that placed it in the framework of Jewishness and anti-Semitism, whose roots lay in the Christian culture of the West, the Holocaust thus proving that the only solution open to the Jews was to return to the Land of Israel and there to build their state, which would be a normal state like any other.

"What do you mean, 'a normal state like any other'? We are the light of the nations!" Yakov said. "You are adopting the anti-Semitic discourse that called for a final solution. The Nazis proclaimed that their means for a final solution to the Jews was their extermination, and you say that the final solution is their migration from their countries."

"Their countries! This is their graveyard, not their country! Their country is the Land of Israel!"

"But most of them considered those countries theirs," Yakov said.

"So why did you migrate to the Land of Israel then?"

"I didn't migrate. Or at least, I was small and came with my sister, and we were afraid."

"Are you against the establishment of a Jewish state?" Uri asked.

"On the contrary," Yakov said. "I stand by the rights of the Jews."

"So what do you want then?"

"I don't want anything. I want to say that I agree with you in essence but disagree with you over how to express it, because I'm using a different language."

"Language is of no importance," Uri said.

"Differences in language can lead to calamities, and you are leading us towards a language close to Fascism."

"I belong to the Workers' Movement and served in the Palmach! You think you're more of a socialist than me?"

"I too am a socialist, but I know that the most important Jewish socialist experiment was here, in Poland, and was embodied in the Bund."

"They were traitors and assimilationists and they led the Jews to their death!" Uri said.

"Why do you resort to calling people traitors in that harsh way?"

"Because I can't stand that kind of flabby thinking. You're an odd bird, old chap. What made you come on this trip? We brought the students so we could teach them to be aware of their Jewishness and that they belong to the heroic generation that came to expunge the shame of the crime with the sword."

Uri looked at Varedka and said disapprovingly and in a loud voice, which he wanted everyone to hear: "You messed up, my dear. What made you choose this idiot professor to lead the students on this trip? We didn't come here to listen to the philosophy of a failed literature professor. All literary critics are failed writers."

Yakov felt incapable of replying. How was he supposed to reply to the accusation of being an idiot? Plus, who says that being an idiot is a crime? After Dostoevsky, idiocy has become another name for innocence and the idiot a metaphor for the Messiah, who embodies sacrifice.

That was what the professor used to teach his students, in the hope that they'd read literary texts as bearers of a different language, employing the same words as the writers of other kinds of texts but turning the semantics of meaning upside down and causing the reader to discover the meanings hidden beneath the meanings.

Prof. Yakov felt that the representative of the ministry of education had damaged his image. He'd become the "idiot professor" to the students, and it was no longer in his power to explain to them the virtues of idiocy, or to invite them to accompany him on a visit to Marek Edelman at his home.

MAIA TABET

Discovering Elias Khoury

I discovered Elias Khoury's writing in 1983 through a series of columns he wrote for *As-Safir*, the left-leaning Lebanese newspaper where Khoury was then an editor. The columns, appearing under the rubric of "Zaman al-Ihtilal", or "Chronicles of Occupation", were a free-form but in-depth commentary on the Lebanese (and Arab) condition in the aftermath of Israel's 1982 invasion of Lebanon.

At the time I discovered Khoury's columns, we used to scan the newspapers on a daily basis, following political and security developments closely during the years of Lebanon's so-called civil war. For me, the newspapers were only marginally interesting: most articles seemed long-winded and predictable, but every time I read one of his columns, Elias Khoury's writing made my heart skip a beat. His deceptively simple but powerful language, his unwavering commitment to what we would now call a liberatory politics, and his poetically charged lyricism devoid of any sentimentality gave me feelings of pleasure mixed with excitement. As a result of various accidents of history, even though I was born to Lebanese parents and raised mostly, but not entirely, in Lebanon, my language of literary expression was English and not Arabic. And because of the way I experienced myself as being truncated between the cultures of the two languages, whenever I read an Arabic text that struck a deep chord, my first thought was, and to this day remains: "I must bring this into English so that all my non-Arabic speaking friends can understand the ineffable beauty of the culture I belong to."

And so it was that I began to translate some of Khoury's columns. I quickly discovered that being a literary translator was very different from being a proficient technical translator – which I already was. Finding the equivalent English word or turn of phrase was the least of it: capturing the feeling of the text and evoking the universes the writer invoked, those were the true challenges. Cleaving close to the Arabic, the source language, often delivered fidelity but not beauty; taking liberties meant I could convey the connotative if not the denotative meanings of words but how much was too much? Thirty-five years later, I'm still working on the "perfect" rendition, imagining it as some kind of dance that I could execute flawlessly.

It turned out that I knew several people who were acquainted with Elias Khoury personally, and although I no longer remember who introduced us, the introduction took place after I had shared my enthusiasm for his "Zaman al-Ihtilal" columns, which I was working on with no purpose or endgame in mind. I had not the slightest idea what might come of the translations, and the notion that they might be published, or that anyone would be interested in them, or their publication, was utterly irrelevant. Looking back, I could describe this as an exercise, one that might have been an assignment in a university-level class on translation.

Once Elias and I met, we became friends. We socialized, I met his wife and children, we went out for coffee, and we talked. Elias is what might today be described as masculinist – a man intent on performing his masculinity in the vicinity of women in ways that can sometimes be unpleasant – but I think he was flattered by my attention to his work and, thus indirectly, to him. He was and is a charismatic figure: erudite, brilliant, funny, sharp as a tack, both intellectually and emotionally. Although he dialed up the magnetism and charm, he was also warm and approachable. He could undoubtedly be overbearing and dismissive at times or come across as condescending and engage in vulgarity with the glee of a schoolboy. But his unwavering political integrity and his deep sense of loyalty to his friends marked him as one of a kind for me, flaws notwithstanding. And he writes like a dream. I was in awe of his writing then, and remain so to this day.

Our conversation progressed from discussing translating the columns to undertaking the possible translation of *Abwab al-Madina* (*City Gates*), one of his early works that is genre-defying. It appeared in 1981, the same year as *Al-Wujuh al-Bayda'* (*White Masks*), a book that conformed much more closely to our understanding of a novel.

I worked on the first chapter of *City Gates* but found it frustrating: not having the literary skills or maturity I have now, the poetic prose and completely surrealistic and non-linear narrative – if one can call it that – just flummoxed me. I tried and tried to reproduce the beauty of the text but couldn't fully grasp its sense and therefore couldn't do it justice. How was it possible to translate a text whose discrete words I understood but whose overall arc eluded me?

At some point, Elias suggested I read *Al-Jabal al-Saghir* (*Little Mountain*), a book with a strong autobiographical undertow that had come out in 1979 to considerable acclaim.

By now, it was 1986 and I was getting ready to leave Lebanon with my newly wedded partner for what seemed to me like a life of exile. We were going to Yemen, where my husband would head the country program for an international NGO, and where I knew no one and had no connections. I was going to be a "wife" and, in the fullness of time and God willing, a mother. Translating *Little Mountain* would be my project.

While we awaited our Yemeni visas as we "honeymooned" in Cyprus in June 1986, I sat scantily dressed at a table on the balcony of our hotel room in the crisp and sun-filled Troodos Mountains and began on my first book-length literary translation. We had no laptops or computers then, and I worked with pen and paper, filling yellow legal pads with my handwriting. By July we were in Sana'a, and as soon as I'd found my bearings, and in between obligations incumbent upon me as the new "mudir's wife", I returned to my project. My husband would leave for his office each morning, and I would sit in our Yemeni house, with its white-washed walls, traditional reception room, and brightly colored stained-glass domed windows, a dictionary and a Thesaurus at my elbow, translating. In time, I became pregnant with our first child but truth be told, *Little Mountain*, as the book would be called in English, felt like my first baby: it was only after I had put the final polishes to it, typed it all up, and sent it off to the publisher that I was able to give birth to the flesh-and-blood baby I had carried for nine months. In the interval between starting the book and finishing it, I had returned to Beirut for a visit, meeting several times with Elias to go over the English text. I returned to Sana'a to produce a final draft and Elias secured a publisher with the help of Edward Said, who wrote the foreword to the English text. Minnesota University Press (MUP), which had recently launched its

MAIA TABET

Emerging Writers series, was interested in publishing *Little Mountain* and they were going to pay me! When MUP told me the amount, I calculated that I would earn less than the hourly wage of what Americans refer to as janitors. I was aghast and indignant at first but quickly learned that it was par for the course. Like writers, poets, and other authors – except for the famous, commercially successful ones – translators are not remunerated commensurately with the labour they perform.

By mid-1989, I had two thriving babies: my daughter Yusra, who was by then going into her second year, and a real pages-and-ink book published by MUP, which went on to be reissued several times. But there was also another move, this time to Cyprus, where I would have the luxury of a living situation as an expat with domestic help, and despite various obligations would be able to see through a proper, book-length, project. Although Elias had been consistently producing a novel every two to three years since 1979, I decided on *White Masks*. The book had appeared in 1981 and marked a significant milestone since it was the first novel written by an ally and "activist" that was openly critical of the purportedly progressive political forces involved in the war. (Interestingly, the difficult *City Gates* appeared in a translation by Paula Haydar in 1993, the year I started working on *White Masks*.)

In 2008, I received an email from Elias telling me that he had a publisher for *White Masks* in English, if only I would finish the translation. By this time, he had garnered an international literary reputation, had a dozen or so books to his name, almost all of which have been translated into other languages, and Humphrey Davies had in effect become his "traducteur attitré" in English. Thanks to the Internet I was able to get it finished, going over revisions with Elias long distance. I had not been back to Lebanon for twelve years and would not return until after *White Masks* came into in being, thanks to Archipelago Press, a small publishing house known for its beautifully crafted books and its commitment to foreign literatures.

In a satisfying closure of the circle, I am today Elias Khoury's colleague: he is the editor of the Beirut-based *Majallat al-dirasat al-filastiniyya* and I am the associate editor of the *Journal of Palestine Studies*, the flagship publication of the Institute for Palestine Studies, which produces both journals. Over the seas and across the ether, our collaboration endures and we continue to talk.

MAHER JARRAR

Language and Textual Strategies: A Reading of Elias Khoury's Novels

At times when the pain of the Arab people has become unbearable, Elias Khoury has proven himself a critical thinker with command of diverse forms of expression, whose voice emanates from a mind committed to liberation struggles and who incorporates these struggles into his everyday work. In this sense, he exemplifies the three characteristics that Edward Said called for in an intellectual: daring to speak truth to power, bearing witness to oppression and suffering, and being a voice of dissent in the country in which he or she is based during clashes with ruling powers and institutions.

How do we enter the world of Elias Khoury's novels? As readers, we are drawn into their space by the familiar voice of the first-person narrator, who weaves us into the fabric of the tale and implicates us within the narrative web, making us live witnesses to events as they unfold. Entering Khoury's world necessitates multiple re-readings of his texts, as each reading adds a new dimension to how we take in, savour and participate in the aesthetics of the creative act.

Khoury's novels are preoccupied with questions of fiction and modernity: among them – Is writing an illusion? Is the truth of the story to be found outside of it? These questions are also pertinent more broadly to the reality of Arab intellectuals in the contemporary Arab world since the novel, as a mode of storytelling, recalls moments lived by the individual subject in the midst of collective social processes and through particular linguistic codes, pushing them into the dialectics of the mechanism by which the future is manufactured.

What is storytelling? Khoury asks. Are stories to be found strewn among the streets of memory and the pathways of the imagination? How do we gather them to create an archetype where all other archetypes have been destroyed? What is death? Can a story actually vanquish death like Scheherezade (if we understand her to be a story herself) did? If we understand a story as an act of recollection, then is this recollection separated from reality only by 'the twinkling of an eye'?

Here, we must stress the nature of the novel as a genre. In spite of the fact that in terms of both form and structure the novel is the aesthetic output of a linguistic-semiotic system, it aligns closely to the social environment it springs out of, as it carries within it objective semiotics that express the traditional and emerging values of its host society. These values by necessity reflect the power relations implicit in its social structures and also indicate the challenges these structures may face. In this sense, the novel is a written artefact that imitates a set of social transformations determined by language, writing and reading/reception. The novelist writes from outside – or even against – the static history of power; he writes the history of change in societies still in their formative stages. When we transfer these general considerations from the narrow context of a debate over the historical accuracy of the text into the open possibilities of language and textual structures of speech, we must be cognizant of how things exist inherently independent of language in the physical space of the world, whereas within the text, their existence must be based in language.

Khoury's novels always open with a death and proceed to tell stories of the lives and dreams of ordinary people and their pain. The death creates holes in the plot, which pave the way for marginal characters and ordinary heroes to narrate their stories. They always emerge from a recollection that works through a forward-moving dynamic. In this way, the end explains the beginning, which itself can only be understood through a 'recollective' dynamic. But this recollection commences from a beginning that is in and of itself the story.

SPECIAL FEATURE – ELIAS KHOURY

Since 1975, Elias Khoury has written thirteen novels and one collection of short stories. Let us take a look at the sources of inspiration that have played a formative role in his texts:

Firstly, his solid knowledge of the Arab tradition of oral narration in Arabic, in both its official and popular versions: the latter embodied by *The Thousand and One Nights* and the popular *sirah*, or oral epic in verse.

Secondly, a firm grasp of the history of the Arabic novel, from the works of Jurji Zaydan to Naguib Mahfouz, and a willingness to engage in dialogue with post-Mahfouzian Arabic novelists: the 1960s and 1970s generations in Egypt, and Emile Habibi, Youssef Habashi al-Ashqar, Ghalib Halasa, Ghassan Kanafani, Anton Shammas and many others besides. He combines all of this with an intimate connection to both classical and contemporary Arabic poetry.

Thirdly, Khoury is well read in novels from all over the world, having begun with reading Camus and Sartre at the age of 15, and having taken in the masterpieces of the major contemporary novelists since he began.

The intellectual corpus that has nourished Khoury would not be sufficient in itself to compel a new, seismic shift in the Arabic novel, were it not for Khoury's stance as a critic and intellectual striving daily for social justice and the struggle against imperialism, especially Zionist settler-colonialism. It is there on the ground, among the people and bearing witness to the emergence of a revolutionary consciousness, that the language of Elias Khoury the novelist matured and he was able to sharply hone his techniques and textual strategies.

Language

Perhaps it is no coincidence that Khoury considers himself a literary descendant of Ahmad Faris al-Shidyaq (1805/6-1887) in the lineage of modernists and innovators. Shidyaq is considered one of the very first to have worked to make Arabic literature more flexible and accessible vis-a-vis the spoken language, preceding even Maroun Abboud. Does this mean that Khoury is a mere disciple of this school? Yes and no; yes, because as a journalist and modern novelist he cannot but be influenced by the Shidyaqian approach to the Arabic language, and no, because he also relies upon other sources, drawing,

Bab al-Shams (Gate of the Sun)

for example, on oral forms of expression as in the popular *sirah*, as well as on the works of writers contemporary to and preceding him. Among them are diverse figures such as Emile Habibi, who worked to deconstruct language by punning on words, using satire and blending formal and colloquial Arabic, and Sami el-Baroudi with his use of religious language and symbolism. Khoury is also influenced by Sonallah Ibrahim and his distinctive style, which deliberately imitates journalistic reports and patches together various registers of speech, both official and popular, into a sort of collage, as well as by the musicality of Edwar al-Kharrat's language, which is based on religious poetry and chanting that constructs its own particular mythic code.

Furthermore, Khoury can himself be considered one of the pioneers of innovation in language. His novel *City Gates* depicts a city closed to the outside world. Its circular form brings to mind the story of the city of brass in *The Thousand and One Nights*, and also establishes an intertextual relationship with the stories of the Argentinian Jorge Luis Borges. Stylistically, it deploys poetic technique such as enjambment, repetition, advancement and deferment (*taqdim* and *ta'khir*), as well as plot interruptions and slang, in an attempt to break with the constraints of form and create a language that had first begun crystallizing in Khoury's mind as a young man. These elements have remained central to his subsequent novels despite the fact that the experimentation with language is different in each novel and gives each one its own special linguistic flavour.

The novel *White Masks* can be considered a quantum leap in modern Arabic fiction, in which Khoury borrows from the journalistic register with its straightforward sentences and blank, matter-of-fact tone, and from the oral cadence of unrefined speech as spoken by ordinary people. With the multiplicity of narrators, the different linguistic registers also multiply for the novel to become a polyphonic dialogue. These techniques capture both the language of everyday life and the fragmented parlance of the civil war, which re-scatters its fragments within the arbitrary mushrooming of urban space. For instance, *The Journey of Little Gandhi* is a retelling of the same story over and over again, alternating in focus between the minor characters one by one and retold in a different voice and from a different point of view each time. This circular trajectory does not lead to the text collapsing in on itself; on the contrary, it creates new outlets for speech through a proliferation of different registers and perspectives, and consolidating meaning.

Khoury's experimentation reaches maturity and becomes a spontaneous, almost poetic dialogue in *Yalo* and *Gate of the Sun*. In *Gate of the Sun*, which is based on real-life testimonies, Khoury adopts the technique of the frame tale from *The Thousand and One Nights*, where telling one's story is, in a sense, an act of overcoming death: one that in this case opens up aporias in the individual and collective memories of dozens of ordinary people uprooted from their historic homeland of Palestine. Khaleel, the principal narrator, is unable to distinguish one story from the next and keeps losing track of things, until he retreats into an interior world characterized by a stream of consciousness, an outpouring of emotions and a disconnection between real time and that of his own subjective world. He keeps handing over the reins of the story to other narrators in overlapping tenses. Each one of these narrators is haunted by his or her own perennial worries and has their own particular language, which indicates the geographic region and social class they belong to. The fragments of their stories come together to redraw for us the map of the Palestinian tragedy as it relates to present-day conditions. *Gate of the Sun* is effectively a counter-narrative that confronts the history written by the conquerors, by relating the history of their racist violence in the language of ordinary people.

In *Yalo*, we continue to experience the freshness of Khoury's language through the pangs of its birth from the mouth of Yalo, the mentally disturbed eponymous narrator and main character. Yalo is reminiscent of Dostoyevsky's Idiot, who tries through writing and recounting his story to prevail over his ego, which has been crushed and dismantled under torture in prison by agents of the authoritarian, repressive security apparatus.

In *As Though She Were Sleeping*, Khoury makes an informal contract with the reader based on references that run parallel to the text, which aim to alert the reader to the writer's variegated textual influences – which branch out in all directions. The title of the novel itself is an allusion to the Bible. It is divided into three parts, or three nights, as their titles show, which stand in for the three days and three nights Jesus spent in the grave between his crucifixion and resurrection. His choice of 'nights' over 'days' appears to be a means to smoothly draw attention to the dreamlike nature of narrative, enticing us to enter into its structure, which the narrator has crafted like a web. The narrator imagines himself to be Scheherezade as he weaves his story patterns in the still of night, making of the novel one uninterrupted dream. Meelya, the main character, is hostage to the world of dreams on 'the royal road to the unconscious' to borrow from Freud's *The Interpretation of Dreams*. The narrative is framed by two dreams: it begins with Meelya as she closes her eyes again to resume her dream, and ends with her dreaming of the white lamb crawling over her chest, which renders the novel a dream that goes in a circle. There are literary dreams too, embedded within the text, which play a role in the novel's cultural context. In this way, the state of dreaming – and daydreaming – links the Biblical past to the present moment, especially as the dreamlike state itself is a borderland or nebulous threshold that rests temporally in rituals of transition, suspended between the borders of worldly time and what lies outside it. The narrator himself in *As Though She Were Sleeping* is inconsistent and non-homogenous in his style and register, assuming disparate roles as he speaks. He goes from taking on the persona of the omniscient narrator who knows all about every character, especially Meelya, to speaking more like a historian. But he also keeps hinting at his own presence in the narrative, until he finally reveals his identity shortly before the end: he is Iskandar, Meelya's nephew, who has become a journalist.

In the first two parts of the trilogy *Children of the Ghetto*, Adam comes out of his 'circular metaphor' which caves in on itself to become a truth that goes beyond symbolism and stands alone, like an ancient Arab poet on the *atlal*, or deserted ruins, that make up Palestine. Named symbolically for being the first baby to be born in the ghetto of Lydda after its occupation, Adam is, in a sense, a witness to the beginning of the massacre as well as the last person to experience the paradoxical enigma of these *atlal* across the geography of the rubble turned by Zionist colonialism into a chasm of violence and madness. There, Adam stands guard to watch over the devastation and preserve the voices of the dead. As a symbol for the beginning of man, Adam is a 'present absentee' abandoned at the crossroads of memory in a liminal, deterritorialized space of departure and deracination. His psyche is haunted by the phantoms of two characters from two previous Palestinian novels: Dov/Khaldoun from Ghassan Kanafani's *Returning to Haifa* and Saeed, Emile Habibi's *Pessoptimist*. Like both of these protagonists, Adam happens to be a Jew by circumstance, or, shall we say, a Jew caught unawares. The *atlal* that honed the contours of his consciousness with their cutting pain, anxiety and memory are rendered an enigma, perhaps by Adam himself, when he associates them with the ghetto of Warsaw and the Auschwitz death camp instead of his own ghetto of Lydda.

In the third and forthcoming part of Khoury's trilogy, this paradox comes to make his character a different person to Dov and Saeed. His character will come out of the metaphor of Arthur Koestler's novel *Thieves in the Night* (cf. Kanafani) and step out of his exile and nomadic life into the future paradox of those *atlal* "whose resolution needs a war to be resolved". This is how, in his novels, Khoury develops a language that operates at the centre of contradictions, based on deconstructing official and mythic discourses. This newly-created language inflames our consciousness and amplifies the voice of the marginalized, re-telling the history of the silenced who are confounded by the challenges posed by their mode of existence.

Narrative strategies

In his texts, Khoury avoids using the voice of the omniscient narrator who dominates the entire space and is in control of its chronological progress, and of describing the characters and their inner conflicts. In Khoury's novels, the implied narrator – à la Wayne Booth – is always one that uses the first person. We do not mean here the monotonous, repetitive tones of a single self-absorbed "I", but rather an open or focalized angle of view – akin to a shoulder-borne 8mm camera – which presents to us views from multiple angles, as different narrators pass on the lens to each other. The changes in narrative voice and pronouns necessitate changes in the levels of narrative and the points of view, which open up to one another like reflecting mirrors. This makes the narration of plot events jumbled, as dialogues overlap and intersect, and the standard process of description is absent. Therefore, the plot is repeatedly reproduced through different possibilities for the outcome of any set of actions, and we have a set of secondary discourses that coexist with each other, helping to complete the structure of the novel's textual space. The textual space is divided up through the cinematic technique of montage, which fragments and chronologically jumbles the tale so that it no longer progresses in a straight line. Repetitions, backstories, recalls, flashbacks and flashforwards all lead to intensifying time in the text, which varies between actual historical time, the time of the narration and the psychological time experienced by the characters.

We can deduce here that the nature of Khoury's experimental language, which is based on deconstruction, fragmented sentences, the use of a blank, matter-of-fact tone, the oral cadence of unrefined speech, and the coupling of standard literary Arabic with the spoken dialects of the Levant is not something contrived, or mere playing with the visual form of language. Rather, it is the natural outcome of a storytelling that is built through the juxtaposition and overlapping of the focal points of speech.

Another element worth nothing among Khoury's textual strategies is his outstanding ability to create characters that are suited to storytelling, making his novels lyric dialogues par excellence. By avoiding direct description and not using the omniscient narrator, he avoids creating ready-made, pre-packaged characters; his characters are complex, multifaceted and formed completely only with the resolution of the story they are in. And given that these are realistic characters who seem to spring from the real world, with universal, humanist dimensions, they possess an ability to linger on in the minds of the reader-receptor. Perhaps Khoury's talent for creating iconic imagery and constructing symbols that have universal significance – Christ, Mar Elias, *L'Etranger*, Palestine as a universal metaphor – is what gives his characters a life of their own outside of the text of the novel.

This leads us to our last item in these remarks: the historical and geographical space that Elias Khoury's novels are so firmly rooted in. His novels take us back to pivotal events in the history of the Middle East, such as the violence that engulfed Lebanon from the 1840s through to the 1860s and extended as far as Damascus, and the ethnic cleansing of Armenians and Assyrians in the early 20th century. These two major events reshaped the Bilad al-Sham, or the Levant, through the violence, death, mass uprooting and forced migration that they engendered. Then came the assault of the Zionist settlement, driven by the ideology of a mythical narrative, to uproot the Palestinian people through slaughter and expulsion from their lands and complete the circle of death by founding a 'kingdom of strangers' (to use the title of one of Khoury's novels) on top of the ruins of the Levant. And indeed, Khoury's novels give voice to these strangers and those dead, to let them tell us, from their own spaces, those stories that history paid no heed to.

The crucial observation here is that it was the Lebanese civil war that led to the true birth of the Lebanese novel. And Khoury himself does not look at the civil war in isolation from the dialectics of historical progress since the mid-nineteenth century, and the founding of the autocratic model of the Arab nation-state. He calls this model the New Mamluks, since our history is the direct outcome of the Mamluk dynasty, and the questions posed about the Lebanese civil war begin from there. Wars have no victors, his work seems to say; we are all losers in war. We are all killed in them and are all strangers; to be alienated is what it means to be human. And at the heart of the existential questions raised by Khoury's texts is Palestine, beset by bloodshed, political debauchery and betrayal. In them, Palestine becomes the central question, an issue that can fuse together all peoples and all strangers in their search for meaning, freedom and human dignity.

Elias Khoury stands apart from the other writers of his generation, and can truly be counted among the great names in Arabic literature. His engagement with novels from all over the world, and strategies that might be construed as 'postcolonial' in nature, also makes him a luminary among the novelists of world literature.

Translated by Suneela Mubayi

ABDO WAZEN

Elias Khoury and the Lebanese Civil War

Novelist Elias Khoury is deemed a trailblazer in the writing of the Lebanese war novel, as well as a pioneer of what might be termed the Lebanese novel's 'second beginning'. The pre-civil war novel was the province of a mere handful of writers, foremost among them the late Tawfiq Yusuf Awwad and Yusuf Habashi al-Ashqar. Awwad anticipated the war's outbreak in his celebrated novel *Tawahin Bayrut* (1972, *Death in Beirut*, 1976), while al-Ashqar foresaw the period of change that would accompany the war in his equally celebrated 1971 novel *La Tanbut Judhur fi al-Samaa'* (Roots Don't Grow in the Sky). Not long after Lebanon's civil war erupted in 1975, the features of an entirely new Lebanese novel began forming on the horizon. This 'new' novel took as its starting point the realities and contradictions of the war and the thorny questions it raised on the intellectual, ideological and sectarian levels.

Elias Khoury, who fought on the side of the Leftist front that sought to change the sectarian, classist and tribal system and defend the Palestinian cause, appears to have been the first to take up the writing of war literature and, more specifically, the war novel. Based on narrative sequence, Khoury's novel *Little Mountain* was the first building block in the foundation of the new novel. This was followed by a succession of novels by Khoury and other writers, both veteran and emerging, for whose work the war provided the impetus, the raw material, and the temporal and spatial setting.

A number of Khoury's works have been viewed as particularly significant for the way in which they reread the war's tragedies, contradictions and absurdities, while drawing on the battlefield for their characters and events. Among these pioneering novels are *White Masks* (1981), *The Journey of Little Gandhi* (1989), *The Kingdom of Strangers* (1993), *Majma' al-Asrar* (1994, Complex of Secrets), and

Yalo (2002), which marked one of the all-time high points of Lebanese war literature.

In *The Journey of Little Gandhi*, the individual unconscious overlaps with the collective unconscious, such that the individual who lives (or dies) on the fringes of society becomes the image of a group which itself lives a marginalized existence. For the group is a set of scattered individuals who fail to realize the ties of unity that bind them, and who make no attempt to interpret their encounters, be they momentary or enduring. The individual has a profound sense of his 'individuality' or 'aloneness,' which is the ideological (or, perhaps, the metaphysical) face of the loneliness which he suffers within the community. Individuals only encounter one another via their differences, where difference is the hidden essence of the movement of separation which causes the individual to be anxious in a locale whose parts do not hold together. It will thus come as no surprise that 'place' in Elias Khoury's novel becomes a kind of mosaic which is in constant danger of disintegrating. The city of Beirut is the more refined exemplar of the jolting and scattering of place, and the ideal expression of the mosaic-like nature of an entire homeland.

Elias Khoury records "little Gandhi's" life story as told by Gandhi to Alice, and as told by Alice to the writer – the narrator – as though the narrative were a missing link within other missing links. The life story of Gandhi the shoe shiner is, above all, the life story of the city, which becomes apparent through the eyes of Gandhi and his simple, inconsequential relationships. Alice's memory, which recovers the threads of stories, events and faces, appears to be part of the city's lost memory. Thus, if Alice's memory has been scattered and has lost a clear sense of time, this is because Beirut's memory has likewise been scattered, having lost the ability to recover the past with its fragmented images and features. Relying as it does on Alice's memory, which is threatened with failure and oblivion, the novel is the narrative of "lost memory", as Khoury has stated in more than one context.

Not surprisingly, then, the novel's structure is scattered among memories, as images fly every which way in the storm that has blown up over the city and left it in ruins. Even so, when the writer steps back from Alice's account, he weaves a narrative fabric which, despite its torn appearance, is nevertheless cohesive. The memories which are not joined by a single temporal context, but which overlap and evoke one another via a state of temporal chaos emerging from the depths of oblivion, quickly coalesce into a single semantic context which transcends its narrow temporality into a broader psychic-existential time. This broader, psychic-existential time is the time of the lost characters, the time of Beirut, which may never have been anything but the illusion of a city. After all, Beirut is "a city without a history", Alice admits. Through Gandhi's story and the relationships that connected him to the other characters who surrounded him during a certain period of time, the writer attempts to create a history for the city whose history is being lost.

So Beirut, then, misses a single specified time, and drowns in an ambiguity of times, with history repeating itself, and one decade blurring into another. Time quickly loses its logic, alternately closing and opening, slowing down and speeding up, advancing and retreating as dictated by the act of remembrance and the presence of memory with its countless dimensions. This is the Beirut of varied faces, the Beirut of night and day, the Beirut of sects, the Beirut of obsessions and successive wars, the Beirut of the East-West mosaic, a refuge for misfits, and for big ideas that clash to infinity.

Characters and faces multiply as though they were phantoms peering out from the darkness of memory, and when memories emerge from the inner darkness, they are naturally disposed to be hazy and ambiguous, causing actual places to appear illusory, imbuing events with an air of mystery, and rendering faces little more than dimly lit silhouettes. Gandhi's character, however, remains central – albeit counterbalanced by that of Alice, who embodies a second axis which overlaps with Gandhi's.

At times Gandhi's life appears to be a muddled expression of that of Alice, who recounts his story mingled with her own, yet with neither of the stories completing the other. Different as they are, the two stories are both important parts of the city's history. The numerous characters that emerge, develop, and fade on the margin of Gandhi's story are quite interesting: at once realistic and bizarre, typical and atypical, clinging to the city's reality even while distancing themselves from it. Corrupt, backward and hackneyed, however pristine they appear at times, they live through the city's transformations and suffer from both inward alienation and genuine exile. Some of them are rooted in the geographical spot, while others have no roots. Characters, or ghosts of characters with nebulous features, appear and disappear like the stuff of dreams or – rather – of nightmares. Given the feverish rush that permeates the novel, and the vertigo that afflicts the "investigation", it would have been possible to invent other characters, any characters, and to have made them say anything.

Were we to pause before little Gandhi's story as narrated by him, by Alice, and by the writer, we would find that it is nothing but the dull story of a dull man who exhibited no heroic qualities. Rather, he was an insignificant person, defeated, who recalled nothing of his absent past apart from a few scattered images and who, during the last phase of his life, worked as a shoe shiner at the gates to the American University of Beirut. If the novel's opening scene is that of Gandhi's bullet-ridden corpse during the 1982 Israeli invasion, this is because his death embodies that of the witness who has seen everything in utter silence. Alice has pronounced him dead and, bullets filling the air, has covered his body with newspapers. The narrator assumes that before dying as a martyr for a cause that mattered little to him and that he hardly understood, Gandhi "had opened his eyes and seen nothing", and that "he didn't know anymore whether he was seeing, or dreaming". While Beirut was under siege, little Gandhi had nearly lost his memory. The narrator tells us that "all he remembered about the days of the blockade was that he had forgotten everything". In fact, "he'd begun forgetting everybody's name", as though in anticipation of his gruesome death. He kept saying that "all it means to live anymore is to be waiting to die", and at the moment of his passing, Gandhi knew that "the bullets weren't aimed at him. Rather, they were aimed at the heart of a city that had destroyed itself."

As the narrator reminds us, Gandhi had witnessed Beirut's day-by-day destruction. In fact, he had sensed it deep down before it actually happened, intuiting the gloomy end that threatens all things.

Translated by Nancy Roberts

SAIF AL-RAHBI

Testament on the Lebanese Civil War

Elias Khoury's path as a writer has steered clear of the familiar conventions and landscape of the Arabic novel. His journey has been one of experimentation and discovery in search of new territory for the language and stylistics of the novel. He is one who makes use of new avenues of expression for the devastation that trampled Lebanese life.

Such devastation had to inspire its own unique and powerfully expressive language with which to speak about this country that was rippling to the rhythm of crime and murder. A place too complex and ambiguous for any literary work, discourse, or solution to deal with naively and simplistically.

In novels and short stories, Elias Khoury has shaped landmarks on the path of Arabic prose. From his first novel, *'An 'ilaqat al-da'ira* (On the Interrelations of the Circle), the features of his writing begin to take shape. He transforms reality into a nightmarish tunnel and sifts the moral values of extreme and crass oppression. This nightmare reality is not given expression as deadpan narrative, but is transformed into the very fabric of the work, its overarching and ambiguous structure. Khoury creates what might be called "the language of nightmares" without falling into a Kafkaesque trap, as some Arab authors have. The language of nightmares, with its difficult inflections and an imagination freed of prior models of form, reaches its peak in the novel *City Gates*. Here we encounter the destruction of the civil war and the shredding of dreams and intellectual and political standards that were stable and carefree before the disaster struck. In this setting, it is as if the hero of the novel is sleepwalking or afloat in a mythic sea.

City Gates expressed the obliteration of dreams and the alienation of people in the face of a war that no one chose but were pushed into as if by mysterious accident. Dozens of novels about Lebanon have been written in a spirit of analytical certainty, whereas *City Gates* gives no clear indication of time or place, as if Elias Khoury has created a new myth of human killing. In this painting-like novel, the author shatters language. His sentences are often incomplete stammered articulations, but in their combined weight they say much about the obsessions of the nameless hero, racing in the wastes of the soul.

In the structural features of his novel *White Masks* we read a different style of writing. This time destruction is recounted in its everyday details, in a language without linguistic abstraction or mythologizing. This stifling of language makes room here for the heroism of destruction, which speaks through characters Khoury has drawn from the experience of the Lebanese civil war. These characters reveal their inner lives from multiple reflections and perspectives in a language that eschews conventional rhetoric and is more like journalese. "People these days have more important things

Abwab al-Madina (City Gates) and al-Wujuh al-Bayda' (White Masks)

to do than read stories or listen to tales. And they are absolutely right. But this story really did happen. The truth is that it did not happen just like that. One morning, I saw in the paper a short piece entitled 'Dreadful murder in UNESCO district' and, don't ask me why, but whenever I see the word dreadful the word 'wonderful' springs to mind. So the phrase stuck in my mind like this: 'Wonderful murder in UNESCO'."

This wonderful dreadful crime is the murder of Mr Khalil Ahmad Jaber in mysterious circumstances that appear to create a detective story, but the novel remains open to various possibilities and has no conclusive ending. The structure of the novel is also far removed from that of a police procedural.

White Masks comprises a harsh indictment of the civil war period. It is crammed with every social and political type and level thrown together in a bloody hall of mirrors as they try to conceal their secrets. The horrors of the war are exposed as it violates people's humanity in a bloody quagmire that only leads to mutilation, destruction, and sadism. The war, here, produced degenerate values, not the "purification of peoples" as claimed by the abstractions of those spectating from calmer shores. In this way, Elias Khoury gave his testimony on the events and sides in the war. After the investigation and trial of the criminal circumstances of the war, represented by the murder of Mr Khalil Ahmad Jaber, the reader does not reach a conclusion, only painful objective truth.

White Masks reveals the defeat of all by a dark destiny and the explosion of a centre of hostility in the human soul. Destruction remains the only master, the only honest voice.

Barricades for fighters on the streets of Beirut

AIDA FAHMAWI WATAD

"Literature above History": Elias Khoury as the moral intellectual in the *Children of the Ghetto* trilogy

Elias Khoury and the linguistic excavation project

In a perfect world, truth and justice would go hand-in-hand and literature would be composed for purely aesthetic reasons. However, in a world of chaos, violence, fighting and oppression, the equation no longer holds, and the relativity of truth stands helpless before the immutability of justice. What can language do in this situation? The first two parts of Khoury's *Children of the Ghetto* trilogy, *My Name Is Adam* (2016) and *Stella Maris* (2019), prove that it can indeed do quite a lot.

The more we apply ourselves to peeling off the layers of *Children of the Ghetto*, the clearer we see the ingenious way in which Khoury constructed his trilogy. Its multiple layers (narrative, meta-literary, linguistic-philosophical, documentary, intellectual and prophetic) shift it away from the traditional genre of the novel.

Khoury delves into the essence of language and maintains a dialogue with both truth and justice from a literary perspective. In *Stella Maris* he writes – "the literary text is your home". He exam-

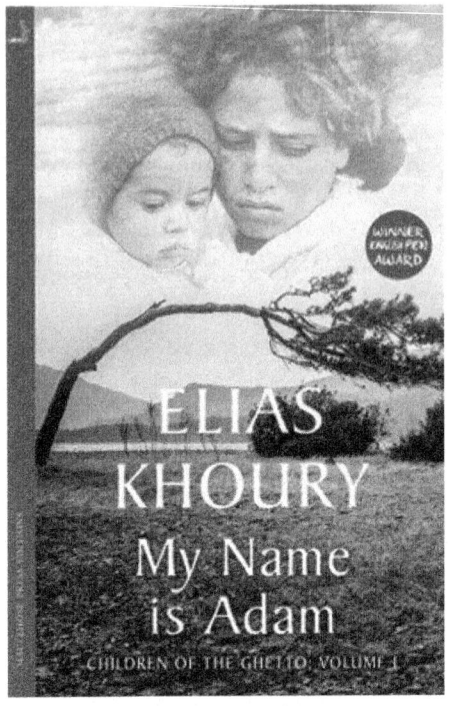

ines the relationship between language and silence, and literature's ability to face the erasure of one's humanity, identity and memory. In this way he becomes "a student of literature, one who makes literature his memory".

Khoury's project in the trilogy is based on the idea that "literature is the record of the fearful" – the worn out, the marginalised – and that "language illuminates the spirit". Here the author is transformed into an intellectual who, in addition to writing for aesthetic effect, also writes in the spirit of morality. Khoury digs for unrestored stories, which deviate from history in the sense of a chronicle of the victors/heroes, and from the canonical novel.

In the first two parts of *Children of the Ghetto*, the protagonist Adam Dannoun documents both his own story and those of others. Adam is a Palestinian, born in the ghetto of Lydda in the year of the Nakba. He flees from the trauma of the Nakba and the home of his mother Manal and her harsh husband and seeks refuge in forgetfulness, concealing both his Palestinian identity and his tragedy to this end. He visits Warsaw, hiding behind this attempt to forget and to become assimilated into the new Israeli society, where he constantly finds himself face-to-face with memory/truth. The truth transforms Adam Dannoun into the Scheherezade of the Nakba; a narrator of its stories from Lydda to Haifa to Jaffa, to his final place of exile: New York.

When Ma'moun "the blind", his friend and former teacher whom he considers his spiritual mentor, tells him that Manal is not his mother, and that his father is not a martyr, but that it was he, Ma'moun, who found him lying over the body of his dead mother under an olive tree during the Nakba, Adam decides to become a writer and emerge from his shell. He drags out with him all the silent stories of the Nakba; stories he had stored away for forty years. His decision to put the stories in writing matured in the first part, *My Name Is Adam*, as a defence mechanism against three forms of linguistic impotence: rage, forgetfulness and silence. Taken together, the first two parts of *Children of the Ghetto* confront two profound questions concerning the role of writing with respect to justice and truth: who writes history? Who writes literature?

Language in the face of justice and truth in *Stella Maris*

The second part of *Children of the Ghetto* follows a historical line through which three tragedies pass, each different and each with its own victims and executioners, but all centered on the Palestinian Nakba, accompanied by the Holocaust and the tragedy of the Arab Jews who were forcefully evicted from their homes and sent to the "promised land". Khoury uses these tragedies to bring to light the moral choices made by nations to create the present and the future. Khoury uses real testimonies which he heard, read or witnessed in person, and grounds them in an appropriate aesthetic context in order to conjure ideological dialogues which break through the genre of the novel, transforming this work into "an attempt to stand up to literature, rather than being a work of literature".

1. The Holocaust:
"Linguistic nudity and the death of civilization"

Adam Dannoun the Palestinian visits Warsaw and is confronted with "man's bestiality, which leads to . . . a divestment from language". His language becomes disconnected and he comes to identify with the victims' silence, "because sacrifice announces its last protest by giving up on speech". Adam evokes Heidegger's linguistic philosophy and his concept of "speaking nonsense" when he says: "when the one who is murdered is silent, the murderer's language becomes meaningless babble".

Accompanied by his teacher Prof. Yaqoub, Adam meets Marek Edelman (1919-2009). The author uses Edelman, a real historical figure and unsung hero, to represent the moral stance of a certain group of Holocaust survivors – those who chose to stand up to the historical trend and refused to emigrate to Israel. Edelman is quoted in the novel as saying: "To emigrate? To leave my homeland? Warsaw is my city, where I learned Polish, Yiddish and German . . . and learned that a man should care for others. Here I was slapped because I was a Jew . . . I will remain here and die here, because someone has to stay at the side of those who have disappeared".

However, when Prof. Yaqoub discovers that Adam is a Palestinian he accuses him of lying. Yet Adam confronts him with the truth: "There were ghettos in Lydda, Ramla, Haifa and Jaffa, surrounded by barbed wire. But you put Palestinians in them, not Jews . . . the barbed wire still stabs my eye. I came to the university in order to grow, but you insist on reminding me of the truth . . . You don't want the truth, but try to falsify it". Here is a dialogue which embodies the cry of those who live in fear, which can be falsified or ignored by so-called 'intellectuals' – and by history.

2. "The captives" and language implantation: The Arab Jews

The second tragedy which has received scant attention in Arabic and Hebrew literature is that of the Arab Jews who were sent to Israel when the state was established. This tragedy is exemplified in the story of Haskil, the Iraqi Jewish writer. In the latter's conversations with Adam, we experience his grief and sense of alienation. In his words: "I am an Iraqi who lives in exile." The story also reveals the fact that Arab Jews were forced to emigrate to Israel, and tells of the grand conspiracy that led to their having to abandon their respective homelands, as Haskil says to Adam: "I don't like to use the words 'ascent' (Hebrew *aliyah*) and 'descent' (Hebrew *yerida*) . . . I was forced to come and lost the ability to return to my country."

The existential identity crisis experienced by Haskil, former Iraqi and now Arab Jew, is highlighted by the fact that he does not consider himself a citizen: "We are prisoners, which means that you find yourself stuck in a *ma'abara* (immigrant camp) . . . your feet in the mud and your head bowed." He also suffers from linguistic alienation: "The hardest thing is that you forget your language. Here I had to forget my language . . . Tamar is the one who helped me in the painful language implant operation that I carried out on myself."

Yet Haskil does shed his Arab identity to a certain extent. He decides not to use Arabic for his first novel, in which he narrates his travails. To Adam he makes the ironic statement that "If the Jewish identity is defined by exile in the existential sense, then you are its true heirs", reminding us of Edward Said's famous statement: "I am the last Jewish intellectual."

3. "The present absentees": Adam Dannoun/Elias Khoury as the Scheherazade of the Nakba

The implicit author asks: "How will the absentees write? Can someone who is absent tell his story?". Here Khoury touches on the harshest of the Israeli laws aimed at erasing the Palestinian presence. He says, through Adam, that "the Israeli legislator who came up with the term 'present absentee' was a genius, because he surpassed the imagination of all playwrights of the absurd and transformed the name of an entire nation into a title for the absurd".

Palestinian refugees during the Nakba

In this novel Khoury succeeds in turning the linguistic equation upside down by his powerful evocation of the 'present absentees' through language. The stories begin with the victim's silence and end with attempts to silence the victims. For the "desired" Palestinian is either one who is silent ("We were all silent with respect to the *khawaja* ['sir']. You are the only one permitted to speak, because the *khawaja* wants you to become a Jew like them"); or "good", as an Israeli author says in the novel – "I want a different protagonist, a polite one, who does not speak with such arrogance".

On the other hand, the Palestinians are aware of their silence, as Abu Ghassan says: "Do you know why we're a silent people? Because our speech lacks a land to receive it. Without a land there is no speech". Perhaps that is why the implicit author asks, with respect to the bloody stories of the people of Umm al-Zayyinat, Sablan and Haifa: "How will Adam tell the story . . . the Israelis prevent us from burying our dead in our cemeteries? Why don't we build a large grave . . . that we'll call the grave of stories and put in it all the stories of Palestine and cover it with the soil of our words?". Yet Khoury does not bury the stories; rather, he revives them through his writing.

***

In conclusion, although the Nakba is the story, "the narrator cannot narrate the story sincerely as long as he does not take us to the stories that lie behind his stories". For the Nakba is not only a Palestinian story, but must "incorporate the story of those who have occupied their land and driven them out in their own story. Their story is not enough for us, but our story is enough for us, for them and for everyone."

Khoury attempts to mould the story of history, not to write it. By declaring that when victims do not adhere to their ethics they may become criminals themselves, he shatters the ideological pretensions of the perpetrators of these tragedies. Elias Khoury, the great writer and moral intellectual, who has left his distinguished mark on the literature of the Nakba, uses the essence of language to preserve the human spirit: "When truth meets art, we shall be able to express human experience." Only then can "literature above history" be realised.

YEHOUDA SHENHAV-SHAHRABANI

Swapping Geographies, Mixing Languages:
The Hebrew-Speaking Universe of Khoury's Palestinian Novels

Elias Khoury is possibly the most prominent of modern Arab authors who, within the Arab world, plays a major role in the tradition of the post-Mahfouzian novel, as Edward Said has once coined it. In this essay, I turn the spotlight on an additional layer of his creative writing which, hitherto, has been absent from discussions of his oeuvre. Khoury essentially invented a unique literary space-time continuum in which languages mix along spatial and temporal planes – a universe best observed in the Hebrew translation of his Palestinian novels.

Khoury has published fourteen novels to date; five of which I have had the privilege of translating to Hebrew; three novels in the context of the Lebanese Civil War: *White Masks* (1981), *The Journey of Little Gandhi* (1989), and *Majma' al-Asrar* (1994, Complex of Secrets); and two in the context of the Palestinian Nakba: *Children of the Ghetto 1*, *My Name is Adam* (2016) and *Stella Maris (Children of the Ghetto 2: Najmat al-Bahr*, 2019, Beirut). Albeit artificial, the distinction between the Lebanese and Palestinian novels is pivotal to restoring Khoury's unique fictional universe in this essay.

In the Lebanese novels, Khoury holds a broken mirror to a society's face on the verge of collapse. Typically, he recounts the horrors of the civil war via stories from the peripheries recalling mangled bodies, streets in ruin, and endless bloodshed in battle-worn Beirut. In his Palestinian novels, Khoury shifts his attention to Palestine and again, uses fragmented stories and memories of the Nakba, whether it be 1948, or the still-ongoing cycle of violence. His narratives are based on the stories of random individuals with firsthand experience of the horrors, or ones who have heard those harrowing accounts. The narration is anchored in repetition, as if the narrator needed it as reiterated proof of the inconceivable or were unable to tell a coherent story.[1] Indeed, Khoury believes that the writer is a key witness to their era; a position evident in all his novels.

That said, there is a crucial difference between the Lebanese and Palestinian novels. In the former, Khoury writes about his own society whilst in the latter, he delves into an ostensibly foreign space. For the translator, this holds every bit as true – only in reverse. In the Lebanese texts, the narrative is typically set in a very much alien world into which the Hebrew translator must dive, immersing themself in the culture, historical context, geography, and various local dialects. In the Palestinian novels, the story takes place in the Hebrew translator's native geography, culture and sometimes, even own language as the narratives are often anchored in Hebrew literature and culture, including whole portions in Hebrew. This inverse scenario creates a universe far less noticeable when these novels are translated to other languages. In such a universe, Khoury is not only an author but also a translator from Hebrew or, imagined Hebrew to Arabic. In his writing, he employs a variety of experimental literary devices, styles and narrative forms that present a head-on challenge to Derrida's concerns about writing and translation.

In *Des tours de Babel*, Derrida acknowledges the limits of conventional translation theory that deals with transitions between two languages, while failing to employ language simultaneity. How to write, and translate a text that mixes several languages, and how to render the effect of plurality?

«Comment traduire un texte écrit en plusieurs langues à la fois? Comment «rendre» l'effet de pluralité? Et si l'on traduit par plusieurs langues à la fois, appellera-t-on cela traduire?»[2]

Derrida also urges the readers to vocally engage in the prospect of one writing about language in general, and about the language of translation in particular:

«On ne devrait jamais passer sous silence la question de la langue dans laquelle se pose la question de la langue et se traduit un discours sur la traduction.»[3]

Using Khoury's latest novel, *Stella Maris*, I show how he tackles these very concerns. The novel presents a simultaneous plurality of languages, showcasing literary techniques that challenge the limitations of language while exploring a unique discourse on translation. This particular Hebrew translation further stands out seeing as how I had translated the novels whilst in Haifa, where the majority of chapters are set. This offers a unique and otherwise rare reading and translation journey, certainly when one is translating Khoury's Lebanese novels into Hebrew. It places the author within the Israeli sphere and like an anthropologist, he translates the fictional experiences and stories that allegedly take place in Hebrew for his Arab-speaking readers. As Khoury's writing simulates a translation, one wonders: how are we to treat a translation of a translation?

Stella Maris follows on from *My Name is Adam*, the first volume of the trilogy *Children of the Ghetto*. Each is made up of multiple layers of space and time, entwined with the history and biography of Adam

l to r: Hebrew editions of White Masks, The Journey of Little Gandhi, *and* Complex of Secrets

Dannoun. *My Name is Adam* tackles Adam's early childhood and autumn years; however, it omits the main chunk of his biography. *Stella Maris,* meanwhile, is Adam's coming-of-age story which seeks to fill in that blank. The story, for the most part, is set in 1960s Haifa, featuring scenes of Haifa life, exposing all forms of trickery employed in Haifa-themed literature, and chronicling the interplay of identities of a young Palestinian living in the Jewish state.

The Mixing of Languages

If the text is to realize its full potential, it must free itself from the vice of monoglot readers who cement the language barrier. It must deal with the dynamic between the two languages simultaneously as opposed to separately. This simultaneity challenges the ideology of a so-called language hierarchy. Defying the notion of diglossia, Khoury mixes (literary and spoken) languages, producing a script that is a blend of both without ever decidedly committing to either. Khoury highlights the fluid nature of language in his polyglot writing:

"The moment you enter a language, you enter with your other language. Languages are open, and in any language, there are layers of another language. When I speak Arabic, when I think in Arabic, using the Lebanese or Palestinian dialect, I discover that I am also speaking Aramaic."[4]

Adam, the protagonist is also a polyglot who regularly mixes languages:

"She told me that that my speech had been slurred and that I'd talked without stopping and would jump from one subject to another, beginning in English, then switching into Arabic or into a mixture of Arabic and Hebrew, and drinking a lot of water."[5]

Khoury's Arabic text occasionally has a transliteration of spoken Hebrew. In one instance, Rabah, the guard at Benjamin Garden, turns to Adam in Hebrew and asks him if he is a Jew: "Atta Yehudim?" In another chapter, Adam tells Rivka in Hebrew that he loves her: "Ani Ohev Otach".[7] Similar examples occur in *My Name is Adam* when a soldier yells at Palestinians who are trying to approach the Ghetto fence: *"Tahzor le-ahor! Asur!"* meaning, "Step back, it's forbidden".[8]

Khoury all the while must provide interpretation to his non-Hebrew-speaking Arab readership. Here is one typical technique from *My Name is Adam*:

> He pointed, laughing, at the people huddled together at the corner of the square and said in Hebrew, "*Khavasim, kmo khavasim!*"
> "What's he saying?" Manal asked the doctor, who was standing next to her.
> "He's just jabbering in Hebrew," Dr Samara said.
> "He's saying we're like sheep," said Mufid Shahada, who'd learned Hebrew from working at the nearby Ben Shemen colony.[9]

When speaking Hebrew, the author occasionally uses Arabic rather than Hebrew idioms, highlighting the many differences between the two. For example, when a soldier says, "Assa batach-tonim!" ("He peed his underpants,") in Hebrew the phrase reads, "went in his pants." ("Assa bamikhnasayim!"). Is this a mere hiccup or rather, a more conscious choice? In the English translation, Humphrey Davies settled this by simply opting for "He's pissed himself!"[10]

Khoury writes through translation and therefore, the translation to Hebrew presents a fascinating role reversal where the original approximates the site of the translation.

The Language of Language

The idiosyncrasies of Khoury's works are heightened by his deep foray into language. The intense preoccupation with language and even more so, language's language (meta-language) paves a long-winded road littered with linguistic, semantic and discursive hurdles that make Hebrew-reading of the Palestinian novels all the more challenging. Every so often, Khoury will turn to meta-linguistic chapters that demarcate how words, grammar and syntax all fall short of signification and therefore, require additional literary illustration.

In *Stella Maris*, the chapter, "The Lovers of Haifa" features an alternate world to A.B. Yehoshua's *The Lover*. In a carnivalesque manner, Khoury inverts signs, representations and names, flipping them on their heads in a polyphonic game of timelines and roles. Palestinian worker, Naim, who can recite Israel's poet laureate, Bialik's *In the City of Slaughter*, becomes Adam who is studying Hebrew Literature;

l to r: Hebrew editions of My Name is Adam *and* Stella Maris

Adam who owns the Jewish-run garage turns into Gabriel, whilst Gabriel himself who owns the vintage Morris car becomes Hebrew author Menachem Zecharia who is at the garage looking for an Arab informant so that he could start work on his novel. In this literary exercise, Khoury not only reconceives *The Lover*'s garage scene but, in his play on timelines, is also ahead of the narrating time, relocating the scene to the early 1960s when Yehoshua was writing *Facing the Forests* where for the first time the Palestinian's muteness is put into words with stark coherence.

Here, the mute character in *Stella Maris* takes Hebrew literature to task quite corporeally, for describing his tongue as having been 'cut out':

> "No! No!" the mute man cried out, shaking his head right and left as he stuck out a long tongue in evidence that no man had in fact severed his tongue.[11]

Khoury repeatedly reflects on local colonial reality, and on the ideological and power implications of its linguistic hierarchy. By that time, Arabic had gradually been erased from the public sphere and less than 2% of Israeli Jews could read or converse in Arabic. The colonial hierarchy that emerged in Israel/Palestine assumes an artificial diglossia between the languages whereby Hebrew is assigned as major and Arabic, minor. In the following example, Hebrew functions as the primary language of the state, thus putting Palestinians at a disadvantage; a reality which culminated in the fatal shooting of an elderly Palestinian man. Supposedly inspired by true events in the village of Saʻsaʻ, a Jewish soldier pointed his weapon at an old Palestinian man who was asking, "Eish hadha?". The Jewish soldier then answered, "Hadha esh!" and shot him. These expressions, though phonetically similar, illustrate the so-called French faux-ami, meaning fake friends. The storyteller explains the source of this bilingual collision:

"Son of a bitch. Fire, 'esh' in Hebrew, is shooting. The poor man asked "Eish", 'what', and they cut him off with fire. This bitch played with the words and the blood".[12]

Discourse about Translation

Khoury also makes sure to reverse the hierarchy, creating translation chapters in which Arabic is the major language and Hebrew, the minor one. For instance, when Adam professes his love for Rivka, he quotes a love poem by the Arab poet Al-Hallaj: "lam yazidni al-ward ila ʻatashan".[13] Adam struggles to translate the line and when failing to find an appropriate Hebrew equivalent, he resolves to abandon the poem's translation altogether and consequently, also his Hebrew readers' prospects of ever understanding it. Should the translator then have translated the poem to Hebrew after all, or were they right to have left it in its Arabic version, as unintelligible to the monoglot readers as it was to Rivka? Here, I opted to leave the poem in its Arabic version transliterated into Hebrew without any translation, whilst acknowledging this choice with a note in the text.

Later, Adam lists to his girlfriend, Dalia, twenty dictionary synonyms for the word "love" – Hawa, mahabba, sababa, huyam, shawq, etc. These are in fact the result of a translative act within language itself. An attempt to endow each of these words with meaning via the dictionary results in a semantic "dictionary loop" where there is no overlap between the words in either language. As the words also do not follow any form of hierarchy in Hebrew or Arabic, or within their own respective language even, the translation task is rendered all the more difficult. There is no way of breaking this cyclical pattern without taking some arbitrary decision, seeing as every choice leads to a simultaneous excess and lack. One's only remaining option is to therefore transliterate the Arabic words into Hebrew, and to decide on the go what their Hebrew markers would be.

"He translated to Dalia the twenty scenarios through which love passes, as described by the Arabs; however, he remained unsure as to the exact meaning of the words, for translating words of love to other languages is not possible, as love itself defies translation. He therefore decided arbitrarily whether the ' sababa' is the portal into the 'huyam,' and whether the 'huyam' is the peak of love, or if it is in fact the other way around."[14]

Ultimately, this multi-layered linguistic universe is embedded in the very art of translation and mandates a re-examination of one's loyalties to the national habitus and its lexicons, for the number of Hebrew synonyms for love at the translator's disposal pales in comparison to their Arabic equivalents. These semiotic and semantic collisions at times do result in a translation impasse that can only be resolved by addressing monoglot readers in one version and one language only.

To sum up, Khoury's linguistic universe undercuts conventional writing and translation for monoglot readers. This is because his writing is already a form of translation (real or imagined,) thereby making translations of his work a translation of translation. The reality of this will stump monoglot readers who expect a fluent, localized text articulated in a single, coherent and familiar language. In doing so, Khoury not only discusses the language that writing and translation are conducted in but also raises the prospect of bilingualism and, ultimately, proposes a political model of bi-nationalism in the space between the Jordan River and the Mediterranean.

Notes:
[1] Elias Khoury. (Arabic) *Lost Memory: Critical Studies*. Beirut: Dar al-Adab, 1982. pp72-76.
[2] Jacques Derrida, "Des tours de Babel," in Joseph F. Graham (ed.), *Difference in Translation*, Cornell University Press, 1987 (Appendix, p.215).
[3] ibid., p.209.
[4] Raef Zreik, Amnon Raz-Krakotzkin, and Yehouda Shenhav-Shahrabani, "Dialogue with Elias Khoury on literature and translation", *Journal of Levantine Studies*, Vol. 9 (1), 2019: 29.
[5] *Children of the Ghetto 1: My Name is Adam*, English version, p.99, trans: Humphrey Davies.
[6] *Awlad al-Ghetto 2: Najmat al-Bahr*, 2019, Beirut, p.48.   [7] ibid. p.140.
[8] *Children of the Ghetto 1: My Name is Adam*, English version, p. 245, trans: Humphrey Davies.
[9] ibid. p.203.   [10] ibid. p.204.
[11] *Awlad al-Ghetto 2: Najmat al-Bahr*, 2019, Beirut, p.102.
[12] ibid. p.328.   [13] ibid. p.128.   [14] ibid. p.429.

RAEF ZREIK

Writing and Guilt: Thoughts on Elias Khoury's Project

Does Elias Khoury feel a sense of guilt due to the fact that he is a writer – just a writer, playing with words? The Cambridge Dictionary defines guilt in the following manner: "A feeling of worry or unhappiness that you have because you have done something wrong, such as causing harm to another person."

This unhappiness comes, usually, along with self-reproach. But what is wrong with writing? And were I correct to say that he feels some guilt, then why would Khoury continue to write?

To begin with, let me qualify why it is that I believe that Khoury is wary of words, and feels some unease with the act of writing and with words. This is probably most evident in his novel, *Children of the Ghetto 1: My Name is Adam*. As readers of the novel know, the book opens with a so-called 'introduction', in which Khoury tells us that what we are going to read is the memoir of Adam, which he himself has received from one of his students, Sarang Lee. Sarang Lee obtained these notes from her friend Adam, who explicitly asked her not to publish them after his death. Readers of the novel are in fact presented with a text that was never meant to published or read. By deploying this trick Khoury distances himself by two degrees from the narrative. He is not the writer or the author, but merely a reader, just like us – and the text itself was meant to stay a secret.

This self-estrangement from words and writing continue throughout the book. Silence is portrayed as noble and sublime, compared to the redundancy of words. This begins with the noble image of Waddah, the lover-poet protagonist who goes to his own death in silence, without complaint or crying out. And Ma'moun, in his designated role as stepfather, is shrouded in silence as well. When Ma'moun meets Adam after years in New York and opens his mouth to tell a story, he reveals the secret that shatters Adam's life and self-image in its entirety: he is not the son of Hassan Dannoun as he believed, but rather, the identity of his parents is unknown and he was adopted. Khoury further assigns a sublime status to silence with his choice of simile to describe the beauty of Adam's Jewish lover Dalia: "She was as beautiful as silence"[1].

Elias Khoury

Furthermore, the breaking of silence emerges in the novel not only as a violence, but almost as a sin. When Adam meets Murad – the witness to the massacre in Lydda in 1948 – he refuses to speak. It is only after an interrogation almost akin to psychological torture that he opens up and speaks. Khoury portrays this interrogation through graphic images of violence. He describes it in these words:

"I did not stop posing questions. The man hardly spoke, his voice dived into the back of his throat, and he told the story as if he were suffocating. He looked at me as a drowning man crying for help, but I lost any mercy."

It is no small wonder that Adam feels reproach, almost guilt, for seducing Murad into speaking out and breaking the silence: "Maybe I should be angry at myself for writing down what Murad Al-Alamy has told me," he writes. "Maybe the tragedy should be kept wrapped in silence, for any talk about its details disturbs its noble silence."

SPECIAL FEATURE – ELIAS KHOURY

In several places within the novel, Khoury associates writing and words with death. Words are not the matter itself, but mere abstractions that allow us to capture a fleeting reality. Language, as an abstraction, is almost a form of treason against the particular, the concrete and the real. For this reason Adam remains wary of words and language in general. He is afraid of becoming a mere symbol, a formula, and for this reason he cries out: "I am not a pattern and my story cannot be reduced to anything else but my story, and I do not want to be a symbol."

No wonder, either, that words evoke images of death and emptiness. As Adam explains it: "I feel I am writing with an old dying language . . . language is not made of earth; it is the opposite of all dying creatures. The problem with language is its corpse, for it stays with us; we reject it but it returns in different shapes, and we find ourselves chewing its death in our mouths." This association of writing with death repeats itself at various points in the novel and takes different forms. At one point Adam revolts against writing itself, claiming: "I do not want to generalize and claim that all writing is a kind of death; still this is what I feel now", and on another occasion he associates the arts in general, not just writing, with death, claiming that "art weaves a shroud made of words and colors" and is a form of evasion of life, as for he describes writers as those who take cover behind words: "The woman hid her life between the dead, and I am hiding between the dead corpse of words".

Notably, this suspicion of language and words is not limited to this novel. Rather it is a recurrent theme across Khoury's literary output. Khoury is a hesitant writer that is always reluctant; writing while wondering whether writing is the correct response to life. In his magnum opus, *Gate of the Sun*, which tells the stories of Palestine and of Palestinians, he chooses to put the hero of the novel, Yunis, in a coma: totally silent. It is also the case that others, mainly Khaleel, who tells his story and their stories, position him as if he were the 'event' with the stories growing along the banks of his life. Yunis speaks, without saying a word.

Something similar occurs in Khoury's other novel, *Yalo*. Yalo is arrested, held in a prison cell, and ordered to write his confession. He writes and rewrites his confession time and again, but always feels that he needs to revise it and that there is something missing. After he drafts the final version he comes to discover that the police had already discovered the criminal gang they were looking for: in fact, nobody was awaiting his written confession at all. The words were in vain, gone to waste, and lagged behind.

Arguably the image of anti-writing is bluntest in Khoury's novel *White Masks*. Khalil, the father of Ahmad Jaber, who has met his death at the age of 25 as a *shahid* or martyr, locks himself in his room and falls silent. But the first thing he does on walking out again is to erase. He gathers up newspapers and begins to simply efface the news about the death of his son from newspapers, and when he is asked what he is doing his immediate answer is "I am working". He finds himself in a compulsive state of ongoing erasure of the past, through the erasure of words. This motif of deletion reaches its peak in the novel when Khalil tries to paint all the walls of the city white, obliterating all words and reclaiming the silence.

How might one view this dubious stance toward words, bordering on loathing and contempt at times? And how to make sense of the fact that despite this disdain for words, Khoury continues to write and write, words and more words, as though words were a destiny or a pre-ordained fate?

This abhorrence of words and speech is as old as words and speech themselves. Words assume language, and language is a regime of meanings, grammar and rules. It is a diktat of reason. But to reach transcendence one requires faith, not reason. As one must put limits to reason to make room for faith, one must put limits to words to make space for silence. In this way, silence becomes the key to the sacred. The assumption is that meaning is primordial to words and speech, it is out there, grows with events and actions, feeds on life and love, while words are a consumption of meaning: they drink from its well, running the risk of rendering it empty.

Shakespeare's King Lear knew this very well, but he knew this too late. When his daughter Cordelia was asked about her love for her father, she only replied: "What shall Cordelia speak? Love and be silent"[2]. As she explains later, "Since I am sure my love's more ponderous than my tongue".[3] In his 1953 tome *Scarlet and Black*, R.P. Malagrida expresses this distrust in words, by saying: "Speech was given to men to conceal their thoughts."[4] But probably the most well-known and brutal attack on writing came from Adorno, observing by the end of Second World War: "To write poetry after Auschwitz is barbaric. And this corrodes even the knowledge of why it became impossible to write poetry today."[5]

The paradox of writing, of writers writing against writing, using words against words, lies in part in the simple fact that language does a double work: it reveals and it conceals at the same time. Language cannot conceal thought – as Malagrida writes – unless it has the potential to reveal thought as well. The concealing factor is dependent on the revealing one, just as miscommunication is a parasitic blight on communication. And it is the nature of language that its consumption is tied to its production as well. Language poses a threat to meaning and still it is its existential condition. But if language departs from life it becomes lifeless itself.

This, then, is the fear that Khoury is fully aware of throughout all of his writing. He wants to capture life in his words and knows that life will always evade him, for it is perennially shrewd and recalcitrant. Thus the more he attempts to capture the pulse of life through language, through the novel, the more he feels that in fact he has moved further away from life: that there is more to be said. But we as a community of readers should be grateful for this ongoing persistence of failure on Khoury's part. This failure seduces him into making another attempt to bridge the gap: a gap that is by definition not bridgeable. He writes another novel, aware that he might be committing treason, but feels he must remain faithful to the ongoing attempt to overcome this kind of treason.

This awareness of the limits of writing in Khoury's consciousness is what makes his writing full of life – and his life full of writing.

Notes:
[1] Elias Khoury, *Children of the Ghetto: My Name is Adam*. All quotes, translated by me, are from the Arabic version, published by Dar Al-Adab, 2016, Beirut.
[2] William Shakespeare, *King Lear*, Penguin Books, 1994, 25.
[3] ibid, 25.
[4] R.P. Malagrida, *Scarlet and Black*, Penguin Books, 1953, 152.
[5] Theodor Adorno, *Cultural Criticism and Society*, Prisms (London: Neville Spearman, 1967), 34. Adorno, later on in his *Negative Dialectics*, offers a withdrawal or rather a reformulation of his statement: "Perennial suffering has as much right to expression as a tortured man has to scream; hence it may have been wrong to say that after Auschwitz you could no longer write poems. But it is not wrong to raise the less cultural question whether after Auschwitz you can go living – especially whether one who escaped by accident, one who by rights should have been killed, may go on living." *Negative Dialectics*, Continuum Books, New York, 1995, 363.

FAKHRI SALEH

Narratives of the Nakba and Holocaust or when Palestinian Adam tries to disguise himself as a Jew

In *My Name is Adam* and *Stella Maris*, the first two parts of his trilogy *Children of the Ghetto*, Elias Khoury attempts to relate the story of the Nakba in a manner often reminiscent of his novel, *Gate of the Sun* (1998). In this text, he charted the recent history of Palestine with a particular focus on the Nakba through to the Sabra and Shatila massacres of 1982. In *Gate of the Sun,* widely considered one of the great Arabic novels of the 21st century, Khoury re-appraises the meanings of history, memory, oblivion and love in light of the Palestinian tragedy, ongoing since the fall of Palestine and the establishment of the Hebrew state upon its ruins in 1948, which saw Israel take the place of Palestine and which scattered the majority of the Palestinian people to the four corners of the Earth.

Through the story of his chief protagonist Yunis El Asadi, Khoury shifts back and forth between the topography of the homeland and the Palestinian diaspora. Yunis regularly sneaks across the border from Lebanon, through barbed wires and in mortal danger, to meet with his wife Naheelah, who in turn bears him many children. He continues to do this for more than thirty years, during which the stormy love affair between the uprooted border infiltrator and his beloved who remained in Palestine transforms into a form of demographic resistance – and of incontestable proof of the ties between Palestine's interior and its exterior.

My Name is Adam and *Stella Maris* cannot be read in isolation from one another if we are to grasp the metaphor that Khoury is trying to cultivate. In both parts of his trilogy-in-progress, Khoury strives to understand the experience of those Palestinians who insisted on remaining behind after the Nakba and were thus turned into 'present absentees' on their own land. The implicit suggestion is that this act of resistance preserved Palestinian identity and a future for it, in spite of the ambiguities and contradictions that mark the existence of Palestinian citizens in Israel, and the extreme tensions between their dual identities on the stretch of land upon which the Zionist movement contrived to propagate its own narrative. This was achieved by claiming that the land was 'a land without people for a people without a land', by means of ethnic cleansing, and by means of cultural, historical and geographic erasure.

Through a simultaneous re-examination of the stories of the Lydda and Warsaw Ghettos, Khoury tries to draw parallels between Jewish-Israeli and Palestinian narratives: that is to say, between the Holocaust and Nakba narratives. The character of Adam Dannoun, born in 1948 during the Nakba, is desperate to rid himself of his Palestinian memory and transform himself into a Jew. To this end, he alters his name (willingly 'cleansing' himself of it) and resolves to study Hebrew language and literature (a form of cultural 'self-cleansing') in an attempt to free himself from the burdensome memory of the defeated. This memory is construed as an obstacle to their living in the present, reminding them that they are 'present-absentees' as classified by the Israeli state: present as holders of Israeli citizenship, absent in the sense of having no right to their expropriated land.

Adam is the son of Hassan Dannoun – a Palestinian fighter for the resistance faction *al-Jihad al-Muqaddas* who dies trying to defend the city of Lydda in 1948 during the massacre of its residents by the Zionist Palmach forces – and Manal, a Christian from the village of Ailaboun who falls in love with him. Hundreds of men, women and children were killed during this massacre, with many executed in cold blood after they took refuge in the Dahmash mosque. Adam goes to live in Haifa with his mother, who then marries another man, Abdallah al-Ashhal. He is one of the *mutasallilin,* or 'infiltrators', those refugees who manage to sneak back across the border from Lebanon into Palestine. Abdallah has lost his wife and two daughters during the Nakba and their consequent flight forms a subplot that again links this trilogy to *Gate of the Sun*, which was also based on the theme of 'infiltrators'. But due to the strict regime of control imposed by Israel on those Palestinians who managed to remain, which stripped them of their national identity and labelled them 'Arab-Israelis', Adam also subsequently elects to free himself of his original identity by altering his name to Adam Dannon and concocting a Jewish identity: one in which he is a survivor of the Warsaw Ghetto instead of the one in Lydda.

Like the pendulum of a clock, the narrative in *My Name is Adam* and *Stella Maris* swings between past and present to recount how Adam conceals himself in his newly-invented identity, but eventually discovers that the magic hat he has opted to wear is unable to fully conceal his true identity. Adam is a son of the Lydda ghetto, not the Warsaw one; he is the baby found fighting for his life at his dead mother's breast, discovered by chance by the blind protagonist Ma'moun under an olive tree and named Naji: survivor, as he survived the death of his parents during the Palestinian exodus in 1948.

Khoury himself takes up the mantle of narrator, and we read of Adam Dannoun through the character's written papers, received by the 'author' via Sarang Lee, his Korean student in New York. Khoury the 'author' then publishes them without modification, or so he claims. Although Adam purports not merely to be a symbol or allegory for Palestine, he does in the end stand as a metaphor for all those Palestinians who remained in their homeland: one that embodies the struggle for Palestine with its continual clashes over identity, history and human rights.

Through his novels, Khoury strives to demonstrate that it is impossible for the victim to completely take on the role of the executioner; or to borrow from Ibn Khaldun's terminology, for the conquered to imitate the victors. Or indeed, in the words of Frantz Fanon in *Black Skin, White Masks* (1967), for the colonized to don the mask of the colonizer. Nevertheless, the parallels that might be drawn between the narratives of the Jewish and Palestinian tragedies throw up uncertainties. The narrator comments and reflects on this, on occasion interrupting the plot to indicate that the symmetry between the two narratives could be construed as a justification for the victim to have turned into the executioner. This is arguably what happened: the former victim established ghettos for Palestinians akin to the Jewish ghettos in Europe, and carried out operations tantamount to genocide against the country's native inhabitants. However, on closer inspection this negative contradiction does not hold for long, especially in *Stella Maris* with depictions of Jewish suffering. The ghastly experience of the Holocaust is foregrounded through Adam's attempt to masquerade as a Jew, in order to unburden himself of his own Palestinian memory and its accompanying trauma and suffering out of a desire to let go and live in the present moment.

It is possible to understand Adam's attempts, which occur frequently over the pages of both novels, as him not wanting to be converted into a symbol – even as he tries to write a novel akin to an allegory for the post-1948 Palestinian condition. The novel speaks to the Palestinian desire to turn away from memory, to wipe the slate clean in the context of a new state that treats them as though they were invisible, no more than ghosts. In the language of postcolonial critics such as Homi Bhabha, resistance to being wiped out emerges in hybridity, in camouflage and in mimicking the colonizer. But in the Palestinian case, this defensive subaltern survival mechanism is contradicted by the fact that the Israeli occupation is one that tries to substitute an entire people with another. It is an occupation, characterized by ethnic and cultural cleansing, that replaces one set of humans with another, erases names and histories to inscribe new ones on top of them, replacing the Palestinian narrative with a resurrected mythical narrative from the Torah. This renders Adam's endeavour to assimilate into his fabricated Jewish identity doomed to fail, as he himself ultimately discovers, and as his Jewish girlfriend, Dalia, tells him at the point of orgasm: this is impossible. Elsewhere his Iraqi-Jewish teacher, Ezekiel Katsav, longs for his own homeland and feels alienated in the new one. Like Adam, he manoeuvres and resists by adopting the colonizer's own language and culture, while unable to forget that he is an Iraqi Jew – linguistically and culturally still an Arab.

It might be said that *Children of the Ghetto* is a kind of rewriting: a meditation on the major novels written on the Palestinian cause and its ongoing twists and turns, from the Nakba to the experience of the present absentees and their relationship to the Israeli other, with each new chapter more embittered than the one that precedes it. There is repeated reference to works that address the same burning questions of the Palestinian cause that Khoury himself also posed previously in *Gate of the Sun*: Emile Habibi's *The Pessoptimist* (1974), Ghassan Kanafani's *Men in the Sun* (1963) and *Return to Haifa* (1969), and Anton Shammas's *Arabesques* (1968). By standing on the shoulders of previous canonical authors, Khoury plays a game of intertextuality that seeks to broaden the horizons of the same questions, thus constructing a framework in which to discuss strategies of camouflage and mimicry of the enemy-other. Khoury repeatedly refers to these iconic Palestinian novels in order to engage both their implicit and explicit messages and their symbolic meaning in the course of the conflict and between clashing narratives. But his questions, as well as his answers, stand apart from those of Kanafani, Habibi and Jabra Ibrahim Jabra. Instead, they come closer – subtly – to those posed by the poetry of Mahmoud Darwish, who sought to rewrite the story of Palestine as one of the great tragedies in human history. Darwish says:

> *Whoever writes his story will inherit*
> *the land of words and possess meaning, entirely!*[1]

Khoury also positions himself closer to the writings of Edward Said and to Said's core contention on the role of Orientalism and colonial discourse in suppressing Palestinian identity, in gagging Palestinian voices, a role which served to justify the occupation in the contemporary Western imagination.

Khoury also makes continuous reference to a number of Israeli works of fiction: *Khirbet Khizeh* by S. Yizhar (1949), *My Michael* by Amos Oz (1968) and *Facing the Forests* by A.B. Yehoshua (1968), texts that all enacted a form of erasure upon Palestinians by depicting them as voiceless or treating them as 'present absentees'. By referring to or citing these works, offering critique or contemplating their implicit meanings, Khoury seeks to perform on Israeli and Palestinian narratives what Said would call a contrapuntal reading. He also seeks to highlight Adam's condition, and his attempts to forget and rid himself of his memory by self-effacement. Thus, Adam's dream of being erased – and indeed, his carrying an eraser in his pocket until his death – bear a great deal of significance as symbols that starkly illuminate his experience and operate as an interpretation of the novel from within. Any reading of these two novels without taking into account these crucial references to Israeli texts will blind us to the main motif the writer is working to build.

Khoury also establishes a symmetry between reality and fiction by having the death of Adam echo that of the Palestinian poet Rashid Hussein, who died in a fire in his small apartment in New York in the early 1970s. In a way, this is also reminiscent of Mahmoud Darwish's poem about Hussein: "He was what he was going to become"[2], he wrote of his friend. This emphasizes the major motif of the Palestinian tragedy in both Khoury's novels, and charges them with meaning, by embedding them within the recent Palestinian historical narrative along with the Palestinian imagination and its new cultural semiotics.

The multiple references to *Bab Al-Shams*, with its characters (Yunis, Naheelah, Umm Hassan, and Khaleel Ayoub) and an overlap in some of its key events, can also be considered contrapuntal with the two novels of this trilogy – or perhaps, as a rediscovery of their shared roots. They could also be interpreted as the author picking up the same story where he left off. But if *Gate of the Sun* focused on the role of storytelling in resurrecting a people, these two novels depict Adam going to that land of absolute silence and muteness of his own free will, his tongue severed, mimicking the occupier in both appearance and name. This manifests in his attempt to write an allegorical tale embodied by the poet Waddah Al-Yaman, who remained silent in his trunk without crying out until he was buried alive to preserve the secret of his love. Adam, however, fails to fully conceal himself behind Waddah Al-Yaman, and abandons the manuscript of his novel about the lover who was buried in the trunk along with his secret before finishing it. For this too, ultimately, is something impossible to achieve.

Translated by Suneela Mubayi

---

[1] Darwish, *Limadha tarakta al-hisan wahidan*. Beirut: Riyad al-Rayyes, 1995. Tr. Jeffrey Sacks, *Why did you Leave the Horse Alone?*, Archipelago Books, 2006.
[2] Darwish, *A'ras*. Beirut: Dar al-Awda, 1977.

SUNEELA MUBAYI

A Mentor for the Ages

I made my first proper contact with Elias Khoury when I started my PhD in Arabic Literature at NYU, and in the spring of 2010 took his class on the Arabic novel and the city. With Elias, it did not matter who you were if you showed him a spark of passion and dedication to literature: Arab or non-Arab, undergrad or graduate student. The students, whether they read Arabic or not, all loved his unique and funny mannerisms. For example, he would always refer to the Syrian regime as "our Syrian brothers" and to the Israelis as "our Israeli cousins", jibing at the official discourse that calls Arabs brothers and Jews *awlad al-'amm* [cousins] of Muslims and Christians. His unassuming, down-to-earth attitude with students was best manifested in the custom he instituted of the weekly drink we would have after our graduate seminar in one of the pubs around the corner from NYU because, as he said, talking about literature makes you thirsty! Notably, from his own novels he assigned *Yalo* and not *Gate of the Sun* as everyone expected; when I told him that I enjoyed the former more than the latter, he smiled and said Mahmoud Darwish had told him the same thing! It was a great pleasure for me when he agreed I could write my term paper on *Memory for Forgetfulness* (*Dhakira lil-Nisyan*), Darwish's unique, genre-crossing memoir of the 1982 Israeli siege of Beirut. It was this seminar in which our bond as mentor and mentee was solidified, and which first sparked my confidence to write in Arabic.

We kept in touch and continued to meet whenever I visited Beirut after that. However, the most special period of my relationship with *Ustaz* [Professor] Elias was in the spring of 2013 when he agreed to work with me outside of the formal class framework to help me develop my writing skills in Arabic. Over the course of that semester, I produced three short articles and two translations of short stories

"Rana Issa, a leading scholar on Shidyaq, planned a visit for Elias and Humphrey to Shidyaq's grave, and invited me to join what can only be described as a pilgrimage of devotees to their saint's tomb"

from Urdu (my purported native tongue that I never learned too well) directly into Arabic. Thanks to Elias, who took time to help me, I became a published writer in Arabic. I will never forget the moment he autographed my Arabic edition of *The Journey of Little Gandhi* and wrote in his dedication: "In anticipation of your first book in *lughat al-daad* [ie the Arabic language]".

When I think about my connection to Elias, I think about the question of whether one can belong to or viscerally identify with a culture without being born into it. I have been haunted by this question since I first began my engagement with Arabic fifteen years ago: I sensed an identification with the Palestinian cause, finding a deep affinity between the sense of statelessness and the state of estrangement I felt from my own body. Many people, both familiar and unfamiliar, would ask: why would I, someone who had no obviously strong connection to the Arab world, engage with it so deeply, to the point of claiming it as my own?

I think along the same lines (albeit not identically, given Lebanon's geographical and cultural proximity to Palestine) about Elias, the Lebanese Christian from Ashrafiyeh, Beirut, and his close identification with Palestine and the Palestinian cause. Palestinians celebrate him as one of their own, despite being fully aware of his background and his never having stepped foot on their land. He is considered today's 'Palestinian' novelist par excellence, and is the author of the aforementioned *Gate of the Sun*, the novel which comes closest to being the Great Palestinian Novel, and which has so much embedded itself into the Palestinian collective consciousness that some years ago, the people of the West Bank village Bil'in named their project to reclaim land stolen by Israeli settlers by the same name. How would *Ustaz* Elias respond to "why?" I seek no answer, nor do I have one. Instead, I find inspiration in his identification with a cause he did not belong to by birth; one that many growing up around him would have been hostile to.

Last year, I happened to be in Beirut during a commemoration held for him at AUB where Humphrey Davies, his chief translator, was a participant. More than one contributor to this portfolio has mentioned him in the same breath as the Nahda-era polymath and iconoclast Ahmad Faris al-Shidyaq. In recent years, I too have found in Shidyaq an affinity and inspiration on my journey through life and literature as someone who challenged assumed notions of identity, belonging and language itself in his time. Rana Issa, one of the symposium's organizers and perhaps the world's leading scholar on Shidyaq, planned a visit for Elias and Humphrey (himself translator of Shidyaq's magnum opus *Leg over Leg*) to Shidyaq's grave, and invited me to join what can only be described as a pilgrimage of devotees to their saint's tomb. The grave lies neglected and derelict on a *waqf* [1] property for burying Ottoman-era notables in Beirut's eastern suburb Hazmiyeh (where coincidentally Palestinian novelist Ghassan Kanafani was assassinated nearly 100 years after Shidyaq passed away). The tomb has for neighbours a health food centre and a bank, neither of which had the slightest inkling as to who lay at rest next to them. Both Elias and Humphrey showed great agility for their age by clambering over the fence onto the *waqf* property, but then perhaps the spirit of Shidyaq imbued us all with powers beyond our usual physical capabilities! We paid our respects to Shidyaq and washed off the thick layers of dust and dead leaves from his tomb. The food centre, who controls access to the site, were at first frightened that we had come to dispute their property, but then decided to let this eccentric bunch fulfil their fantasy and allowed us to take water to clean the grave. After laying fresh flowers on his grave, we read out Elias's favourite passage from *Leg over Leg*.

Elias Khoury and Humphrey Davies cleaning the tomb of Shidyaq

This connection to Shidyaq, the irreverent tongue-in-cheek rebel, is another source of inspiration I have found I share with *Ustaz* Elias Khoury. It is my sincere hope that this decade of memories will be the first of many that I have the honour of sharing with this *adeeb*[2], whom I consider nothing short of a mentor.

---

[1] An endowment of property under Islamic law, to be used for charitable or religious purposes.
[2] From the Arabic word *adab*: denotes a writer, but also has connotations of culture, education and refinement.

Chip Rossetti reviews
**Elias Khoury's
The Kingdom of Strangers**
Translated by Paula Haydar
University of Arkansas Press, July 1996
ISBN: 978-1557284334. Pbk, 112pp.

Malleable Storytelling

As in many of his other novels, Elias Khoury's *The Kingdom of Strangers* wrestles with issues of Lebanese identity and memory, using a fractured, non-linear narrative to reflect the fracturing of society during the Lebanese Civil War. Originally published in Arabic in 1993 as *Mamlakat al-ghuraba'*, it appeared in English in 1996 in Paula Haydar's excellent translation. In style and setting, the novel evokes comparisons to his earlier novel *Rihlat Ghandi al-saghir* (*The Journey of Little Gandhi*, also translated by Paula Haydar), which is also set during the civil war and evokes the lives of those who died during those years. The eternally recurring present in these novels, in which the same incident is narrated more than once, acts as a counterweight to forgetting by focusing the reader's attention on it.

The kaleidoscopic array of interlocking narratives in *The Kingdom of Strangers* reflects the chaos of wartime life: there is a single narrator, who seems to be a stand-in for Khoury himself, but there is no single plot in the conventional sense. Instead, the narrator offers fragments of detail about the lives of individual characters – friends, lovers, Biblical figures, and others – only to second-guess or contradict his account and then shift to another narrative. Each chapter, in fact, begins with the narrator asking himself (or the reader) a variant of "What am I writing?" and this emphasizes the narrator's own uncertainty about the aim of his storytelling. In his study of Khoury's novel *City Gates*, Nouri Gana refers to this technique as

Khoury's "tirelessly sustained experimental style", reflecting what he calls the "formless form" of contemporary Lebanese literature. Haydar addresses the novel's unusual structure in her informative preface, noting commonalities between Khoury's literary style and the postmodernist fiction of contemporary Latin American authors such as Carlos Fuentes, Gabriel García Márquez, and Miguel Ángel Asturias.

Among the characters whose stories are presented in recurring segments throughout the book are the Naffaa family, a Christian family in Beirut, and a woman known as "white Widad" or simply "the Circassian," because of her light skin. In the 1920s, the middle-aged businessman Iskandar Naffaa purchases a thirteen-year-old girl named Widad to work as a maid for his family. As we learn later, Widad is in fact originally from Azerbaijan, and had been kidnapped and eventually sold (in what today would be called "human trafficking") in Alexandria and Beirut. In a disturbing turn of events, Iskandar soon abandons his wife and family to marry the much younger Widad. Despite the circumstances and their age difference, Widad and he remain faithful to each other, and by the time Iskandar dies, several decades later, Iskandar's grown son George Naffaa has come to feel a filial affection for Widad, a childless widow now without family of her own.

The pain of Widad's sad story is only dimly hinted at, and Khoury deliberately gives the reader little access to her interior life, while the Naffaa family, including Iskandar, remain mostly incurious about her. They never bother to learn about her past, to the point that she spends her life mislabelled as a Circassian, and in the narrator's words, "As for Widad . . . no one knows what she felt, or what she thought, or what she wanted". We are ultimately unknowable to each other, the novel suggests, and thus the world we live in is the "kingdom of strangers" of the book's title. Only at the end of her life, as a seventy-year-old woman during the early years of the civil war, does Widad's hidden self resurface, to the surprise of George Naffaa. Falling into dementia, she stops speaking Arabic altogether and her childhood Azeri comes flooding out again, although no one can understand her. She escapes the hospital where she has been committed and three days later, she is found dead on the street – an unwitting victim of the war taking place around her.

Much like Widad, the narrator tells us, Beirut was also in the process of losing its memory, as an effect of the civil war. Khoury expressed a similar idea in a 1993 interview with the Lebanese literary journal *Al-Adab* (cited by Haydar in her translator's preface), in which he states that Lebanon has a national tendency to forget its own past, "as if it carried along with it a big fat eraser with which it blotted out its own history".

A recurring theme of the novel, however, is that history – whether an individual's life story or the history of a nation – need not be true to be valid. Ultimately, the telling of the story is what matters, not its underlying factual details. When the narrator recalls his meeting with the real-life Arab nationalist military hero Fawzi al-Qawuqji, he points out that the war stories the elderly veteran tells are confused, since he mixes up his exploits in 1936 and 1948. Nevertheless, the narrator happily asks: "Why not believe him? What's the difference between 1936 and 1948?" The novel presents different versions of characters' lives not to draw the reader's attention to an "unreliable narrator", but to emphasize the malleability of narratives themselves and the relative unimportance of their underlying "truth". Human history is in fact a collective blending of individual stories or agreed-upon myths that take on a reality of their own, and the narrator proposes that memories "get jumbled together and form into a mixture, into a single story with its roots in all the stories".

The most striking example of the malleability of storytelling as a form of communal mythmaking is the narrator's discussion of a Lebanese monk named Jurji Khayri, whom he at one point calls "an Arab folk hero, like Robin Hood". Jurji Khayri supposedly lived in Jerusalem during the British mandate period, and was found murdered beside the Damascus Gate. However, as the narrator tries to research the facts of the monk's life – visiting his home village in Lebanon and searching among his relatives, the true story becomes more elusive. The monk's aged relatives claim not to have heard of him, and the stories about his life vary wildly: he either revolted against British authorities or led a gang of thieves and rapists in the Galilee area, or perhaps targeted Jewish settlers for kidnappings.

Mamlakat al-Ghuraba' (The Kingdom of Strangers)

Even if his existence has passed into legend, the narrator concludes, Jurji "owes his very existence as a story to the popular imagination".

The dialogic nature of stories is also reflected in the multiple portraits of individual lives presented here, from the Israeli graduate student, Emil Azayev, whom the narrator befriends at Columbia University in New York, to Faysal, an 11-year-old Palestinian boy who survived the 1982 massacre in the Shatila camp by hiding among the dead bodies of his family, only to end up killed by a bullet in 1987, at the end of the years-long siege of the camps, prompting the narrator to ask: "How can I write Faysal's story when Faysal died before his story ended?"

Elias Khoury does not see himself as a recorder of history, as simply bearing witness to the dead. (In fact, in a 2001 interview with Sonja Mejcher in *Banipal*, he objected to readers' tendency to approach his fiction as history, even though he acknowledged that histories of Lebanon's recent past are lacking, since "as a novelist . . . it is not my job to write history".) Instead, in *The Kingdom of Strangers*, he suggests that by turning the dead into stories, we betray their historical truth, but ultimately those stories become their own truth. Fittingly, for an author who has long sympathized with the Palestinian cause, Khoury closes the novel with the narrator describing his visit to the mass grave in the Shatila camp where his friend, the Palestinian fighter Ali Abu Tawq, is buried. Like Widad the Circassian or the monk Jurji Khayri, Ali has become a story. In the end, Khoury suggests, the telling of that story is what matters most.

Stephanie Petit reviews
City Gates by Elias Khoury
Translated by Paula Haydar
Picador, Reprint edition, November 2007
ISBN: 978-0312427153. Pbk, 112pp

White Masks by Elias Khoury
Translated by Maia Tabet
MacLehose Press, February 2013
ISBN: 978-0857052124 Pbk, 304pp

Stories of the city

These two books, *Abwab al-Madina* (*City Gates*) and *al-Wujuh al-Bayda'* (*White Masks*), Khoury's third and fourth novels respectively, were published in close succession in 1981, when their author was in his early thirties. Though staggeringly different in content and composition each novel takes Beirut as both muse and canvas, exemplifying Khoury's commitment to chronicling – and providing a creative response to – the civil war (1975-1990) that ravaged his native city. Khoury, famously, has taken on this task with imagination, lyricism and candour – writing fiction, he states, "was very important because it gave me the chance to rethink and to understand what was going on. The imaginary level that is part of every fiction made it possible for me to create some distance from the political practice, and to criticise it."[1] As examples of Khoury's early artistic output the works provide a fascinating insight into the author's creative processes. Indeed, and inasmuch as they are Khoury's real-time critique of socio-political and cultural currents, *City Gates* and *White Masks* are also experiments in *form*, in which the author's wilful contortion of language and of narrative-building display his profound interest in how this critique can be conveyed through art.

City Gates is an enigmatic, haunting novella that speaks to the motifs of trauma, exile and displacement. It concerns a man referred to only as 'the stranger' who, bearing a suitcase containing a pencil, papers and a photograph of his father, searches for the entry gates to an unnamed city, the contours of which are impossible to establish. There is a white square, and an adjacent sea. The city is largely deserted – from the outset one senses a tremendous catastrophe has taken place there. A small host of vaguely drawn, difficult to individuate characters are left to traverse the white space: a 'storyteller' and a cast of women weeping for lost, ghost-like children. There is a king who has been asleep for endless years, another woman made of yoghurt. The city appears completely dislodged from time and space. The narrative, woven into a loose tableau of images rather than following an actual plot, moves slowly between dreamlike sequences reminiscent of a legend or fable. The deafening silence in the city is occasionally broken by wailing that emerges from the sea, and by the sounds of animals passing – snakes and flocks of pigeons "cooing with sadness". Gradually a nightmarish tone envelopes the story. The figures are directionless and confused. They weep, wait, long to escape, are unable to move. The narrative becomes perforated with glimpses of a past that no one remembers, of what happened to the city before it "faded away". Through inexplicable hallucinations the stranger starts to see "bodies stacked on top of one another, women weeping over bloated corpses", "bodies running in every direction and voices rising up". A cry, "the dead were everyone, and this thing killing children we know no reason for, this thing that kills will kill everyone" reverberates as a terrifying warning. With nothing remaining, the city then perishes in an epic inferno before becoming engulfed by the sea, where "everything was floating, and nothing remained of the city except weeping voices coming from the entrails of the fish and rising to where no one can listen to them".

Speaking about the novella, Khoury explains "I do not think I can go back to *Abwab al-Madina*, which was written in 1979/80, when I was feeling as if I had gone through a nightmare. It was a personal experience about things that were totally closed and language that was totally destroyed, to a degree that nothing could be seen and said anymore." *City Gates* does indeed convey this despair, this desire to denounce the conventions of storytelling in favour of a disordering of the senses in order to convey human suffering in the context of war. Though Beirut is never truly revealed, one feels that Khoury sought to convey the mood of the tremendous devastation that the city suffered. A graceful translation (published in 1993) by Paula Haydar further captures, and recasts into English, the strangeness of the Arabic text in eerie, jagged sentences that cut off and dissolve into nothingness:

> The woman was white, she spoke and she was white, like the white sand that filled the place, then the colors began to ooze out of her eyes. There were hands stretching out and black daggers and a woman changing into trembling red pieces in the middle of the square.

Precisely because it is such an unusual work, it is regrettable that *City Gates* has become somewhat sidelined in Khoury's oeuvre, even, as the quote suggests, by the author himself. As an artistic achievement it really is quite stunning. But at the same time, and though it readily invites a multiplicity of readings, the novella does speak its themes in a way that is remote, fantastical, and in this sense it does not pack the close-to-the-ground punch of the author's later output.

In contrast, Khoury's subsequent novel *al-Wujuh al-Bayda'* (published as *White Masks* in an English translation by Maia Tabet, in 2010) brings Khoury's own politics to the fore much more clearly: "My criticism became more explicit in *al-Wujuh al-Bayda'*," he explains, "which was considered to be very heavy criticism of what we – our leftist and Palestinian camp – were doing". *White Masks* revolves around the death of Khalil Ahmad Jaber, a middle-aged father of three whose corpse is found by dustmen in a backstreet of Beirut. Only partially clothed, his body bears the signs of torture: bruises, abrasions and puncture wounds to the chest and face. The gruesome discovery makes a splash in the local newspapers ("Dreadful murder in the UNESCO district") where it is picked up by the novel's unnamed narrator, an aspiring journalist. Though the killing is hardly unusual in a city gripped by war – the narrator, with striking nonchalance, acknowledges that there are many similar cases in Beirut, it comes to occupy him to near-obsession. "Although I tried, I couldn't place the man's name, but I seemed to remember that I had come across him somewhere," he explains. He starts to research the circumstances of Jaber's death, and interviews those who might be able to shed light on it. Accordingly, the bulk of the novel is constructed as a compilation of anecdotes and testimonies by people who knew, or are in some way connected to, Jaber: his wife and adult daughter, various acquaintances, the pathologist who performs the autopsy on his body. Through their myriad voices – committed to the page in an ostensibly verbatim style and bearing all of the repetitiveness and inconsistencies that are inherent to everyday speech – a portrait of the dead man emerges. All his life Jaber had been "a most transparent man", an ordinary postal worker with no obvious enemies. Jaber's quiet life is shattered when his only son Ahmed, a promising young boxer, dies in combat shortly after the outbreak of the Lebanese Civil War.

This appears to set in motion his father's slow, agonising descent into madness: In the months following Ahmed's death Jaber becomes a recluse, initially refusing to leave the confines of his bedroom where he obsessively arranges and rearranges press cuttings and photographs bearing the image of his dead son. Later on we hear of his final months on the streets of Beirut where, caught between a confused stupor and feverish madness, he is observed pulling down posters of the city's martyrs, chewing and swallowing the paper strips as they tear away. A kind neighbour tries to intervene. The authorities take him away for questioning. But, ultimately, the accounts remain fragmented, the circumstances of his death shrouded in mystery.

"This is no tale," the narrator discloses, and indeed, without a final unravelling, Khalil Ahmad Jaber's story is left hanging. Initially bearing the hallmark of a literary murder mystery, the novel instead unfolds as a moving portrait of grief, of a father incapable of letting go and refusing to abandon his son's memory to the anonymous mist of war. The meek ordinariness of the man makes this all the more affecting. Indeed, subsumed under emotional pain, tortured, shot and left on a rubbish heap, Jaber is too small, too insignificant to count in a city portrayed as gripped by a horrific reality, with civilians maimed, raped, displaced. Lives such as his, the narrator appears to say, will not be remembered.

For its unflinching depiction of violence, *White Masks* is at times a difficult read. Hard-hitting too, in its portrayal of militia leaders' hackneyed gestures towards the bereft families of martyrs who died "for the just cause of the nation", and of aspects of the Palestinian revolution that, as Khoury admits, were largely considered beyond the reach of criticism among his cohort of leftist intellectuals. One of the most moving side-stories in *White Masks* concerns a young Palestinian: Moeen Abbas, a medical student based in Cairo. Deported while in the middle of his studies, Abbas is abandoned in Syria with nothing but some pocket change and a few cigarettes. After some weeks sleeping on the floor of a mosque, a collection raised by the local community helps him obtain a passport and visa for Sweden. On the night before his departure, Abbas is robbed of his money and papers and, overwhelmed by the utter hopelessness of his predicament, commits suicide in a toilet cubicle at the airport.

White Masks is undoubtedly a compelling novel, though its style, the rambling digressions, the self-referentiality and ultimate lack of resolution, demands a certain commitment from its readership. A skilful translation by Maia Tabet brings the novel's mosaic of voices and registers to Anglophone readers. Most remarkably, the book continues to read with a sense of immediacy that transcends its locality – though the passing of time has changed the perspective from which it is read, the emotion and the senseless brutality that inflects the otherwise ordinary lives of its characters remain recognisable. As in *City Gates*, Khoury imbues *White Masks* with a certain confidence, a boldness in method and execution. As a writer he is measured, humane and unafraid.

In this sense it is a testament to their continuing relevance that his *City Gates* and *White Masks*, first released nearly 40 years ago, read as fresh and as urgent as if published yesterday.

---

[1] Mejcher, Sonia. "The necessity to forget and remember." *Banipal 12*, Autumn 2001

ELIAS KHOURY

A CHAPTER FROM

On the Interrelations of the Circle

TRANSLATED BY PAULA HAYDAR

1

'An 'ilaqat al-da'ira *(On the Interrelations of the Circle)* is Elias Khoury's first novel. It was published in Beirut in 1975, and has not been translated into English

The chair moved forward. To its right, the long, black robe undulates, and wide eyes encompass me all about. I don't know why I cried. The shots fired forth from my open mouth and my nose without my grasping what was going on. I take a glance. The chair moves forward, and a bald man with a big belly now stands beside the long robe. Two eyes stuck along the bottom of his chin. Two large moles and a beard like blackthorn – small in size but strong in odour. I look towards my legs. My shorts are a bit dirty, but they move in the direction of the chair. The black robe lowers its head. The face is big, and beneath the nose is a huge wart that moves as it makes a sound I don't understand. I begin to wail. The robe takes me into its arms, picks me up and speaks calmly to me: "You are going to sit in this chair now. The celebration will begin, and St. Elias will be the one to adopt you." I understand everything. My father will come. The

ON THE INTERRELATIONS OF THE CIRCLE

long robe said so. I put myself in the chair, and I begin to hear a new tune. I look up high and see the two big moles next to the robe. "The celebration is about to begin. You must cut his hair and then take him to the church." This is the first instance of its type. The chair rocks and the two moles move downward. "We don't usually accept children your age." The scissors begin to make a strange new sound. "Why didn't you wash his hair?" The long robe sways on its way out.

The window of the spacious room overlooks an open-air playground. The sky is blue. I look at my fingers and notice the white lines under my fingernails getting bigger. I hear a creaking sound. I look up. The black animal opens its mouth in very slow motion. It doesn't have teeth. It falls on my head, and the music begins to blare while the rain falls from all directions. I look at the very blue sky. The rain isn't falling from it. I look at the ceiling. Drops of black rain fill the sky of the room and pour down in a torrent. The black robe is in all directions. The black rain is in all directions. The white lines under my fingernails rise in very slow motion, and when I put my hand on my head I begin to cry. The belly jiggles as it lets out a loud bellow and the black robe comes next to me. Out from its right side comes a white hand holding a tissue that begins to wipe my tears. Then I hear a tender voice. "Don't cry, child."

The robe picks me up from the chair, takes me outside the room into a long hallway.

"Name?"

(The child trembles.) I sit on the floor.

"Sister Barbara, Sister Barbara. The boy doesn't know his name." And the laughter starts.

"What shall we call him?"

"Ibrahim, George, John . . ."

"No, no. His name is Mansour. We will call him Mansour."

"Mansour is a beautiful name," the robe shouts and comes towards me.

"Your name is Mansour, little boy."

The robe takes me by the hand and walks across the long hallway before turning around to the left and opening the door. We enter together. A shower head on the ceiling and down low beside me a water faucet. The floor is yellow. He begins removing my clothes and then sits me on a wooden table. He turns the faucet on, picks up a bowl filled with water, and the cold water begins to stream down my body. The flow of water stops. "I will be back in five minutes." The black robe leaves, and I am left alone. I am naked on the low bathing table. I look at my body. It appears to me that I have twelve toes. I count again. Ten toes. I start to laugh. He opens the door. The black robe comes in wearing an apron. He looks at me, then leans down over me. There are three black hairs moving constantly. They're clustered around the big wart. He picks up the soap and starts rubbing it on my body. He pours the cold water. Then he gets a big towel. He gives me trousers and a yellow shirt. I put them on.

"Mansour, my boy. You're going to eat now with the children. Come with me. I'll tell you the whole story from the beginning."

We enter a new room. The black robe goes and sits at a table. I remain standing.

"Sit down, Mansour, my boy. Here's a chair."

I approach the chair and put my hand on it. I see my fingers and the white lines. I try to sit, but I can't – he becomes a piece of wood – I put my hand on my hair. "Where is my hair, Mr. —?" The black robe gets up and hugs me to his chest. "Sit down Mansour, my boy."

"We are a monastery. This house is an orphanage. The orphanage is a home. We bring beautiful children to it. They study. They live in love and affection. And then they go out into the world when they grow up. They are . . . Mansour, you know a lot of things. The children here don't know much. We don't usually bring children in from off the streets. But you are a special case. Of course, you remember, Mansour, my boy, that you were sleeping on the sidewalk with your right arm bent beneath your head. We felt sorry for you. We said what a nice child. We can take him into the monastery. I'm sure you remember how Sister Barbara came and carried you here crying. My dear boy, Mansour, we love children here, because God loves children. You will go to our school. You will learn to pray. We will teach you a trade, and then you will leave the orphanage. Yes, of course, in ten years you will become a man, and then you will remember us fondly. Now, Mansour, enter into the church and pray in front of the large icon. Then, come and eat with us."

Mansour understands everything. The icon. The church. And most importantly, the food. "I'm hungry."

ON THE INTERRELATIONS OF THE CIRCLE

The ancient tranquillity mingles with the smell of burning candles. Darkness. On both sides of him, it illuminates the eyes of the saints, and the antiquated fragrance. Mansour looks at the ancient place. The nun's hand leads him towards the entrance of the altar. Mansour kneels. All the voices stop, and out from the scent of the incense comes the sound of the litany for the souls of the dead. Mansour is still hungry, and the voices of the saints emerge from the mouths of the cement covering the church floor. Mansour looks straight ahead. The darkness isn't dense. It is still daytime, but the dust of the icons gives a sharp feeling of night-time. My fingers tremble. And he kneels before the altar.

"The book. Hold the book."

"Armies of ants."

"Read the words."

"Armies of ants."

The words are ants, Mansour thinks. Something nice. A sidewalk, a book, and ants. "Father, Son, and Holy Spirit," the nun says. "One God, Amen," repeats Mansour after her.

The book falls from my hand. Its ancient black cover tears apart. Mansour stands. "Go, child, in front of that wide icon. Stand before it with humility and pray. It is the icon of Saint Elias the Living One. Saint Elias is not dead, does not die, and it is he who is adopting you."

The icons move in a long procession. They turn to the left and encompass Mansour. On the right, the icons sway, and on the left, their backs are hunched over a little, while Mansour holds the censer in the middle. And God appeared to His people in a great voice. "We cut your hair, so it won't become a breeding ground for bugs. Where do you think you are? You're in an orphanage. An orphanage isn't a fancy hotel for tourists. It's a place of work. Don't say what did I do wrong. Your crime is the sidewalk. The sister hit you. Next time, she'll break your neck. Where do you think you are? You won't go? You'll go whether you like it or not. You must work. A dead person is a piece of wood."

The procession of icons turns, speeds up, but the rhythm doesn't stop. "Remember, Mansour. Remember. You are a smart and well-behaved boy. You were sleeping on the sidewalk. The sister came and picked you up. Before that, where were you? Who is your father? Certainly, the sidewalk didn't give birth to you. It must have been a woman who gave birth to you. Come on, boy. Remember. Okay, your name is Mansour. We got that. But what's your family name? Come on, remember! Don't cry like a baby. You're a big boy. You're smart. Such a strange case you are, boy. How could you forget? Were you selling chewing gum on the streets? You mustn't have gone to school, because you don't know how to read. Come on, Mansour, remember!" The black robe sways. It starts shaking beneath the icons' queries. "Dear boy, the past is important. If you don't remember, listen. Just listen, at least. Why are you trembling and crying?"

The icons dance upon the ropes of incense spread about, and the book is not in my hand. The book fell to the floor. The cement is cold. It starts etching black marks on my knee. I reach with my right hand below my knees and wipe them. They're smeared with tears and matchsticks. He comes towards me, emerging from the picture, with a water basin in his hand. The door slams shut. I'm hungry. The saints fall silent as they leave the courtyard. One of them breaks a leg on his way back to the wall.

PAULA HAYDAR
Translating Elias Khoury Full Circle

Translating the first chapter of Elias Khoury's first novel, 'An 'ilaqat al-da'ira (On the Interrelations of the Circle) has been a meaningful experience for me. I have come full circle, so to speak, in translating Khoury's earliest work, as my translation of City Gates, another of his early works, was my first foray into the world of literary translation. "On the Interrelations of the Circle" exemplifies his early writing style, which is that of an impressionist painter. He starts with broad strokes, adds touches here and there, then goes back to the beginning and starts again. Very circular indeed.

Khoury's early narrative style goes against all the norms, seems intent on tearing readers out of their comfort zone. He makes it

ON THE INTERRELATIONS OF THE CIRCLE

He holds the large spoon, lets it dip into the bowl of rice and opens his mouth. He is sitting on the right side of a long table. There is total silence. The wooden seat hurts his thighs, but the smell of food is wonderful. The silence is absolute. The angels are present at the dinner table. That's what the black robe says to the children. I eat a lot. Why are they looking at me? One of them laughs, and then the whole table breaks out in laughter. Why are they looking at me that way? Their eyes are stuck to the side of my mouth. The sidewalk walks on my spoon. The taste of water beneath my teeth. We resume eating. The spoons move towards the target and come back empty.

"My name is Mansour," I answer him with my mouth full. "I am happy and love you very much."

The spoon shines in my hand. The bell rings and we rush out to the big playground. The sun is hot. They run. I run and then walk slowly. All the heads look alike. I rush towards them, and I put my hand on my head. The black rain begins to pour down. The forest is a garden with organized sides. The trees turn around but are standing in place. The trees are stuck in the soil. They all look alike.

difficult to determine if the scenes or inner thoughts of the narrator are reality, a dream, or the reliving of some sort of unclear memory from a real or imagined past. At the level of sentence structure, fragments abound, along with illogical or unfathomable descriptions, endless examples of personification and a constant fascination-cum-preoccupation with death.

The verb tense is always shifting, as is the point of view. The narration is often interrupted by another voice – the author's, perhaps. It is difficult to know since dialogue is not always set in quotes or in paragraph breaks. While there is an absence of a clear plot structure, poetic moments are striking and serve as a kind of substitute for rising and falling action.

"Have you ever seen a black forest?"

"I've never seen a forest in my life."

"The forest," says the nun, "resembles your heads. The forest is composed of hundreds of trees that look alike. One tree by itself is not worth a thing. One tree on the sidewalk doesn't give shade. But when lots of trees gather in one place, then it becomes a forest. And a forest gives shade. This is why we brought you all to this house, so you could be a forest.

Yes, yes. The children on the playground and the trees move in all directions. A little tree runs behind a big tree, and the cement touches the roots.

"Enter the forest, Mansour, my boy. Don't be afraid. You will become a tree. By the power of the Holy Spirit, you will. Go play with them."

Mansour runs towards the playground. The khaki school uniform is the symbol of the new tree. The uniforms mingle and blend, and so begins the jumping and playing and tug-of-war. The tree is not little.

I stand in the middle of the playground. The trees beckon me to join them. One of the children comes up to me . . . "You're the new boy Mansour. Come play with us." They rush over in large numbers. I thought they were going to hit me, but they like me. I do a little dance for them and they swarm around me. Then another tree dances. We always think the new one will be left out and the story will be written about his pain and sorrow amidst the forest. The new one is not sad. The forest is everything. The sad forest doesn't allow its trees to be sad. Sadness is not a condition; it's a position one takes.

I look at the sun. Its little black circles remind me of the three moving hairs. I walk towards the playground. My forehead enters, and a long hallway opens up before me. We all go in together.

The teacher stands up. "Today I will tell you a nice story. We will enjoy ourselves while learning a fruitful lesson. The Prophet Jonah was sailing on a big ship. Then there was a terrible storm, and all the passengers thought the ship was going to sink into the sea. The captain gathered everyone together and said, 'We must throw one of you into the sea, so we won't all die. Who volunteers to die?' No one volunteered, so the passengers decided amongst themselves to throw the Prophet Jonah into the sea. One of them approached him

ON THE INTERRELATIONS OF THE CIRCLE

and threw him into the waves. Jonah began to cry because he was going to drown. And he did begin to drown. Then along came a whale (she draws a whale on the blackboard), opened its mouth, and swallowed Jonah. Jonah cried and cried and began to slide around in the belly of the whale until he finally settled there inside its stomach. Then Jonah prayed to God, and the whale opened its mouth and spit Jonah out safe and sound. Jonah is the man who loves God. He didn't fight the whale. He went down inside his belly and came out alive. The whale is harmless."

"Mansour, you are new here."

Mansour stands in front of his desk. "Yes, I am."

"Tell us. Do you like Jonah?"

"Yes. I like Jonah."

"And the whale?"

". . ."

"Speak, boy. Do you like the whale? The whale is harmless."

"Yes, it's harmless. I like the whale."

The belly jiggles. And the toothless whale took care of everything. And erased all the evidence. The whale is harmless. Jonah came out of the whale safe and sound.

"Does the whale have eyes?"

"The whale cannot see. God put the sense of smell in his nostrils. He smelled Jonah and swallowed him into his belly."

The boy wiggles his toes, and an awful smell emerges.

"What's that smell? What's that smell?"

"The whale can smell," the children shout. "He smelled Jonah and swallowed him up." "And Jonah can smell," says Mansour. "He smelled God, and so the whale spit him out safe and sound." The teacher claps her hands. She draws a whale on the blackboard and asks: "Who is this?" "That's the whale." "Where's Jonah?" "Jonah's in heaven."

"And the whale?"

"The whale is still on earth."

"Yes, I saw a tree."

"I'm asking you if you saw a dead man."

"Yes, I saw a tree."

"Why are you tormenting me, son? Go to class. You will practise. I wanted to tell you, so you wouldn't be shocked. Go on to class, you and your tree."

Mansour carries his head and goes into the classroom. He sits in the back row. The belly comes. Mansour looks up and sees a fat face and black, bald head. He looks at his eyes, and then he runs out of the classroom.

"Yes, I saw a dead man." The boy trembles.

"Where did you see him?"

"In there. He was standing in front of the blackboard with a heavy staff in his hand."

"Go back to class, boy. A dead man doesn't stand up and doesn't hold anything in his hand. A dead man lies there. You and your friends can carry a dead man. A dead man doesn't do anything. Just lies there and sleeps."

"Does he dream? I dream when I sleep. I dream of Jonah and the whale."

"A dead man doesn't dream. He's dead."

"How so?"

"Go back to class."

Mansour carries the tree, enters the classroom, and sits in the back row. He hears a loud screeching sound. "We will divide you into two groups. The older ones will be in the music group and the younger ones will be pallbearers. Why are you sitting in the back, boy? Come to the front. You are little. You will be a pallbearer. Now I will explain the story again. The music plays what we call a funeral dirge. A funeral must include a dirge. When a person dies he turns to dust, and the music helps him enter heaven. This is why you must play well. When you play the funeral dirge, it helps the deceased's family to forget.

"The deceased forgets his condition when he hears the funeral dirge. For this reason, your assignment is of great importance. Go out of the hall now and practice the dirge music. Horns, drums, cymbals. Instruments of all shapes and sizes." The older children go out and the younger ones stay behind. The older children run for the musical instruments and jump for joy. One of them runs, reaches for his head with his body bent forward. He takes a step back, and then he continues forward. The music fills the air. A celebration of music. God loves music. God commanded us to play music. Did God command us to play it over a dead man's head?

"He commanded us to play it over the heads of people, so they can forget that they're dead. They remember nothing but the little hands hitting the drums and the cymbals being carried by the trees and the horns whose wailing sounds rise up to the living."

"The pall cloth is black. We wrote the name of the orphanage on it. The orphanage participates in the mourning. We mourn whenever anyone dies. But we are filled with joy at the same time. We are joyful because God opens his arms to those who love him.

"Your job, children, is to walk. To bear the pall and walk down the road. This is why you must walk in an organized manner. Then people will point at you and say how organized you are. Order is the basis of life and the basis of death. People must die in an orderly fashion, so that we can walk in an orderly fashion at the funeral, isn't that so? I am sure you understand completely. You all understand. But there is a very important matter. You will go inside the dead man's room before the burial and pray briefly over his head. That will help him a great deal. Cleanse him of his sins.

"Yes, it is true. He goes to hell. The fire that is never extinguished. He stays there his whole life. And there a lifetime never ends. How can it be, after a thousand years, two thousand years, ten thousand years, that a person doesn't die? Forever and ever he doesn't die while the fire roasts him."

The nun laughs, and the knees tremble.

One of the children sticks out a finger, and so the other children stick out their fingers. When they take hold of the pall the nun's voice emerges encouragingly. Night approaches them. The children slowly listen to the massive, jiggling belly. The belly moves forward and opens the desk drawer. He picks up a black rag with a cross on it. Everyone stops. The rag comes forth. It walks along the row of desks and then stops in front of Mansour's desk. The children shout. Mansour cries. Then he screams in a booming voice. The black rag widens. Night has come, the children say. We must go to sleep.

In the spacious room, the beds are lined up next to each other. The children put on their pajamas. Each gets into his own bed and makes the sign of the cross. He closes his eyes and the voice comes. To the right of the spacious room, the icons hold a meeting, and to the left the telephone rings. "One of them has died!" screams the long, black robe. Relief has come. And the children sleep.

"Who ate the bananas? There was a kilo of bananas for the Bishop's visit. One of you snuck in and stole them. Who stole the bananas? No answer? Whoever stole the bananas, his face will turn red. (No one's face turns red.) Whoever stole the bananas will go to Hell. (None of the children goes to Hell.)

"Listen, you little imps. We picked you up off the street. We prayed for you. I clean you up every day, and in return you steal the bananas? The bananas will get caught in the throat and choke the one who eats them. Who stole the bananas? Listen carefully, children. I will tell you a story. The story of Saint Elias the Living One. Stand up for Saint Elias. (The children stand up.) Sit down. (The children sit down.) Saint Elias the Living One will come at night and strangle whichever one of you ate the bananas. Saint Elias is strong. He's not a wretch like your fathers who tossed you out into the streets. Saint Elias comes at night. (The nun's voice slows down.) His beard is white as snow. He will slip in through the window, come into your beds, and sniff your mouths and teeth. Whoever's mouth smells like bananas will die. Saint Elias will grab his neck and choke him until his spirit leaves him. It's your choice. If the one who stole the bananas comes forward now, he will not die."

One of the children comes forward. "Here is the criminal!" shouts the nun. "No, not me. I didn't eat the bananas. But my mouth smells a little like bananas. Every night I dream of eating the bananas. I'm afraid Saint Elias will come and strangle me." "Go back to your seat, boy. Saint Elias knows."

The children stand in front of their desks. Incense rises from the priest's mouth and the children begin to chant hymns. Then the priest's beard yawns, and the children's heads tremble.

I was afraid. I am afraid. Night has come. The white beard approaches. Who is standing before me? Mansour looks out the window. He doesn't see the tree; he sees black. He thinks he is going to die. I'm going to die now. I broke the sister's rules. The bananas will come out of my ears. Mansour is terrified. His right hand starts trembling. The sidewalk tiles emerge from his eyes and start leaving for the seashore while the white beard trembles. Who is standing there?

The bird moves forward. Its sorrow spreads all over the tree. A yellow feather comes out and builds a nest for itself in the corner of the carob tree before coming towards the window. It circles around it. Then the yellow colour becomes the symbol of his forehead and moves forward.

ON THE INTERRELATIONS OF THE CIRCLE

Who strangled the bird? Who strangled the bird?

No one answers. The bird is on the treetop, and the tree is on top of the earth. The earth didn't strangle the bird. The bird strangled the earth. The circle widens. The children sing. One runs towards the tree. He carries a branch and starts to eat. Then a herd of swine comes to the bank and hurls itself into the sea. And Mansour cries. He closes his eyes and the white circle widens. "Who is standing there!" the little boy shouts. The white robe comes forward. Signs fill his forehead. Crosses, icons, censers, voices. Mansour looks. His limbs shudder: the bananas. They come towards his neck. His hands reach out and squeeze very hard. The child opens his eyes. In the corner of the spacious room is an icon of a woman with her arms wrapped around her son. There's a lit candle in front of it. He plunges his head beneath the covers. The black robe moves forward, carries death in his right hand, and the black rain pours down.

"Keep practising. You will all wear navy trousers and white shirts. You'll walk in organized lines. You'll be the pallbearers and chant the funeral hymns. People will point at you and remark how organised you are." The belly jiggles, and the children's cries come from all directions.

"We will study history. We study history to learn about the past. Just as you learn arithmetic and learn carpentry, we study history. History is a window we open onto the past."

"Where is the past?" asked a child who was crying. I remember. My father sold watermelons on a vending cart. And my mother did laundry for rich people and mopped their floors. One time my mother came home very tired, and she was wailing: "He got run over by a car! He's dead. Five children. Where am I to go with them? Damn this life! He put five children in my womb and now he's dead." The wheels of the vending cart rolled in front of our house, and people rushed in, crying. Then they came and took my father. He was laid out inside a wooden box. We didn't see his eyes. Everyone walked to the cemetery, but I stayed at home. Days started giving birth to nights, and nights gave birth to sorrows. Then a woman came to our house and told my mother: "We are going to take the child to the orphanage." I cried when they took me away in a car. And when the teacher came and cut my hair, I knew I would not become a watermelon seller. I would become a respectable man. But my mother doesn't visit me very much. I dream of her every night. And when she comes with candy-coated almonds wrapped inside her handkerchief I ask her why she doesn't come every day. But she doesn't answer. She kisses me on the cheek and says this boy looks like his father. And she leaves.

"History, my son, is not the past. Not any past. It's the past of great men. Not stories about the watermelon seller. It's stories about men who made history. We study the stories of kings. King George and Alexander the Great and the Crusaders. And great men from our land. Habib Bey Abu Shahla and Riad al-Solh. That's history. The watermelon seller was a pitiful man. He got hit by a car. What happened after he died? Did people stop eating watermelons? Then he didn't make history. History is the past of great men.

"Long ago . . . (The grass comes onto my forehead. The birds suspended from the treetops swallow their sorrows. And when the red watermelon becomes pregnant, it gives birth to red water. Washes my face. And so, I weep for history, and history weeps for my tears. The street moves forward. The street moves forward, but the cart does not retreat from its sorrows, and in summer the watermelon rolls onto the red Beirut asphalt.)

"Long ago, the crusaders came to our lands and occupied them. They occupied Jerusalem and built an important kingdom there. They stayed in our lands for ninety years, and then they left. A mighty man forced them out, whose name was Saladin the Ayyubid. And when they returned after World War I, they were kicked out again by Habib Bey Abu Shahla and Riad al-Solh. That's Independence Day."

"Why did they give them that name?"

"Because the cross was their emblem. But they did not carry out Christ's teachings. It was because of that that the great wars took place. The Arabs defeated them. Then the Mamluks came and defeated the Arabs. And after the Mamluks came the Turks, who ruled our lands for four hundred years. And when the Turks were defeated in World War I, the French and the English came. The French took Syria and Lebanon, and the English took Iraq and Palestine. And in 1943, the French left and the Lebanese Christians came to power. This is our history."

The children shake their heads down low. The watermelons roll along their shoulders and fall onto the wooden benches. The watermelon seller stands on the table. "When I used to sell watermelons, every morning my voice would be cleansed by the eyes of my five children. The sidewalks and the streets beckoned to me, and people would see the watermelons and buy them. One time my wife said that my head was shaped like a watermelon, and down went my head under the wheels of the speeding truck."

(The playground is teeming with voices. When we forget, we play the game of life with the wooden boards. And when we remember, we play the game of death with the grass.)

One of the big boys stops and asks me to follow him. I follow him. My leg shrinks as it walks, and my fingers make a sound like the creaking of the old church door. But we play. Every day we invent a new game to play after lunch. It's a wonderful thing to eat delicious food. Sister Barbara always makes delicious food, so we always eat and thank God.

In line . . . the line of "soldiers going up to Bhamdoun to get drunk . . ." He jumps onto my shoulders and laughs. Everyone laughs. We take the nails and start hammering the wooden boards onto each other. Carpentry lesson. Then we invent a new game. Wreath lesson. The nun comes with flowers. We wind them on top of each other and wrap them around a wood frame or shape them into a cross. We plant the flowers. They become a wreath or a cross. The flowers walk in the funeral procession, and the children walk behind them.

"There weren't any children at my father's funeral."

The watermelon seller walked to his burial on his own two feet. Then his hand rolled off. It shook the coffin and fell asleep inside it.

The sun comes out and bathes us in sweat. The sun sweats on our bodies, and we savor the smell of fire. We play. When Mansour opens his mouth to lick the sweat his mouth is dyed the colour of blood.

We enter the spacious room. Mansour puts his body on the bed. He lifts his hand and makes the sign of the cross. Tomorrow, after tomorrow, is a burial . . . we will walk in an orderly fashion. He shuts his eyes. The bird suspended at the top of the tree weeps. He holds tightly to the covers. He puts the bird in the corner of his eye. And Saint Elias lies down beside him in the bed.

International Prize for Arabic Fiction
The six 2020 shortlisted novels

The Spartan Court by Abdelouahab Aissaoui

The novel follows the interconnected lives of five characters in Algiers from 1815 to 1833. The first is a French journalist covering the colonial campaign against Algeria and the second is a former soldier in Napoleon's army who finds himself a prisoner in the city and then a planner for the campaign. The other three Algerian characters have different attitudes to the Ottoman and French colonial powers. Ibn Mayyar thinks that politics is a means of building relationships with the Ottomans and even the French, whilst Hamma al-Salaoui believes that revolution is the only means of achieving change. The fifth character, Douja, is suspended somewhere between all these: she witnesses the transformation of Algiers helplessly and is forced to become part of this changing world. For one must live according to the city's rules, or one must leave.

The Russian Quarter by Khalil Alrez

The novel tells the story of a neighbourhood that for many years resists being dragged into the war going on around it, but is finally compelled to get involved. However, it enters the war with stories rather than weapons. The book's characters include a giraffe from the zoo, a poodle, a female Afghan hound and a sparrow made of wool. Its human characters include the narrator, a translator living in the zoo in the neighbourhood's Russian quarter; Victor Ivanitch, a Russian former journalist and now manager of the zoo; Abu Ali Suleiman, French teacher and owner of a clothes shop; 'Isam, a popular hero working in a cabaret; Rashida from Morocco, former oud player in the cabaret; Arkady Kuzmitch, a little-known Russian writer; and Nuna, daughter of a clarinet player, who knits wool and lives with the narrator in the zoo.

The King of India by Jabbour Douaihy

In mysterious circumstances, the body of Zakaria Mubarak is found at the boundary of his village, Tel Safra. He had just returned from a long exile in Europe, America and Africa, carrying with him a painting by Marc Chagall, the "Blue Violinist", a gift from his girlfriend in Paris. Suspicion falls on the cousins who may have killed him to get a treasure supposedly buried underneath the house built by their grandmother when she came back from America. This absorbing novel tells the story of Zakaria's murder, intersected with fables of gold, sibling strife, the love of French women, the fake promise of revolution and sectarian enmities which have been flaring up from time to time in Lebanon for the last 150 years.

Firewood of Sarajevo by Said Khatibi

In *Firewood of Sarajevo*, Said Khatibi compares and contrasts the sad destinies of two countries. At one time tied by bonds of friendship and ideology, both have become embroiled in futile civil wars, descending into hell and reaching a state where pain is the only common denominator uniting people. In Algeria, as in Bosnia Herzegovina, the twentieth century had a bloody end as people were torn apart by issues of religion and ethnicity. The novel's protagonists, Salim and Ivana, both fled destructive war and hatred in their countries, and went on to build a new lives in Slovenia. Through them, the ugliness of conflict between brothers belonging to the same land is exposed, now brothers only in pain. Even in exile, the smell of war lingers in their nostrils and its effects are felt in their everyday lives.

The Tank by Alia Mamdouh

The novel explores the relationship between human beings and the places which have been taken away from them. After four decades of exile, the writer imagines her return to Iraq and begins her journey of observing the huge changes experienced by the country and society. It is a literary return with a tragic undertone, and interwoven with the text is the life of the writer who has shared with her characters the upheavals which have shaken her homeland.

Fardeqan – the Detention of the Great Sheikh by Youssef Ziedan

The novel depicts the life of Ibn Sina (Avicenna), or "the Great Sheikh", the Muslim polymath whose work has had a profound influence over the last thousand years. It takes the reader on a thrilling journey from Ibn Sina's birthplace in a village near the ancient Uzbek city of Bukhara, until his death in Persia after an eventful life. Although he became a vizier twice, Ibn Sina was detained in the remote fortress of Fardeqan, where he wrote some of his philosophical works.

INTERNATIONAL PRIZE FOR ARABIC FICTION

ABDELOUAHAB AISSAOUI

The Spartan Court

EXCERPT FROM THE NOVEL
TRANSLATED BY RAPHAEL COHEN

Dupond
Marseille, March 1833

In this world, my esteemed friend Dupond, God is the Devil, yet you still believe that all women are Mary Magdalene, every leader an epiphany of the Saviour. Your mind is so deluded that I feel sorry for you. Wake up, Dupond. Wake up, or go back to Marseille.
Your archfriend, Caviard

Twelve years after Napoleon's death and three years since the fall of Algeria, those words still resound through my head. In not one letter did my old friend want to retract them.
Roaming the streets of Marseille, I sense that people have become oblivious to the turmoil of the past few years and that visit by the Dauphin. Ah, sorry, there is no Dauphin anymore, not since they revolted against him and he too became an exile, just a pale and fleeting shadow in feeble memory. In kingship, twenty minutes is much the same as twenty years; Louis XIX or Napoleon, pas de différence! Who, I wonder, still preserved the dreams of the madman who wanted to be crowned king of the world? His name had continued to stir in the memory of the people, but of them all, the most impassioned and inflamed by the mad leader's life story was my friend Caviard. I liked to call him the fallen Saul, and he laughed when he heard it. He agreed with the merchants of Marseille that remaining in that Spartan city rising beyond the sea would benefit the French. Surely, merchants in Marseille did not only want it as a

memorial to their past glories, but for other reasons. Money, as Saul would say, is a new god, and how many gods there are! Gods at sea and others on land.

"Dupond . . . Dupond!" his voice calls me from beyond the horizon, mocking my fantasies. Imagining him behind me, I turn around suddenly and see faces I do not recognize, their bodies hidden in wool overcoats, hurriedly roaming the streets. My gaze stretches to the end of the road, to the blueness and the harbour. My friend is standing there smoking his pipe, or so it seems. Could Caviard really have returned? But Caviard chose his fate when we parted two years before in North Africa. He blew smoke in my face and said: "My dear Dupond, go back to Marseille and your newspaper. People like you won't do for life here. One bout of dysentery would be enough to kill you. I know more about this land and these barbarians than anyone else. You can't possibly believe that what you are doing or what you think are more than figments of your imagination." So I went back.

Maybe my friend was right, although I now realise that those delusions were once facts. In my despair I was easily fooled, despite the pleadings of Ibn Mayyar, and even his friend al-Sallaoui. They clung onto me like Mary Magdalene to Jesus, but rather than reassuring them, I ran away. My despair led me to abandon them, just as I abandoned what I believed.

A cold gust of wind brought me out of my reverie and I stood observing the harbour. My friend was not there. The blueness went deep into my memory and the cold pricked me like a needle. I returned to my original path, urging myself on as I turned right into a side street, then left down another. I came to the large theatre, counted off its six columns and fled it for the remaining alleyways, which I hurried down as if pursued. Past the theatre, I went down a wider street and the second turning took me into Rue Venture. As soon as I entered it, I saw the sign for the newspaper. I pronounced its name, Le Sémaphore de Marseille. Before lowering my eyes, a disembodied arm extended from behind the door and pulled me inside. Then it led me down the passageways to the editor's office. The editor glanced between me and a man in his fifties seated opposite me. "It seems your old friends," he said to me, "now they've run out of gold, have filled their pockets with bones!"

"Who do you mean?"

"Your officer friends, Dupond. Were you not the correspondent with the campaign that sought to turn Sparta into Athens, only for a Roman city in North Africa to take us by surprise?"

If only you were here, my friend Caviard, you would have known that I'd been right all along. But you preferred the triumph of your soul, which the years of captivity and slavery had filled with black emotions. May God illumine your soul, my friend. My silent prayer for you was interrupted when the manager said, "Do you know the steamship *La Bonne Joséphine?*"

"I might have heard of it."

"She's bound from Algiers, and there's not much time before she drops anchor in the harbour. You will accompany the doctor there." The manager threw the words in my face as he indicated the man opposite me. Then he picked up his overcoat and left the office, leaving me to introduce myself to the doctor.

The doctor gave me a long look then spoke. "It's said the steamer is carrying human bones."

"Are they those of soldiers, who requested to be brought home?"

"No. They're for the sugar factories'. For use as a whitener, apparently."

His words astonished me. "Are you aware of what you're saying, my good Doctor?"

"That is why I am here. All you have to do is accompany me to the harbour."

When we left the office I felt exuberant, as though I would prove to myself, or to my old friend perhaps, that the events of three years before had been a mistake. A mistake I had been trying to purge myself of by any means, even if doing so would force me to return to Algiers.

From the newspaper doorway we spotted carriages at the top of the street and ordered one to take us to the harbour, where we would wait for *La Bonne Joséphine*. As we rode over the cobblestones I went over the doctor's words. Marseille had been under a cloud of rumours for days. Then it had rained a white powder that made people feel sick. But human bones, was it credible? I only knew that I had seen the doctor's expression change, and I thought about asking him whether he really believed the rumours. I sensed his growing disquiet as we neared the harbour, and I almost suggested that the coachman stop for a few minutes, but the doctor broached the subject. "I want to convince myself not to trust these rumours, but my conscience compels me to see for myself. I am afraid to bear such a shame."

"You know that it is not our only shame. All nations have their flaws."

"For all of them I have found justifications, but what justifies the sale of the bones of another nation, and for the reason doing the rounds?"

"Money is a new god. For many reasons he tempts you to dig up graves and consume the bones of your brothers. I am certain we will find them in the steamer. Not because I am clairvoyant, but because I knew them truly and intimately."

The carriage jolted around the last bend and I tried to regain my seat. I raised my head to look out of the window and saw a few sailors wandering around. Their expressions changed whenever they looked out at the deep-blue expanse of the sea. Did they have the same opinions as a politician in Paris? The south had often caused problems, but sailors were not politicians. The sea makes you believe that some certainty exists; even if it is vague, it strikes you when you long for dry land. Politics, however, is something else, given that the only certainty you have to embrace is uncertainty. I realised that the carriage had stopped and heard the shouts of the coachman telling us to get out. I opened the door and stepped down, followed by the doctor. His eyes roved the area. All he could see was the horizon. "So *La Bonne Joséphine* hasn't arrived yet?" I said.

He turned to me and his face adopted a more serious expression. "We'll just have to wait then."

An hour, perhaps more, passed. The bustle of the sailors quietened down, and a few merchants left once they had loaded their goods. Others remained, occupying the benches like us. Then the steamer appeared on the horizon. I could not tell whether it really was *La Bonne Joséphine*. I suspected it was her when I spotted them standing in another corner. Their clothing and headgear gave them away as soon as I saw them. The atmosphere of anticipation and excitement confirmed my remaining suspicions.

The doctor stood at the edge of the quay in wait for the ship. As soon as he saw it, he knew it was her. His eyes had expressed it from the beginning, while I was distracted by my pathetic analyses, as my friend Caviard called them. "Dupond, hey, Dupond, why bother yourself with those ridiculous ideas? Do you think you'll side with these barbarians?"

Had Caviard been here, I would not have waited long with the doctor. He would have taken a bone out of his pocket, perhaps the bone of a small child or an old woman, and given it to me: "Here, take it. It's good for carving into a cross to hang round your neck."

And why not, Caviard? What's the difference between my wearing a cross made of bone or my turning bones into sugar? Isn't it the same? Whichever god you believed in, he wouldn't be pleased. In the past, people believed in numerous gods who fought one another. Today people believe in one god, and buy and sell people's bodies for his sake! Isn't that what you wished to say, my friend Caviard, every time we argued heatedly about your critique of the city you called Sparta. Didn't you say that you had been enslaved there and that the likes of you weren't fit to talk about it? Yes, I respect your suffering, but you don't cleanse yourself by torturing others. Suffering gives birth to knowledge, not hatred; to wisdom, not spite; to faith, not apostasy.

When the sails were lowered and the ship had cast anchor, the doctor suddenly took a few steps back. Had he predicted that the steamship he was awaiting would be well armed with cannons? Or had he guessed that it would be a ship under the merchant flag? I saw how disappointed he was when the tremendous irony sank in as he compared the number of traders flocking in front of him with the number of soldiers onboard the ship. After a few moments he resumed watching a few of the passengers disembark. The area between him and me was soon filled with people: the petty traders of Marseille awaiting the goods *La Bonne Joséphine* had brought, and the agents of others who had sent them and continued to sit behind desks on the other side of the city.

A sailor approached, and standing next to the doctor, I steeled myself. I didn't catch the first few words of the exchange, but I saw the doctor's hand holding out a document. The sailor inspected it, then ran up the gangplank. He was gone a few minutes before signalling to us from above to follow. We went up till we reached the main deck. The sailor went a few steps ahead of us, halted suddenly, and addressed the doctor: "The Captain's cabin."

The Captain was standing at the far end of the room, his face pressed to the porthole. On the small table that stood between us were charts, a compass, and an enormous logbook. He turned around and stared hard at the doctor. He leafed through the document, seemingly unconvinced by its content. "The civilian prosecutor sends a doctor to inspect us. That is why you've come, isn't it?"

"It's not like that, Captain. It's an inspection that can only be carried out by a doctor. The civilian prosecutor wants to limit the scandal if the rumours are true."

The Captain was silent for a moment, then said: "You've come for the crates of bones?"

"Why, is there anything else onboard?" I inquired.

"You have no business apart from what's specified. If you want to see them, that's my condition."

"We're not looking for anything else," replied the doctor.

The Captain shouted to the sailor, who immediately came into the room. I watched the captain fold up the warrant and slip it into a pocket. He asked the sailor to accompany us below deck. The doctor stepped in front of the sailor, who told him to get back behind him and led the way to the hatch leading below deck. He opened it and descended the steps, motioning for us to follow. The doctor went next, with me behind. As soon as my feet touched the floor, I caught sight of the crates, which were stacked up carelessly. The sailor remained standing by the steps behind us, while the doctor went over to the crates. He tried to open one, but large padlocks prevented him. He looked from me to the sailor at a loss. My eyes, however, were searching for any implement that might help.

The sailor only gave me a few moments, during which he disappeared behind the steps, before returning with a hammer. He went over to a crate and smashed the lock. Then he went from one lock to another, as if caught up in a game. The sea, as Caviard would say, sometimes makes its habitués prone to folly. I always remembered that madman at odd moments. I wished he were with us. Would he have been surprised by what was in the crates? What would I say to him if they were just full of animal bones? He would laugh and repeat a favourite saying of his: Dupond, you're a good man. You remind me of an altar boy. I find it amazing that you've seen soldiers drowning in blood, yet you're still such an innocent.

Caviard was always the more eloquent, but always admitted that I was the more stubborn. That's how we left each other: both unable to change anything about his friend.

INTERNATIONAL PRIZE FOR ARABIC FICTION

JABBOUR DOUAIHY

The King of India

A CHAPTER FROM THE NOVEL
TRANSLATED BY PAULA HAYDAR

Mahmoudiyya Orchard

On page 34 of *An Eyewitness Account of the Mount Lebanon Crisis*, a book about the calamitous events of 1860, published in Alexandria in 1892, it reads:
"People's intentions have become corrupt, and man's baser self now thirsts for blood in every corner of the land. The strife found its way to the village of Tel Safra, located fifteen miles east of Beirut and inhabited by Christians and Druze. Fighting broke out between the villagers, and the Christians were not known for their bravery or appetite for battle. Consequently, many were killed in al-'Abbadiyya and on the road to Zahleh . . ."

That's all it says. Those broad generalizations are the only published account – the only written account in fact – of the massacre that Zakariyya Mubarak's town witnessed a century and a half ago. However, the farmers, especially the Christians among them who had suffered defeat at the time, made sure to pass down the various chapters of their struggle to their children orally, from one generation to the next. Voices from the heart of the tragedy bear witness to the sufferings of individuals, which are of little consequence to historians more interested in narrating their 'spin' on the events than in recording their actual details.

One of those hushed and concealed voices was that of Bahiyya al-Murad. After washing her daughter Philomena's hair and braiding her two pigtails, she would take her by the hand, walk her down to the overlook at the edge of the pines, and start talking. Mostly when she spoke it was as though she were talking to herself. She chose to entrust Philomena with the safekeeping of her life's tragedy. She saw in the eyes of her eldest daughter what she did not see in the face of Philomena's innocent younger sister Katarina. Bahiyya would start talking within earshot, and Philomena would listen. Though still at an age when the meanings of some things were difficult for her, her mother's deep sorrow found its way into her young heart, along with that anger of hers that no amount of time could extinguish. Bahiyya told her how beautiful the old days had been, how bountiful and prosperous. They had lived a life of ease and comfort, because her father was a business partner with the Abi Nakad family in the Mahmoudiyya Orchard.

"That is what you see there before you. It extends all the way to the bottom of the valley."

He had uprooted the ancient olive trees and planted mulberry trees in their place, in order to raise silkworms. Silk production was very popular at the time, and Bahiyya was of marriageable age. Relatives and neighbours praised her beauty, so a young man from one of the nearby villages came on two occasions to their house for evening gatherings. He was a zajal poet-singer who wore a striped vest and red keffiyeh made of pure silk: a gallant, well-mannered man. He waited for her a few days later on the road to the village bakery just so he could walk a few short steps with her and tell her in all seriousness and brevity that if she did not accept his marriage proposal then he would enter the order of the Mariamite monks. Her heart would start pounding whenever she caught sight of him in town or at Mahmoudiyya Orchard where he worked with her father during silkworm season and otherwise learned the tailoring trade the rest of the year. She persuaded her mother, who consulted with her father, and he in turn consented. Everyone agreed to have the wedding on the Feast Day of Saints Peter and Paul. Bahiyya started counting the days as she prepared a trousseau of her own handiwork. But early in May, the townspeople were drawn out from their homes by sounds of shouting and clamour outside. Some peasants were carrying the body of a young man from the town who had been murdered along the cobblestone road to Damascus. He had been travelling with three government soldiers who didn't raise a finger to stop the Druze from beating him with sticks and stoning him to death. The townspeople prayed over him and buried him. A delegation of the town's Druze community came the next day to condemn the incident and declare they had nothing to do with it. They made an agreement with the Christians not to fight with each other and that whosoever was bent on causing problems should go join the rest of his faction outside Tel Safra. Tensions were defused. People went back to their work, and Bahiyya busied herself once again with preparations for her wedding day, until the news of Sheikh Abu Saeed Hamdan came along. He was one of Tel Safra's socialites, and a powerful and influential man. He'd fallen prey to an ambush set up for him by the Christians in the Hammana district. It was said that they tortured him before killing him and that one of his assailants was a young man from Tel Safra who wasn't heard from afterwards, nor were his whereabouts ever known again. The Druze did not react immediately but waited until their messengers got the word to their relatives and supporters in the neighbouring villages. They assembled outside the town in the morning before the church bells for the First Mass rang out, attacked the Christian quarter and began burning the houses and property. Nayfeh, the sister of Sheikh Abu Saeed, marched at the front of the line, singing war songs that called for revenge.

Bahiyya went outside barefoot, worried about her father and fiancé who had set out for the orchard at dawn. Three or four of the Druze were mounted on horses while the rest were charging on foot. She raced ahead of them to the orchard and tried to face them off. "We have never fought with you!" she shouted. "We want peace. Let us be!" But one of the mounted men charged right at her on his horse and nearly trampled her, causing her to fall down on the side of the road. Her father and fiancé refused to flee like the other Christians, who were not in the habit of aiding each other as they were scattered and lacked leadership. The moment they got within the crosshairs of the Druze's rifles, they were shot at from multiple directions. They had no chance of survival. They fell in the middle of the mulberry orchard, while all their assailants disappeared in the blink of an eye.

Whenever Bahiyya reached this part of her story, she would stop walking, in order to let her beating heart quieten down so she could bring back the scene and hold it steady in her mind. She would finish the story, hugging her daughter to her chest.

"I was left all alone with my father and my fiancé in the mulberry orchard. The breeze from the sea was cold that morning. The first time I ever kissed my fiancé he was lying dead on the ground. Completely unarmed, he stood to face them, refusing to leave my father all alone. I embraced my father who had never once in his life embraced me. My mother used to say I was his favourite. He wouldn't sleep all night if I had the slightest fever, but he was embarrassed to hug me. I started crawling on my knees and clutching at the soil. I thought I was going to die, too. In fact, I wished I would die. I started rubbing my face in the mud. I rolled my father onto his back, with his face looking up to the sky. I did the same with my fiancé. I clasped their hands across their chests to be as I imagined the angels were in heaven. I prepared a spot on the ground between them and lay down on my back like them. I remember hearing the chirping of birds before falling unconscious. They got to us around noon. They picked me up and sat me in the shade of a tree. My mouth was full of mud. I didn't see my father or my fiancé. I didn't know where they had taken them. I tried to weep, but the tears burned in my eyes."

French soldiers came to shore from their warships off the Lebanese coast, and life returned to normal in Tel Safra. Bahiyya al-Murad remained inconsolable. Her mother thought she might go mad and that the only cure was marriage. They married her off while she was practically unable to speak, to a poor young man who in less than two years' time gave her Philomena and Katarina before falling into Hajal Valley where they discovered his body two days later. The mule whose back he had fallen from led them to his corpse after wandering in the streets weighted down with the sacks of flour he was carrying. People said that Bahiyya al-Murad did not weep for her husband because she simply could not mourn any more. They didn't even dress her in black, out of fear for her life. It was also said that someone had 'written' a spell on her, and there were stories about a woman of Turkoman origin who'd married into the town and was envious of Bahiyya's beauty. It was as though whoever had 'written' a spell on her had done the same to her daughter Philomena, who resembled her with her pretty figure and big eyes.

Their lot in life was beauty and bad luck. However, where Bahiyya had succumbed to her grief, Philomena fought against her fate and ultimately defeated it. She too fell in love with a young man who did not possess many worldly belongings. In winter, he was asked to clean and prune the trees, and at the start of spring to graft the cherry and apple trees. He pocketed a small income with which he could support himself and his wife. One day a representative from the Abi Nakad family came to ask him to clean up and till the orchard. However, Philomena, whose mother's terror-stricken voice had made its impression on her, begged him not to do it and not to go near Mahmoudiyya Orchard. She offered to compensate him with her small savings and what she could get from selling her two gold bracelets that had belonged to her mother.

Mahmoudiyya Orchard has been known for a strange story that persists even in our current times. It started with the murder of Philomena's grandfather and her mother's fiancé. They had been buried secretly at the bottom of the orchard, because getting to the Christian cemetery in town had been impossible at the time due to the presence of armed Druze in that direction. In fact, the matter had been concealed even from Bahiyya, who had always assumed they had been laid to rest up in the cemetery.

The authorities punished the Nakad elders for their participation in the attacks and murders. They confiscated their properties, including Mahmoudiyya Orchard, which encompassed over a hundred dunums. It was left neglected, and for years, no one went near it, until the High Authority of the Mount Lebanon district decreed that personal properties be returned to their owners, until work was underway to restore them via partnership contracts. The orchard had withered, and the nearby silk factory had been shut down, so the only solution was uproot the mulberry trees and sell them as cheap firewood. Following that came a mugharasa contract, whereby the lessee earns half ownership once it turns a profit. It was a fifteen-year contract signed by the heirs of Salman Abi Nakad and a

INTERNATIONAL PRIZE FOR ARABIC FICTION

Christian partner who began planting various types of fast-growing trees, while his workers looked after irrigation and cultivation. He promised himself to start reaping a harvest in three years. During the long-awaited spring season, a hot khamsin wind – never known before in those parts – blew in. They said that it had come all the way from the distant Libyan desert. All the blossoms shrivelled up and the fruits and branches became worm-infested, causing them to turn black and wither. In less than a week's time it destroyed years of constant work and tireless effort. All the townspeople came to observe the disaster with their own eyes, the likes of which they had never seen in their lives and for which they could not fathom a cause. The murabi' – quarter-partner – complained about his situation to the Abi Nakad family who sympathized with him. They reclaimed the orchard from him without making him pay a penalty for breach of contract. History repeated itself a few years later. Bahiyya looked up into the heavens and muttered, "How great you are, Oh God!" Then along came another partner, convinced that the problem wasn't with the land but rather with his predecessor who hadn't been good at caring for it or cultivating it. He planted Mahmoudiyya with grapevines and watched over them night and day, nurturing, irrigating and pruning them, until a cold snap hit along with heavy rain, followed by a morning freeze that burned the tender shoots of the mirwah and 'abeedi grapes, dashing all the second partner's hopes. After that, the Abi Nakad family couldn't find anyone to make the land profitable for them, neither as a murabi' quarter-partner lessee nor as a mugharis half-partner lessee. They neglected it and it became overrun with brush. Snakes and moles and wild mulberry bushes, whose fruit people were afraid to eat, multiplied and resulted in parents warning their children not to go near it.

During that time, Philomena's husband Masoud Mubarak decided to flee. He donned his clean black striped sirwal pants, white shirt, and his tall boots – the only thing of value he had inherited from his father – and walked off with the clippers in his pocket as if on his way to prune trees at one of the orchards. He set out and all trace of him was lost forever. He had been silent about it and hadn't divulged the secret of his sudden departure to anyone. It didn't take Philomena's mother Bahiyya al-Murad long to follow the departed ones. In her final years, she lost her ability to speak, causing her to sink deep inside herself, and she never come back out. She died just a few days before the birth of her grandson Gabriel.

Philomena realized that if she stayed amidst her broken family there was no power in heaven that could help them. Alternatively, if she did stay near her husband's relatives, who had not shown much concern for her situation, she would find neither sustenance in life nor the least bit of joy. One morning, while she watched her son crawling around on his knees and trying to get her attention so he could grab onto her and stand up on his feet, she decided to fight the death that was on her trail and cast off the heavy burden of grief from her shoulders. Without actually looking out towards the sea, which was hidden from view at the time by a thick white morning haze, she knew her only option was to go far away. It was common in those days for people to travel to America, even for women to go on their own. And so, she went.

During her absence, the Great War took place. There were shortages and people were poverty-stricken. They were terrified by stories that came from the north, from towns in Byblos and Batroun, of people dying of starvation. Mahmoudiyya Orchard was still overrun with brush, not bearing a single fruit. So, the townsfolk banded together in the fall to plough and plant it with wheat in the hope it would provide enough bread to sustain them. Katarina alone – who raised her sister Philomena's son Gabriel as one of her own children – knew that nothing planted in Mahmoudiyya would grow, because blood is heavy, and because there is divine justice in the world.

And indeed, when the wheat stalks grew and the green of the sprouting spring carpeted the entire vast area, they started hearing news of locusts storming over the slopes of Mount Lebanon. It didn't take long before they arrived and covered the sky, blotting out the sunlight. They devoured everything in sight in a matter of a day or two. Mahmoudiyya reverted once again to an arid orchard. Many Druze fled to their relatives in the Hauran region, and the Christians tried to manage despite the shortages and the spread of typhus.

The owners of Mahmoudiyya Orchard gave up all hope for it after the war ended and they were unable to find anyone to partner with them in developing it. Its reputation spread to the neighbouring villages, and all sorts of stories were concocted about the land being tainted and how it had been the object of the wrath of Astarte, the goddess in whose honour the Roman temple had been constructed.

INTERNATIONAL PRIZE FOR ARABIC FICTION

ALIA MAMDOUH

The Tank

EXCERPT FROM THE NOVEL
TRANSLATED BY NANCY ROBERTS

Mr. Samim, family name unknown

As in old picture albums, we all thought: We, The undersigned, are the family of Ayyoub Al- who will gradually appear with us here before long, either directly in front of us, or a bit to one side. It would be best to leave the mother, Makkiya, seated on a chair, since she can't stand up for long even if it's just to get a picture taken. Next to her is Aunt Fathiya, then the younger aunt, Saniya. The grandmother, Bibi Fatim, isn't among us, since she stayed upstairs. Now, in order for us to be properly dignified, it's preferable that we men – including me, father Ayyoub and my brother Mukhtar – stand behind them. Here it would be advisable for us to leave a place for Hilal, our oldest son, and for her – our daughter Afaf – whose case we've entrusted to Mr. Samim. Come on, brother, take the task off my hands, and let me go back to my place in the album.

Well, Miss Afaf's ghost appeared just as I was writing your name. Dear Doctor Carl Valino,

I am Samim, a secret writer and I operate under a code name. I'm the man who came with her in 1986 to your private clinic on Rue de Jasmin in the Sixteenth Arrondissement. I hope your memory doesn't fail you. As for her, Miss Afaf, she was leading the way with her short, slender frame. In her hand she held a square painting she had done, which she presented to you without a word. My wife Tarab, the sculptor, was her friend and colleague at the Academy.

Ma'ath Alousi, my friend and Miss Afaf's engineering advisor, is the architect whose initial design of 'the cube' Miss Afaf was so taken with that she enrolled in the Faculty of Engineering, and studied there for two years before changing her major and transferring to the Academy of Fine Arts in Wazireya. Ma'ath may have 'corrupted' her when he said to her one day: "We'll design 'the cube' together, and we'll invite our favourite people to view it."

Perhaps based on the course of that cube and fine arts in general, and the context of our whole city, it was Miss Afaf – and I insist on using this prefix to her name at present, setting aside nostalgia or anything close to it – who was always the first topic of conversation.

Then there's the lawyer, her uncle Mukhtar, who may provide us with some legal rationale and administrative advice so that we might find some consolation in the archives.

And her brother Hilal, whom we continue to write letters to, urging him to act quickly, but which he has yet to reply to. Who knows? Maybe, during the final hours before the curtain closes on the last of our faces, he may show up and be part of this manuscript, or whatever you want to call it. Ma'ath says that Younus's smile has changed of late. It's become perplexing. He asked him if he'd been thinking of joining us, since he could report on what's been going on inside him. Ma'ath added: "These entries will take on special importance, even if it doesn't happen right away. If we knew the address of Mr Yassin, we would send for him and make him join us . . . We would also provide you with some footnotes and additions, and things we don't have a title for. Our letters might draw in Aunt Fathiya, and she might speak out . . . We'll manage the situation, our situation. And, wise sir, you for your part will go from monopolising some, or all, of the truth, to sharing it with us – the family members that you expect to look for her before it's too late. You'll be required to certify everything that you know and find out, what you've heard, and what has come to your attention, whether by coincidence or design, so that you can confirm the perpetrator, whether you, or us. Every one of us references their stories to her trail, wary of disturbing their certainty of a deceptive innocence. Of course, we know about some eras and what they achieved and engraved in us. They're going to expose both us and you to criticisms on all fronts, and from every direction. They'll cause us to start betraying principles in a case, or cases, of tentative or final elaboration of all the facts, both confidential and public . . . You will observe this, sir, all of our tracks, as we surprise ourselves even more than we do you. After all, we would have preferred that the secrets remain between us. But now, we'll face hardship and some danger, each of us in his own way, as we place them in both your hands and our own: those that remain in our hands, and on our clothes. Before anything else, we thought this might be the only way we could regain contact with her or get her back in person, that is, if we implicate each other on account of our legal, linguistic, intellectual, religious, artistic, sexual and political records. We thought that if we recovered ourselves, we who are on the verge of drowning, then some day she might dream, just as we do, of herself unexpectedly appearing before us. Ahh . . . How often we've thought of keeping certain secrets hidden, and disclosing others. Each one of us has to act according to the dictates of his own circumstances.

Ma'ath assigned me the task of recording this manuscript.

He told me encouragingly: "You have clear, bold handwriting, and your letters are fully formed. This will make it easy to read and translate. I'll supply you with scraps of paper to work from, either typed, or in my own lousy handwriting."

And Tarab!

She's still hesitant. She has reservations about letting all the secrets out. She said: "Some of us make them up and weigh ourselves down with them in order to come across as high class. And some transport them to the world of art and literature, where they take unexpected paths."

It was Uncle Mukhtar who supported our efforts in that nonchalant way of his, which Miss Afaf liked so much that she brought him on board with us. He isn't the conversationalist that he needs to be and he's usually drunk, the way she likes to see him. So if he works with new tools, he won't feel any inhibitions. On the contrary, he'll overcome his stutter and the parallel account he narrates about her will start to get ahead of ours. The Ayyoub Al- family may not take to all these types of narrative tracks, since this might block the steps required to search for her. On the other hand, it might have the opposite effect. We don't know, Doctor. But there's one thing the family wants in a hurry, as it hangs over all of our heads. Come on, start telling the story right now. Look for our daughter. The time since she went missing can't be compared to the natural cycles of childhood and youth, or to periods of lasting health or imagined illness. Come on. Sing like her, or whisper like her so that the echo can sound, all the way to the ill-omened lands of westerners that led our daughter astray. Come on – move to the same place. There . . . have you begun to see her? That's our daughter herself, or nothing but a character inside the pages of a book that you intend to write but that doesn't lead you to her. Don't ask questions you'll never find the answers to, since all you have are words and dry paint on a handful of canvases that have been lost among her friends. But all of us are evidence of one sort or another, are we not? Good. And as nobody would suspect us, don't avoid taking us into consideration. Scrutinize us. Come and talk with us. Scrutinise yourselves too, or others. We don't know your plans. Are you going to open a police-like report, or will you content yourselves with an announcement? Is she gone for good? Why do you go to other people's lands? Huh? It's nothing but a pain in the head, in her head, that's playing the murderer. This isn't a legal problem as her uncle Mukhtar keeps saying, but we, her family, disagree over what to call it: Is it a crime? Or a general state of panic that's making the rounds of the world's continents and capital cities? We didn't see a drop of blood on our daughter's clothes as she disappeared from sight. We didn't see that. Oh! She's so far away from us now. Yes she is, yes she is. The lines and roads that might lead to her have been blocked for a long time, and not just because of wars.

We miss her, and we don't know what to do with the longing, or how to manage it amongst ourselves. We don't know where to put it, or how to spread it around. Did some of us get a bigger share of it than others? Can we put it off, or hurry it up so as to get over it all at once? But it was sucking up half our lifetimes, so we don't know where the years went, or how they passed.

The foreign doctor may be in good health, and his heart may have stopped pining. We don't know why. Maybe that's the reason he's busy earning his living, and you all are like him. You said, "Missing her doesn't do any good," and then you relaxed and felt better. True, longing is an obnoxious thing, and your doctor doesn't bother to look for the right diagnosis for it. True, it has no entry in any medical textbook. Even so, it's a deadly disease, and it's the only chance we have left to put some warmth back into our blood.

Come on now, tell me: What have you been doing with all those pencils, papers, cups and drinks when our daughter has been gone for so long, Mr. Samim? What are we going to do with all these caravans of bitterness when the road to her is unsafe, when parts of it are blocked, and when everyone knows the reasons? We aren't going to be able to hold onto our daughter when we don't even know how old she is now. Every day our longing grows more intense, and weighs more heavily on us than it did the day before. We also don't know how to distract ourselves from these things, or with whom.

How does there come to be this inseparable link between disappearance, longings, roadblocks, and wars? I thought you all knew the reason, and that you would be able to tell us. Hah . . . you're looking here. The roads that lead to her are closed, and there's no hope of healing there. So then, who's going to look for her? It won't do to manipulate us or exploit us, or to flatter the westerners and play the hypocrite. So long as you carry on in your lazy way, even if you moved and took all the references and volumes, working until your eyes couldn't see any more, we would never find any trace of her. That way won't bring her back to us, or to you. Don't you realize that she left you before the streets were closed! She left Tarab, and Younus, and Yassin, and you, Mr. Samim, and that engineer who considered her his confidante. In the end, she developed an aversion to him and took his secrets with her.

And we the aunts: Yes, I'm Aunt Fathiya. I got sicker and sicker as I formulated the simple sentences she loved in hopes of her coming back. I started talking to her every day, calling out to her in the way stories usually begin and the way we want them to. We could stop the girl right here, bringing the camera up close to every face in the family. Remind me, Mr. Samim, whether I've forgotten one of us. Your doctor will give a faint smile, since she was the youngest in the family when we moved to Tank Street. Yes, I'm the one who divided her name in two. Whenever I looked up and saw her in front of me, I would say:

"Affou, clean the table really well. Some society lady might drop by. The neighbours around here aren't like the people on the ship. I checked both ordinary folks and the elite, and wrote everything down in my diary, darling."

As soon we'd settled into our new home, I took her by the hand and said to her: "Come out for a walk with me. Let's check out the streets, the houses and the amazing mansions around here. Store in your head the colours of the sky, the feel of the ground, and the scent of the bitter oranges as they burst open on the tree. Take it all in with your nostrils, Affou. Then sit down and color and draw."

It's true, Mr. Samim, that Affou wouldn't answer when I called. So I would repeat myself, more loudly than before, and as a way of teasing her, I'd draw out her name a bit, like this: "Affouooooo . . . !"

But she wouldn't respond, since she knew what I wanted. I'd talk to myself with her standing behind me, saying, "Come on, sweetie pie, draw pictures of all of them. I have them ready for you so that you can see what they looked like and what they were wearing, with their King Faisal I-style sidara hats, their tarboosh and their turbans. Come now, I want to see them decked out in full regalia. Make their shoes as shiny as their bald heads, make their suits look brand new as though they'd just come from the tailor's shop, and their collars snow-white. Now, sweetheart, what would you think about putting on an exhibition for the Iraqi ministers? See? I took the illustrations from the book that shows the members of the Iraqi Cabinets and I had them enlarged at the Sabah bookstore at the beginning of Ishreen Street. See how chic they are, and what good taste they had! Here's Prime Minister Abdel Muhsin Saadoun with his sidara and bowtie. You know, Affou, they were all so well groomed, I could smell cologne wafting off their clothes and their moustaches. Heh heh! Back in those days, they had nice customs related to eating and dressing. They also had certain ways of holding their hands and posing for the photographer when he came to take their pictures. They were real gentlemen."

She would grow quiet when I called her by her nickname. It bothered her, and she would clam up. Was I the only one who didn't know it upset her? Did my use of the diminutive make her feel diminished somehow? That's the kind of misunderstanding that ruins relationships, maybe even for generations. I thought it was a way of showing affection or approval. Don't you agree, Mr. Samim? One day I stood her up in front of me and explained it to her.

I said: "Don't believe them. Your mother had wanted to name you Afifa after our mother. But your father, a man of refined taste, settled the matter. 'No,' he said, Afaf is prettier.'"

INTERNATIONAL PRIZE FOR ARABIC FICTION

SAID KHATIBI

Firewood of Sarajevo

EXCERPT FROM THE NOVEL
TRANSLATED BY PAUL STARKEY

The genie's eyes

In this trembling, apprehensive city, one catastrophe begets another. All at once disasters emerge from their hiding places to fall on our heads and shatter them. The embassy had refused my application for a visa for Slovenia and the following day, I woke up with no job and no income. A lost and broken object of anger, not knowing where to turn my face.

After the publication of an interview with a member of the political opposition living in London came the catastrophic decision, banning the publication of the paper. The order wasn't sent to the chief editor or the publications manager but instead to the printing house, where we were informed by an employee that an order had been issued by the Ministry of Communications withdrawing the newspaper's licence without telling us the reason. We only had to think for a bit to conclude that the reason for the decision must have been the interview.

"I'm just following orders," the employee told us.

"And I'm unemployed," I told Malika.

"I'll employ you as my personal guard and pay you a salary each month!" she replied sarcastically.

Her sarcasm struck me as misplaced. I was in deep shit and she was joking like a schoolgirl trying to set my mind at rest, though her intentions were innocent. She wanted to make a joke of it to change my mood and relieve me of my nervous tension, that's all. Her intuitions had been right. When I told her on the telephone I'd been assigned to an investigation in the village of Sidi Labka, she replied coldly: "You're giving yourself trouble, you won't achieve anything!" I was cross at her reply at the time, but later I understood what she had meant. Sometimes I had a strange feeling about Malika. I could detect in her the smell of motherhood that a man looks for who has lost his own mother before he's been weaned from his dependence on her. After Hajja Fatima's body had grown thin and she had lost her appetite, she suffered from continuous vomiting. As the cancer sapped her spirits, I looked for her smell in one of my aunts without success. I couldn't find it in any other woman I had met before, apart from Malika, in whom I could sense a lost warmth, a light leading me back to the woman whose presence I needed.

With my tall stature, light skin, and calm features, I looked like a younger brother of Malika – whose brow had become covered in light wrinkles – rather than her personal bodyguard.

"Why don't you go to another newspaper?"

"Advertising revenues have dried up, and with them employment opportunities."

The year I was orphaned, after I'd got my degree in media studies, I got a position on *al-Hurr* newspaper. For the first three months I worked as an editor on the 'Correspondents' page'. I took over from a female editor in her thirties, who had gone on maternity leave then resigned to live with her husband and young child in a coastal town in the east of the country. Every day I would receive dozens of faxes and phone calls from young correspondents about routine and sometimes unimportant news items. News to fill a couple of pages about the repair of the pavements in some out-of-the-way village; a forestation drive in another village; a citizen looking for some lost medicine; someone else with some money who had given a donation to build a mosque; a Christian graveyard whose graves had been desecrated; dogs forming packs behind a school and terrorising the pupils. Assorted new items, sometimes not even worth a mention, which I would re-read, re-edit, choose headlines for them, then send them to be typeset and published the following day. After three months had passed, the chief editor transferred me to the cultural department, where I met Fathi. We became friends and he awoke in me a passion for writing and literature. I started to undertake some assignments outside the office, covering events on location. Sometimes the paper would receive new books, in Arabic or French, which I would look at with Fathi, discuss their contents and the lives of their authors, and I would write reviews of them. But I only stayed in the cultural department a year and four months. The manager decided to scrap the cultural page and replace it with a page of jokes and crossword puzzles, which changed during Ramadan into a recipes page. So I moved with Fathi to the politics department. I found myself writing about death and the dead – the monster that was lying in wait for us – and about the pronouncements of state officials with broad faces and thick moustaches, whose names and faces I knew, but had never ever met any of them. From time to time I would be charged with investigating places where blood had been shed, either in the capital, Algiers, or elsewhere.

"You're a bachelor, the only one who can be entrusted with this," the chief editor commented on one occasion.

I was given those jobs because all my colleagues were married with children, and people were afraid for them, but I was also afraid for myself. It's true that I had lost my mother, and my father – who'd developed Alzheimer's – was becoming more distant from me, but I wasn't ready to lose my life for the sake of people I didn't know. I had sympathy for them, but none of them would have any sympathy for me if I died because of my eagerness to write about what was happening to them.

"It's water under the bridge," said Malika, trying to reassure me.

I looked into her brightly coloured eyes, blue with brown, and said to myself that perhaps she had been struck by a genie while she was still in her mother's womb. Perhaps she herself was a genie, an ill-fated woman, and I didn't know it. I lowered my eyes to her lips, which she was constantly moistening with her tongue. I waited for her to smile and reveal her white teeth but she refused and went back to her jokes.

"If you'd accept a job as my personal bodyguard, I'd pay you the same and look for a suitable wife for you."

I brought a bottle of cold water from the fridge, went back over to her and asked: "Won't you be going to visit your family?"

"I don't want to visit them, and have to confront their repeated questions about my private life. Huriyya visited them and told me that my aunt wants to marry me off to one of her sons! Imagine!"

"Why not?"

"I'm not the sort of person who wants to marry a relative!"

"If you continue to refuse, you'll never marry at all!"

She fell silent for a moment then gave me a look full of anger. "What's that got to do with you?' she suddenly asked me. "You rascal," I muttered. The signs of joking disappeared from her face and her eyes became bright as cherries.

"Have the 'guardians of the soul' started corresponding with you again?"

I expected her to answer no – I had put the question just to relieve the atmosphere.

"Who will guarantee that they won't do it again?"

Once they sent a former female colleague on *al-Hurr* newspaper a piece of white cloth like a shroud, with some soap, and wrote on a small piece of paper: "If you come back, we will come back." What if they get to me, and threaten me, I asked myself. I could find no answer. I was consumed by fear for a whole day, secretly praying that God would spare me anything like that.

Malika and I hid ourselves away in a corner of her small room, arranged as befitted a faithful reader of John Steinbeck, Anais Nin and Ernest Hemingway. Everything was clean and in the right place: window curtains, covers, a bed, two wooden chairs and a small desk, crammed full of novels by her favourite American authors. We sat opposite each other, saying nothing. The silence was broken only by the voice of Cheb Khaled coming from the tape recorder. When he burst out into his old songs, we felt that the earth had stopped turning.

If you find my love combing her locks, cover me with her hair
If you find my love crying, quench my thirst with her tears
If you find my love dead, bury me opposite her.

As Khaled sang, Malika closed her brightly coloured eyes and rested her cheek on the palm of her left hand. She got up from her chair and, with her bottom on the floor, leaned her back against the bed then pushed back a stray hair behind her ear. She sighed as though she wanted to say something but left Khaled's voice to speak for her.

Khaled Hadj Ibrahim, to give him his full name, was the salt of the desert, the spring of travellers, and our national memory. Intentionally or otherwise, the dark man from Oran spoke to me, describing me in his songs better than I could describe myself. In these bloodthirsty times, people's voices turned to tears and lamentation, except for that of Khaled, who spoke of love and freedom. The 'negro', as the inhabitants of Oran called him, knew how to play on the hearts of his listeners. I saw him on television some time ago, singing with his eyes shut, standing in front of the microphone like an obedient soldier, with a radiant smile, and an untidy moustache that was quite unique. A certain writer said that a man without a moustache was like a woman with a moustache. Did this mean that I was not a complete man? Would Malika really like to see me with a moustache but was hiding her wishes from me? Malika had never commented on my appearance but she loved Cheb Khaled, and Khaled did not trim his moustache. Perhaps she liked to make me listen to her favourite singer to convey to me a message she was unable to express openly.

> *I don't care what people say about me*
> *God willing, I will always be okay*
> *Those who gossip about me*
> *Take my faults from me*
> *I believe in fate*
> *And will accept my destiny*
> *I don't like to worry*
> *I don't care about gossip*
> *It's in my nature to hate scoundrels*
> *I aspire only to God*

Khaled carried on singing, as Malika passed her right hand gently over her hair, which had grown long. She had dyed it black, like Isabelle Adjani's hair in the film One Deadly Summer. Had she dyed her hair for me? To gain my attention? But I didn't say a word or praise her beauty. I swear that I am no romantic, and incompatible with romantic women. I continued to stare into her face, licking my lips just as she did and listening to the sound of the Rai coming from the tape recorder, ascending to a heaven that was more merciful than the earth we lived on. As she looked away from me, I felt confused: Should I embrace her? Stop the music and talk to her? I sat on the ground beside her and put my arm around her waist, waiting for a suitable moment to take her lips by storm.

Malika didn't buy records or cassette tapes and avoided going into shops that sold them, for fear of rousing suspicion, so she said. She also avoided going to the women's baths on Fridays, or to the hairdresser's. Instead, she got a friend of hers to style her hair or dye it from time to time, and recorded both old and new songs from the radio, which broadcast evening concerts on Mondays, Thursdays and Fridays. By night, she danced with the living, while by day she had mercy on the dead.

When Huriyya came into the house, we got up, Malika switched off the tape recorder. I regretted that I had wasted the opportunity to flirt with her. We left the room to greet Huriyya, and she slipped her veil down so that her blond-dyed hair could be seen, tied in a ponytail, like Steffi Graf's. Then she kissed me on the cheek. I was on the point of leaving when Malika tried to persuade me to stay and have supper with them, but I insisted on going back to my apartment.

"Imagine if the 'guardians of the soul' were to visit us at night and found me with you, with no family connection between us!" I whispered to her, jokingly.

"I guarantee we'd die together and you wouldn't deceive me with another woman!"

I went back to the open books scattered around my apartment, to my clothes and the other things lying all around the place. I looked at them with a feeling of disappointment in my heart. I wasn't the same person I had been before. I was an unlucky man. Fate was against me and I hadn't got a visa to travel. I was unemployed, an out-of-work journalist. My staying in the building was a matter of time, nothing more. I might not be able to save enough money to make another advance payment.

My mood changed and I lost my appetite. Faruq contacted me to ask how I was and I told him that the embassy had refused my application for a visa. He encouraged me to try again. I wanted to tell him that I was unemployed and that the paper had stopped publication, but I hesitated. He would find some reason to criticise me again, for neither he nor al-Hajj were happy with my choice of job as a journalist, and I think that Si Ahmad was also unhappy with my decision. My aunts, Zuleikha, Sa'diya and Sharifa, said nothing, and had no view on what happened to their nephew. After I had finished university, al-Hajj suggested to me that I should go to the desert to work in a petroleum company, through the good offices of a friend of his, but I refused. He and Faruq considered my decision to be illogical, and thought that I wasn't looking after my interests. If Faruq found out what had happened at the paper, he would be like a broken record, insisting he understood my interests better than I did. Sometimes Faruq treated me like a juvenile, as if I were his son. There were only five years between us but he wanted to impose his advice on me, like those scout leaders who arouse revulsion in those who consult them, because of the severity of their advice.

"I'll submit another application for the visa!" I said, without much conviction, then put the phone down.

I turned on the radio, brushing away the flies with the palms of my hands. The insecticide had been useless. I heard the announcer mutter something about Widad Tilmisan's team, who had won the Republic Cup, then changed stations to the French-language channel, where I heard the announcer speaking about the anniversary of the Soummam Conference. He talked about it as a pivotal event in the history of the state and the War of Liberation. 'The Soummam Conference was a compass that changed the history of Algeria', said the announcer in a tone of triumph. If only the martyrs could return and see where the compass has led us. I changed the channel to a Moroccan station playing Egyptian and Lebanese songs and stretched out on the bed like a debilitated dog, stinking of sweat. I shut my eyes, and across my mind there floated the pale faces of my colleagues, frowning and gloomy after they'd learned of the decision to cease production of the newspaper. I decided that I would go the following day to a popular café in Martyrs' Square, on Fathi's advice, to meet an 'agent', and negotiate with him for a forged visa. Getting out of a counterfeit country like this, where I no longer had a job, needed serious, resolute forgery.

INTERNATIONAL PRIZE FOR ARABIC FICTION

KHALIL ALREZ

The Russian Quarter

EXCERPTS FROM THE NOVEL
TRANSLATED BY SOPHIA VASALOU

1

The Russian Quarter, the roof terrace overlooking the zoo. On a table not far from where the muzzle of the giraffe was nestling, scenes from a match replay between Spain and Uruguay were flickering across my 14-inch TV. I could hear the rumbling of artillery fire somewhere in the vicinity – it had been going since early morning – as we sat there, the giraffe and I, watching black-and-white shots of dusty old goals scored 50 years ago in Madrid. I was sipping at a cup of tea that had gone cold, my mind on the apple pastries which would soon be arriving, courtesy of Denis Petrovich, the clarinet teacher at the Music Academy. The nearby artillery guns were pounding the Ghouta district from their base inside the gardens of the Russian Quarter. But all my senses were straining toward the long flight of stairs running up to behind the settee where I was lounging, and where any moment now Nonna's lithe footsteps might come tearing. She had popped out to the city centre to pay a visit to her dad at the Russian Cultural Centre.

The full moon was bathing me in its luminance. Images from the TV screen were flashing across the giraffe's large black eyes, their silver light catching the thick frizz around its lips that was almost mingling with the forms of long-gone football players, long-gone spectators, and long-gone turf on the football pitch.

KHALIL ALREZ

The amount of space allocated to the giraffe in the zoo had always struck me as disproportionately small for its size, which stood out in its sheer enormity whenever one viewed it against the backdrop of the other animals and the other parts of the zoo that surrounded it. Passers-by on the neighbouring street had grown accustomed to seeing its lofty head swaying over the wall of the enclosure and its fringe of shrubs ever since I'd taken up residence in the former room of my friend Saleh at the top of the zoo's warehouse. Saleh had vanished from the Russian Quarter without trace a few months before the war broke out. At that point my wife had given up on me, as had my father-in-law, owing to what they saw as my numerous "defects" – a topic which this is neither the time nor the place to get into. In any event, as soon as I realised I'd ceased to be of any use or consideration in my home – the formal property of my wife and her father – I lost no time in clearing out, and I left them to its exclusive enjoyment, harbouring no regrets. At the time, the place that Saleh had formerly occupied at the zoo still stood empty, so I quickly stepped in to fill it. I did so under enthusiastic encouragement from the Afghan hound President Petrovna and her owner Viktor Ivanich, an old colleague who used to work with me as a translator at the news desk of the *Moscow Daily* 20 years ago, and who now headed the zoo at the Russian Quarter and edited its newsletter, The Wall.

Even before we became neighbours, the giraffe and I were no strangers to each other. I had always met with a warm welcome from everyone at the zoo. Whenever I approached the giraffe's pen, I flattered myself that it singled out my hand for special attention from among all the other hands that reached out to touch it through the fence. I felt it didn't shy away from me the way it usually did with Ivanova, the lady who cleaned its pen daily, and it didn't become all skittish the way it did with the vet Basheer Ghandoura who would stop by to do a check-up from time to time. When I was standing within view, I had the impression it would turn its head about and seek me out. On rare occasions, when it felt me stroking its front legs or picking the small stones out of its hooves, it would bend its head down right above my own.

This is not to say that I was oblivious to the amicable relations the giraffe enjoyed with all of its consorts, be they zoo workers, members of the administration, or fellow animals. It was as if its consciousness of towering mightily above all other entities and exis-

KHALIL ALREZ

tents naturally disposed it to have a sense of care toward them and to treat them with affection. One of the things that always struck me in this connection was that it would sometimes take pains to lean over the fence that divided it from its neighbour, the ostrich, as if to make sure, time and time again, that no constraints should subsist between them. On some occasions it would stick out its long black tongue and it would begin rolling it gently, cautiously, and affectionately over the small patch of the ostrich's forehead, the bottom of its flat beak, and its long hairy neck, while the ostrich stared back goggle-eyed with its usual look of disbelief. As it made its way toward the edge of my roof terrace after nightfall, it would pause and look about here and there in a leisurely manner. If something happened to catch its attention, it would study it calmly and carefully. Perhaps it wanted to make sure that the sickly old wolf and his equally ancient wife were still breathing inside their small pen, that the black eagles hadn't yet collapsed from exhaustion after a whole day spent glaring at the world from their artificial crests behind the mesh screen, or that the rambunctious little lemurs were still hopping about from one artificial painted branch to another.

From among all the other animals at the zoo, it was the Afghan hound President Petrovna that had best discovered how to carve a special place for itself in the giraffe's heart. It lived with Viktor Ivanich in a room on the roof terrace across from Saleh's, later to be my own. Almost every morning without fail, it would jump across to the terrace outside my room and it would post itself at the very edge of the roof, where it commanded an open view of the giraffe's enclosure. It would then start trying to attract the giraffe's attention by uttering a series of low gentle barks. The giraffe would quickly respond to its impassioned calls. It would sway over and with just a slight dip of its head would be standing right before it. Immediately it would lower its eyelids with their long tassels of jet-black eyelashes and surrender in blissful serenity to President Petrovna's attentions as the hound threw itself with zeal and determination into the task of working its tongue over the insides of the giraffe's flattened nostrils, its ridged forehead, its eyelids, its ears, and its stubby horns, and licking them all clean.

Nevertheless, and for mysterious reasons I can't quite establish, I felt that as time progressed, nobody in the zoo was able to compete with me for the giraffe's affection. This impression was fortified by the fact that, already from the very first night I spent in Saleh's room many moons ago, it started to make me the beneficiary of that pure form of silent listening which it afforded to none of its other acquaintances and consorts, not even the closest. It was a type of listening that for the most part wasn't aimed at understanding anything specific I happened to say. By temperament, I'm not a man of many words. From time to time I feel the urge to say something out loud, and I let the words out as the mood takes me within the giraffe's hearing, just so I'm rid of them and they don't linger pointlessly in my mouth. And sometimes in the evenings I find myself picking up a book – it might be in Arabic or in Russian – and reading a few passages out loud in front of it, or just reciting some poem to it from memory. Yet most of the time when I'm in the giraffe's presence, my mind simply drifts, without a single word escaping my lips. And even then, it continues to listen to my silence in that same limpid, devoted way. It's as if it was always communing with some secret bustle that it loved to hear, which it was able to pick up directly from my thoughts and feelings.

It was a source of great pleasure for me, naturally, to be lying there on the settee, my hand fondling the humped forehead and stubby horns of the giraffe while my attention drifted to the moon being momentarily curtained by a passing cloud, to a cat licking itself clean on the opposite terrace, or to a cacophony of honking suddenly erupting one street across. Around other people I'd usually start to feel awkward whenever a certain amount of time passed without my saying something. I'd never feel this kind of awkwardness around the giraffe, no matter how much time elapsed. It made me feel that I was always providing it with something to occupy its thoughts, that it found what it was looking for in me and what was worth listening to at all times.

Sometimes I would pull up a wicker chair and sit down right before its face where I could reach out and stroke the top its mane with my hand, and where it could also listen to my thoughts turning about from up close if it pleased. To see its glistening eyes and perked-up ears, it was as though it were reading off my face some happy time gone by – tasty trees in faraway forests, a whole troop of hooved and winged associates and acquaintances whose cheerful ruckus it hadn't heard in a while. And sometimes, as in a pleasant daydream, I'd feel as if it were searching my features for signs of a calf that had dropped into the world from its lofty womb long long ago, and which it couldn't work out where and how it had managed to lose on some ill-fated day under the sweltering midday sun.

2

One day, Nonna suddenly discovered spring onions. It was as if she were seeing them for the very first time. She went ahead and bought herself a bunch.

Nonna was new to Damascus, and she hadn't yet picked up the habit of eating spring onions, not even with bread and yoghurt. But on that day Nonna realised why she'd bought that bunch, in a single flash, when she ran into me for the first time on the front steps of the Russian Cultural Centre in the old city of Damascus. I was standing there hugging a giant wad of old Russian newspapers to my chest with both arms. I'd just bought them by the kilo at the library, thinking I might use them for the zoo's newsletter The Wall. Nonna was making her way past me, clutching at her bunch of spring onions with evident pride, when suddenly she caught glimpse of me and came to an immediate halt. She began devouring my face as if trying to stoke the memory of past events and faraway places. She looked as if she was about to take a step forward and throw her arms around me, newspapers and all, but at the final moment she faltered and froze to the spot. By that time her face was all red and her blossom-pink lips were quivering; so she thrust out the bunch of spring onions to me as if they were a bouquet of roses. By now, I was also ready to throw my arms around her, newspapers and all. Not because we knew each other, as we could both easily pretend we believed, but because at that difficult time, I'd found a woman like her to take an interest in me.

"Remember me?" she asked excitedly. "I'm Nonna!"

Wedging the giant wad of newspapers against my chest with one arm, I held out the other to take up the bunch of spring onions she'd offered so preciously, receiving it as if it were a bouquet of roses.

"I remember you," she pre-empted me. "Don't go away!" And without waiting for an answer she ran up the stairs and disappeared into the front door of the Russian Cultural Centre.

The truth is I felt I as if I didn't want to remember her. As I stood there with the fragrant stalks of the spring onions brushing into my face, the newspapers felt lighter in my arms, as if the stack had somehow shrunk in size. The people walking on the street around me seemed less sombre, as if there was some beautiful harmony holding them together. I didn't care whether there was or wasn't some prior event that had brought us together and through some incalculable sequence had paved the way for our unexpected intense encounter moments before. Overall, I didn't need additional reasons to interpret or justify her enthusiastic response to me, or to explain why I was now standing happily on the pavement of 29 May Street in front of the Russian Cultural Centre holding a wad of newspapers and a bouquet of spring onions.

All I cared about at that moment was that I was waiting for a beautiful woman, which every fibre of my being was crying for. As the time ticked by without a sign of her, it goes without saying that I didn't begin to doubt my senses and feelings. I continued to stand there, hardly registering the passage of time, all my thoughts concentrated not on her absence but on her.

Then at some point I noticed a blind old man walking along tapping his stick. When he drew up alongside me he wavered for a moment, but he took another few steps before coming to a halt next to a young pine tree. A sweet smile now spread over his face, as if somewhere in the dark void behind his eyes he'd stumbled upon a dear friend standing by the tree. His stick had deftly probed the empty space in front of him and assured him he was there. I didn't wish to spoil the pleasure he was taking in his private spectacle. I made a cautious effort to alert him to the fact that I wasn't standing next to him, and that no-one else could see or was expecting to see his dear friend in the darkness enveloping him, and then I turned my eyes upward to contemplate the pure blue of the sky. That was when I felt his long stick tapping lightly against my knee, as if by accident. I turned around. His smile had broadened, and he was peering through his wizened eyelids toward the entrance of the Russian Cultural Centre where at that very moment Nonna was appearing in the door.

She was now wearing a short sleeveless dress of a golden yellow that showed off her milky-white legs and naked arms; from her shoulder hung a crimson handbag. She looked so ravishing as she gracefully swept down the stairs that I could barely bring myself to recall what she'd been wearing before she went in. She was almost breathless when she came to a halt in front of me. Her blossom-pink lips were parted and her eyes were shining with happiness as they questioned my face to discover where our first-ever steps together in the old city of Damascus would take us. I glanced around at the blind man. He was still smiling radiantly; most likely his smile was intended for us, Nonna and me. Then I was struck by the fanciful thought that his dear friend whom we couldn't see, and who was possibly still standing before him in his ink-black darkness by the side of the pine tree, was also giving us the same radiant smile. I bade them both goodbye with a short friendly nod of my head, and then I flagged down a taxi and we set off, Nonna and I, for the zoo in the Russian quarter.

INTERNATIONAL PRIZE FOR ARABIC FICTION

YOUSSEF ZIEDAN

Fardeqan –
the Detention of the Great Sheikh

EXCERPTS FROM THE NOVEL
TRANSLATED BY JONATHAN WRIGHT

Ibn Sina downed his drink in one gulp and toyed with his cup. He looked dazed, as if drowning in a sea of sorrows. He thought back to the tragic event that had taken place in the month of Shawwal five years earlier in the harsh, vast and merciless wastelands of Karakum. At noon on the day before that tragedy, the emir Maamoun ibn al-Maamoun, also known as the Khwarezm Shah, had hastily summoned all the scholars who lived under his patronage in the capital of his kingdom. He did not disclose the reason for inviting them to the meeting, which took place on a Thursday afternoon, although that was one of the two days on which the council of scholars did not usually meet in the presence of the emir. They all wondered what the reason for haste might be, why the emir insisted that they all attend and why he could not leave it till the usual time on Saturday evening.

Some of them speculated he was going to announce that he had chosen Abu Rayhan al-Biruni as vizier. There were several signs that this was likely, including the fact that the emir had installed Biruni in his palace a few months earlier out of respect for him, and the fact that he had asked Biruni to measure the circumference of the Earth and calculate lines of longitude and latitude accurately. Biruni devised a formula by which he could achieve this. The emir was also very proud of the two books that Biruni had recently completed: An Explanation of the Principles of Astrology, which dealt with the movement of celestial bodies, and How to Determine the Coordinates of Places and Calculate Correctly the Distances Between

Population Centres. The emir's associates also knew that the emir was uneasy that the military commanders were interfering in government affairs and were at odds with his wise vizier, Aboul Hussein al-Suhayli. The vizier was advanced in years and no longer able to bear the burdens of office, let alone handle the resentment the Khwarezmian troops felt towards the emir, whom they accused of complete submission to his brother-in-law, Mahmud bin Sabuktikin of Ghazni.

The forty senior scholars met in the emir's council chamber, seated in the usual order. Biruni's face looked pale and slightly jaundiced, and that puzzled them. They were even more mystified when the emir came in scowling, with a scroll of paper in his hand, and did not greet them in his usual way. The emir looked at the piece of paper and, without any long preamble, declared: "I received this letter today from Sultan Mahmud of Ghazni. In it he orders that you be dispatched to his capital without delay on any pretext, because he wants to boast that you are present in his palace."

The scholars were taken by surprise and there were loud murmurings. The emir interrupted them. "It's up to you to decide what suits you," he said, speaking like a man trying to conceal his embarrassment. "I will not force any of you to do anything, so give it careful thought."

After a period of silence Ibn Sina was the first to speak, in a voice that suggested suppressed anger. "No, by God," he told the emir. "I will not myself consent to go there to entertain the sultan at parties. That is work for dancers and singing girls, not at all appropriate for scholars."

"Ibn Sina, you're a distinguished man of wisdom, as are all these friends of yours. He wants to boast to other rulers that he has people like you in his retinue and that you grace his palace," said the emir.

"No, your highness," replied Ibn Sina. "This sultan of Ghazni is not known to have any interest in learning or in scholars. He is famous for fighting his opponents, and he should seek someone else to boast about. I do not wish to become a mere palace ornament."

"Listen, Ibn Sina," said the emir. "I appreciate you will never forgive him for destroying the Samanid dynasty, razing Bukhara, your beloved home town, to the ground and annexing the area to his vast kingdom."

"Allow me, your highness. Forgive me for interrupting you and for what I am going to say, or . . . No, I shall say nothing and I will not put you in an embarrassing position with your brother-in-law. Instead I shall leave this place as soon as possible."

"Where will you go?"

"I don't know, sir, I really don't, but the world is wide and God's grace is boundless."

"You have every right to do so, Ibn Sina, what does Master Biruni have to say, and what do the rest of you think?"

"I do not know, my lord," Biruni said in a troubled voice. "Sultan Mahmud of Ghazni doesn't appreciate the kind of learning that I do. He doesn't think that mathematics, astrology and the history of ancient peoples are as useful as the religious learning that he favours."

Abu Sahl al-Masihi interrupted him, saying: "He doesn't favour religious learning in general, but only the Sunni school of law, a cause he has recently started to promote to please the Abbasid caliph in the short term and undermine the power of the Buyids, who are inclined towards Shi'ism. He recognises only the Ash'ari Sunni form of Islam, so what would he do with someone like me – a Christian who has worked on medicine and philosophy, which he thinks is associated with atheism?"

In the middle of the gathering the great scholar Mansur bin Iraq muttered something in a low voice. The only words of his that were audible were: "I see disaster coming! I see disaster coming!"

The debate grew unusually heated, noisy and confused. The scholars known for their Mu'tazilite tendencies or their Shi'ism looked alarmed, and there were many of them. Amid the turmoil the emir stayed silent and looked around at the faces of the scholars, whose world was falling apart before its time. In the end he was so distressed that he suddenly stood up and left the council chamber, weighed down by a sense of shame. He understood that his world had run its course.

In the middle of that dark night, Ibn Sina was sitting in his bedroom, awash with anger and racked by insomnia, when one of his servants came and told him that Abu Sahl al-Masihi was knocking on the door. Ibn Sina went to meet him and found him in a pitiful state physically and psychologically. "What's happened, Abu Sahl," he asked, "and why are you shaking?"

"I've just received some news," he said.

"Sit here and calm down. What news do you mean?"

Shivering feverishly, Abu Sahl whispered in Ibn Sina's ear that a trustworthy man from his own Nestorian sect had visited him and told him that a large group of soldiers planned to storm the palace at dawn with intent to kill the emir. Ibn Sina was alarmed. He arched his eyebrows and asked impatiently: "And how did this man find out about this?" He had hardly finished the question when Abu Sahl replied unequivocally: "He's an old informer. I know him well and I trust him."

Ibn Sina was puzzled for a moment, even more so when Abu Sahl asked him if there was a lame servant in his house called Wardan. Ibn Sina was surprised, raised his eyebrows and said: "Yes, but how did you know that?" Abu Sahl told him that this servant had been planted on him by the spies of Ibn Subuk, the derogatory name he used to refer to Mahmud of Ghazni. In an even softer voice, he added that one of his relatives had told him that those who had brought this servant over to their side had promised to give him money if he told them immediately if and when Ibn Sina fled the city, as they expected.

"Then what?"

"Then they would go out after you, arrest you and send you in chains to Ghazni."

"Why?"

"So that Ibn Subuk can put you in prison until you die, because he's annoyed about what happened in Bukhara and he's convinced you're a Shi'ite missionary working for the Ismailis."

"But I've never been a missionary for any religious group, and you know that well."

"It doesn't matter what I know. What matters is what these people think and what they will do to you, and to me. They'll tell Ibn Subuk what you dared to say at our meeting today. They've heard about it and they're even angrier with you now."

Ibn Sina shook his head sadly and recited a Qur'anic verse: "We shall test you with a certain amount of fear and hunger." He believed what Abu Sahl had told him about the servant called Wardan, because he remembered that a few days earlier he had spotted him sneaking out of the house by night and coming back before dawn. When Ibn Sina had asked Wardan about it, the traitor replied that he was looking after some orphans on the edge of the city and had secretly married their widowed mother. His explanation was strange and his behaviour suspicious. Why had Ibn Sina unwittingly trusted what he said?

"We have to leave before the break of dawn," Abu Sahl whispered, trembling again. Ibn Sina took him to his room and on the way woke up a loyal servant called Qunbur who had been working in his house for years. In his room Ibn Sina took out the title deeds to his three male slaves and the old slave woman who prepared his meals. At the end of all four documents he added a declaration that he was setting them free. He attached his own seal and asked Abu Sahl to sign as a witness. He took twenty dinars out of his money bag and gave them and the documents to his astonished servant. "Qunbur," he said, "this is the last thing I will ask of you. I'm leaving now, but don't tell anyone. Take seven of these dinars for yourself and in two days' time give two dinars to each of the others, and their manumission certificates. Don't let Wardan leave the house or meet anyone during these two days, and if necessary tie him up to stop him."

"He's a traitor, sir, isn't he?"

"Yes, Qunbur, and he's been planted on me."

"I had my doubts about him, the bastard. Would you like me to kill him for his crimes and bury him behind the house?"

"No, we're not murderers, and people's lives are not our property, for us to destroy whenever we want."

After Qunbur left, Ibn Sina stood hesitantly in the middle of the room for a moment. He then asked Abu Sahl if he needed to drop by his house before leaving. "No," he replied. "I don't have any children or money there and a friend warned me not to go there, because they're lying in wait for me, just as they are for you."

Under cover of darkness and obscured by the dust in the summer wind, they left through the back door of the house an hour before dawn, wearing ragged clothes with tattered turbans on their heads. They each had long strings of prayer beads in their hands and around their necks. They looked like Sufi dervishes of the kind known popularly as qalandars. In this disguise they hurried eastwards till they reached the harbour on the bank of the Jayhoun, the large river now known as the Amu Darya. Ibn Sina did not tell Abu Sahl that fleeing might be as dangerous as staying until two hours after they had set sail northwards in their boat, when the sun had already lit up the burning sky and Abu Sahl's head had recovered from the clutches of drowsiness. As they sat alone at the end of the boat, rocking from side to side, Abu Sahl asked Ibn Sina in a whisper why they were going north.

"Because they expect us to go west," he replied.

"True. That's wise planning on your part, but what next?"

"By noon we'll be far enough away and we'll cross the Karakum desert until we reach the shores of the Caspian. From there we can sail south by boat, then follow the tracks through the Alborz mountains until we reach the city of Ray. We'll be safe there, under the protection of the Buyids."

"Very well. But crossing this arid desert will take two or three days' riding. May the Lord be with us and spare us from bandits."

Near a remote village on the west bank of the river, they disembarked from the boat. From the caretaker of a small church on the edge of the village Ibn Sina bought two emaciated donkeys and the water and other supplies they would need. They proceeded westwards without delay. The vastness of the barren desert was awe-inspiring and troubling, and the probable dangers were many. What was improbable was what they encountered on the morning of their second day in the desert. The first day had passed peacefully and the hardship had been tolerable, and that night they lit a fire within the walls of a derelict house. They were pleased when the wind picked up and started to whine and moan, which reassured them that the area would be free of bandits and roaming wolves.

Abu Sahl suddenly started to sing a mournful hymn in Syriac and stared up towards the stars that appeared from time to time between the scudding clouds. After a while he suddenly stopped singing and said resignedly that he did not feel they would reach Ray.

Ibn Sina realised that his companion was so anxious and exhausted that his mind was befuddled, so he decided to ask him a question to distract him from his thoughts and the aches and pains in his thin and exhausted body. "Tell me, Abu Sahl," he said, "have you sent your latest epistle, the one on the plague and foul air, to the copyists to copy?" Abu Sahl convulsed with laughter in a way that showed he understood the point of the question, but he didn't answer. After a while Ibn Sina tried to console him by asking him to recite whatever poems came to mind. Abu Sahl immediately recited to him, in Arabic, the first part of the famous line of poetry by Abu Tammam: "The sword is more truthful than any book." He did not complete the line. Instead he started laughing and sobbing at the same time until his eyes filled with tears because he felt so wretched.

Dawn broke but it wasn't like any ordinary dawn. The weather was wild, with dust flying everywhere. They wavered a while between continuing their journey and staying within the shelter offered by the walls. When the wind died down for some time, they set off hurriedly and full of hope, unaware of the fate that lay in wait for them.

In the middle of a desert that offered no shelter or place to hide, the winds picked up again at midday and dust devils danced on the horizon. Soon the winds went mad, howling and lashing the ground until they hid the sky from the ground completely. The donkeys' legs could no longer carry their weight. As soon as the men dismounted, the donkeys panicked and ran off like the wind until they disappeared from sight in the swirling dust. Ibn Sina took off his jelaba, tied the sleeves and made it into something like a column of material to protect himself from the onslaught of the wild storm. He did the same thing for Abu Sahl, but how mistaken he was. The garments could not fend off the stones that came flying with the clouds of dust, and soon the two columns of material were blown away.

Abu Sahl collapsed on the ground choking and shaking. Ibn Sina sat next to him and tried to shield his face from the dust with what remained of his tattered cloak, but it was no use. The storm was wilder than ever and the roar of the wind was louder. The wind picked up pebbles and stones from the ground and hurled them into the air like arrows. Ibn Sina curled up in a heap and wrapped his arms around his poor friend and mentor. Abu Sahl's thin body was shivering and eventually he lost consciousness.

Ibn Sina called out to him in a voice he could not hear. "Hang in there, Abu Sahl, don't give up," he said.

But after a few convulsions, Abu Sahl died, and Ibn Sina lost consciousness too. The wind rolled his body until the sand buried it and the desert almost swallowed it up. When Ibn Sina regained consciousness several hours later, he found himself alone and becalmed. On his face, which had been battered by stones and pebbles, he found streaks of blood mixed with dust. He staggered around in his tattered clothes until he found a pile of sand and spotted the body of his poor friend under the pile. His eyes streamed with tears.

He looked up at the sky and shouted into the void of the desert: "O God, O God. Was it for this torment that You created us? O God, answer me!"

BOOK REVIEWS

Susannah Tarbush reviews
Daughter of the Tigris
by Muhsin Al-Ramli
translated by Luke Leafgren
MacLehose Press, London,
November 2019
ISBN: 9780857056825 Pbk 384 pp
Pbk: £14.99 / $18.77
ebook: 9780857056832 £9.99 / $12.98

The dawn of democracy?

When the English translation of Iraqi author Mushin Al-Ramli's 2012 epic novel of war and love *The President's Gardens* was published by MacLehose Press in 2017, it was acclaimed by critics and readers alike. The translation, by US scholar Luke Leafgren, won the 2018 Saif Ghobash Banipal Prize for Arabic Literary Translation.

The success of *The President's Gardens* encouraged MacLehose to ask Al-Ramli to write a sequel, with Leafgren once again as translator. The translation of the sequel, *Daughter of the Tigris*, was published at virtually the same time as publication of the Arabic, *Bint Dijla*, by Dar al-Mada of Baghdad.

Al-Ramli has lived since 1995 in Madrid, where he is a professor at St Louis University. *The President's Gardens* and his 2009 novel *Dates on my Fingers* were both longlisted for the International Prize for Arabic Fiction (IPAF). His latest novel *Abna' wa Ahdhiya* ("Sons and Shoes"), published by Dar al-Mada in 2018, is one of 13 books on the Sheikh Zayed Book Award 2020 literature longlist.

The President's Gardens depicted Iraq under the dictatorship of Saddam Hussein. The sequel carries various plotlines and characters into the post-invasion years. Al-Ramli is a remarkable storyteller, and in *Daughter of the Tigris* he creates a dynamic, intricately plotted narrative, brimming with stories and a host of memorable characters.

The invaders claimed to be bringing justice and democracy to Iraq, but the country descended into insecurity, violence, hostage-taking and rampant corruption. Al-Ramli has an acute sense of irony, and he lightens the darkness of the situation with humour and fantasy. He brings us characters from different parts of society, paying special attention to the common people – the "salt of the earth" – and their endurance.

Luke Leafgren is Assistant Dean of Harvard College where he taches Arabic and translation. His translation of *Daughter of the Tigris* has clarity and naturalness and reads very well. He has an assured touch in translating a text that ranges in tone from nightmarishly visceral to lyrical, and in finding English equivalents for Arabic idioms and earthy language, and snatches of poetry and songs.

The President's Gardens opened with nine severed heads, each in a banana crate, being sent to the village of Nakhila beside the river Tigris. One of the heads was that of middle-aged Ibrahim. From this gruesome beginning the novel looped back in time to the boyhood of Ibrahim and his two best friends, Tariq and Abdullah, relating their personal histories as time passes in turbulent Iraq.

The President's Gardens ended with Ibrahim's widowed daughter Qisma travelling with her baby son by car to Baghdad in search of her father's decapitated body. She was accompanied by her father's longtime friend Tariq, a religious sheikh whom she had agreed the previous evening to marry as a second wife. Burdened with anxieties and feeling nauseous, she asked Tariq to stop the car.

Daughter of the Tigris begins: "After vomiting by the side of the road on the way to Baghdad, Qisma felt hungry and decided to eat Iraq." Later, when Tariq asks what she wants to eat, she says "Iraq", adding that "she would eat this country that was eating its children, that had eaten her father, her husband, her childhood and her future, that had eaten all her dreams. She had decided, therefore, that she would take it as fodder for a new dream. She had no idea how, but she would search for a way."

The novel chronicles Qisma's odyssey through a changed Iraqi in the company of Tariq. Her search for her father's headless body is the main axis of the plot, around which Al-Ramli weaves an expansive, digressive saga rich in sub-plots.

Qisma is a defiant character with a regal quality, and en route to Baghdad she stands up to US soldiers at a roadblock who are humiliating Tariq. She swears at them, and the American General Adam tells her that Iraqi vehicles must keep at least 100 metres from US vehicles, or risk being shot at. Qisma remembers the rape of 14-year-old Abeer al-Janabi by US soldiers, who murdered her and her family. Images of rape, whether of women or of Iraq itself, recur in the novel.

Qisma's quest for her father's remains contains an element of repentance. As recounted in *The President's Gardens* she had as a young girl recoiled from her father when he returned to the village minus his right leg, which he had lost in the US aerial bombing of Iraqi troops as they withdrew from Kuwait in 1991. She rebelled against her father's fatalistic approach to life and his naming her "Qisma" meaning "fate".

Qisma shunned her father, marrying an officer in the president's Republican Guard and changing her name to Nisma. The couple mixed in the highest echelons of society and lived in an impressive house in Baghdad. And then calamity befell Qisma when, during a party, the president summoned her and raped her. She did not tell her husband of the rape, and when she gave birth she did not know if her baby was his or the president's. Her oblivious husband actually named him after the president. In *Daughter of the Tigris* Qisma changes her son's name to Ibrahim, in tribute to her dead father, and changes her own name back from Nisma to Qisma.

Ibrahim was actually the quiet hero of *The President's Gardens*. He had a job working in the president's gardens where he was ordered to bury victims of the murderous regime. At great risk to himself he started to record in hidden notebooks details of the bodies and the torture they had suffered, in the hope that one day families

Muhsin Al-Ramli, photo by Khaled Kaki

would be able to find the remains of their vanished loved ones and give them a proper burial.

One of those whose details he recorded after a particularly grisly torture and death turned out to be Qisma's missing husband, killed for having been involved in a coup attempt. Qisma realises how bravely Ibrahim has behaved, and her search for his headless corpse is in part fuelled by remorse.

For Qisma, her marriage to the much older Tariq is a practical matter for as a single widowed woman she would be unable to travel alone. But Tariq longs to consummate the marriage to the bewitchingly attractive young woman, and there is comedy in his constant lusting after Qisma while she fends him off. He had planned to tame her, but she proved untameable.

During the journey to Baghdad, Tariq suggests a detour to visit his friend Sheikh Tafir al-Shakhabiti, head of the Shakhabit tribe. He is amazed by how well Tafir is doing under the occupation, and the luxury in which he is now living. Tafir tells him: "We are living through a historic opportunity. It is the dawn of democracy, and anyone can do what he wants and attain the riches he desires.

"Don't you see how many nobodies and scoundrels have suddenly become rich and are now men of power and influence? Even the foreigners! Why have they appeared from every nook and cranny if not to plunder our wealth? It is certainly not to liberate us, as they claim, but rather for the sake of oil."

As for the fund for reconstruction, it is "a great swamp from which billions are ladled out. Countries, companies, political groups and individuals take from it such plunder as has never been seen in the history of the world".

During the visit to Tafir, there is a public debate between Tafir and Qisma on women's rights. Tafir argues that a woman could never be like a man, giving as conclusive proof the inability of women to piss while standing. Qisma challenges him to a pissing contest: he agrees that if she wins he will grant her three wishes.

To the astonishment of all, Qisma wins the wager. Not only does her powerful jet of urine extend to a wall which Tafir's efforts failed to reach, but she manages to write the word "Woman" on the wall with it. Tafir and Tariq are left uneasy about this feat, and start to doubt that Qisma really is a woman.

Tafir urges Tariq to take advantages of the opportunities offered by the new situation in Iraq, as does another key figure in the novel. He is aged Sayyid Jalal al-Din, son of long-ago mayor of Nakhila. He had left the village as a teenager and gone to Iran where he joined the opposition, but following the invasion he returned to Iraq where he has a high rank in a big party involved in power sharing.

Unbeknownst to Qisma and Tariq, Jalal is in fact the biological father of Abdullah, the old friend of Tariq and Ibrahim. At the age

of 17 Jalal had impregnated Zakiya, a mentally disabled orphan girl who was living with his parents. The scandal was hushed up and Jalal's parents sent him away from the village in disgrace. Zakiya was hidden in a cellar and after giving birth she was murdered by the mayor and Tariq's imam father.

In *The President's Gardens* Abdullah learned the truth of his parentage from the mayor's elderly dying widow wife after he returned from 19 years as a prisoner of war in Iran. *Daughter of the Tigris* finds him full of hatred for his biological father, and in the early pages of the novel he vows to kill him. Jalal is desperate to visit the village in order to try and make amends with Abdullah, and tries to use Qisma and Tariq to engineer a meeting with him. Abdullah furiously refuses to countenance such a meeting, but Jalal continues with efforts to arrange it.

Jalal tells Qisma and Tariq that they should get involved in shaping their country's future. His suggestion that they form a party of their own ignites their ambition. The novel traces, at times amusingly, the steps they take to put their plans for power in motion, together with a rascally dwarf named Rahib from the Shakhabit tribe and his Bohemian poet brother Bara.

While Qisma pursues her aims, there are sinister signs that her life is in danger. A masked man in a car looks at her as he draws his finger threateningly across his throat. A booby-trapped whole stuffed lamb explodes in the kitchen of Qisma's house when Jalal comes to call. She is fascinated by the various corpses she is shown in her search for Ibrahim, and by knives. "Qisma's desire to slaughter or be slaughtered like her father grew until it had taken hold of her entirely."

Today, Iraq remains an unstable and corrupt country, as shown by the ongoing anti-government demonstrations held by young Iraqis in protest at unemployment, corruption, a breakdown in public services, and meddling by foreign powers. *Daughter of the Tigris* helps explain their anger, and deserves to be read not only by lovers of literature but by anyone seeking to understand the predicament of Iraq.

BOOK REVIEWS

Barbara Haus Schwepcke reviews
**1001 Buch – Die
Literaturen des Orients
by Stefan Weidner**
Published by Edition CONVERSO,
Bad Herrenalb, Germany.
September 1, 2019. Hardback,
ISBN: 978-3981976335. 432 pages,
€30 / £23.83

All the literatures of the Orient

How do you translate a title? One of Stefan Weidner's previous books was called *Jenseits des Westens* – John Steinbeck's classic *East of Eden* was given the German title *Jenseits von Eden,* and while we all remember Meryl Streep and Robert Redford in *Out of Africa*, German viewers would remember the film being called *Jenseits von Afrika*. Weidner packs a lot of definition into his titles: what lies beyond the 'West'? What is *Jenseits des Westens*? The 'East'? Or something much more intriguing, more complex, and more difficult to define? The title of Weidner's new book points towards an answer: *1001 Buch – Die Literaturen des Orients* (One Thousand and One Books: The Literatures of the Orient). East of the West lies the Orient and out of the Orient comes an infinite multitude, a complex and intriguing literature for and which they will hopefully take delight in discovering through reading this new compendium.

But can we still use the term "Orient" after Edward Said's devastating critique of this Western concept, which in his opinion was born out of ignorance and often condescending illusions about the "Other"? Stefan Weidner makes a convincing case that we can, especially if we want to be inclusive rather than exclusive. No other term offers quite wide enough a remit for this ambitious project: Weidner's new book is a compendium of all the literatures of the Orient and therefore defines what is difficult to grasp. It is vast, and yet within its 432 pages admirably concise; it is a book of reference, providing the curious with a curated choice and knowledgeable critique of a great array of books from all epochs and translated from three major (and several minor) languages into German. How lucky readers of that language are to have publishers who invest in the translations discussed in this book, which vastly outnumber those available in the English language. This is an engaging literary travel guide, an invitation to explore unknown territories and discover something new – an invitation readers can accept even in times of travel bans and social distancing.

1001 Books, The Literatures of the Orient

1001 Buch – Die Literaturen des Orients is neither complete nor objective. Quite the contrary – Stefan Weidner makes it clear that this compendium has been put together through subjective choice, born out of decades working as a scholar, critic and translator, and informed by experts who became friends, and fellow travellers who became companions. It has been influenced by listening to the great storytellers who inhabit his Orient, which for Weidner reaches from ancient Cordoba to modern Cairo, from the Balkans to Bamyan, and from Samarkand to Seattle. By reclaiming and restating the word 'Orient' Weidner is able to build bridges between and within regions and religions, to reach across cultures and centuries and thereby enlarge our horizons beyond the cliché. Used in a post-Saidean sense, he argues, the term has in fact an additional advantage over terms such as 'the MENA region' or 'the Islamicate world'. When Weidner uses the term 'Orient' he is no longer under any illusion that he is talking about a clearly defined region:

> The Orient is increasingly becoming frayed at the edges and, as far as literature is concerned, is now situated in the middle of Europe,

BOOKS REVIEWS

Stefan Weidner, photo by Klaus Ranger/Symposium Dürsten

the seemingly Non-Orient, in the form of the literature of exile and of those authors, who as migrants or colonised write in European languages, whether they live in the West or not.

Critics of Weidner have been quick to pinpoint gaps and highlight minor errors in the work. Shame on those critics, who claim to be experts and are pointing to gaps or minor mistakes! They might be experts on Ferdowsi's *Shahnameh* but what do they know about Jewish poetry of Andalusia? They have not quite grasped what Weidner is trying to do: in *1001 Buch – Die Literaturen des Orients* he is trying to get away from the concept of national literature with national borders, when even the concept of the nation state is a 19th century European phenomenon. The *Qur'an* is not a Saudi Arabian book even if the followers of the Prophet, who wrote it down, lived in the Arabian Peninsula.

In describing these 1001 books and portraying their authors Weidner is writing about *Weltliteratur,* a term coined by Johann Wolfgang von Goethe to suggest the capacity of literature to transcend national, epochal and linguistic borders. Weidner is writing about all genres, about Nobel Laureates such as Orhan Pamuk and Naguib Mahfouz as well as best-selling authors like Alaa Al Aswany; and Stefan Weidner is trying – and succeeding – to draw lines and make connections that ought to surprise even the most finicky critic.

Subjective? Yes! Interesting? Absolutely! It is worth mentioning that it is currently shortlisted for the 2020 Sheikh Zayed Book Award in the "Arab Culture in Other Languages" category. (To follow the award go to www.zayedaward.ae/en/)

BOOKS IN BRIEF

FICTION

Velvet by Huzama Habayeb, translated by Kay Heikkinen. Palestinian author Huzama Habayeb was awarded the 2017 Naguib Mahfouz Medal for Literature for this enthralling book, which the judges said was "a new kind of Palestinian novel". It was also chosen for *Banipal 63*'s list of "The 100 best Arabic Novels". The moving narrative follows one day in the life of Hawa as she plans, after falling in love, for a new beginning that could take her out of the Baqaa Palestinian refugee camp in Jordan where she has lived all her life. Flashbacks unfold hard memories of her childhood in the 1960s and '70s, an abusive father and daily hardships, later working for a Syrian seamstress in Amman, helping to buy beautiful fabrics. In spite of the hardships Hawa finds she is "able to capture joy in the midst of oppression". *Velvet* is Huzama Habayeb's third novel, after four successful short story collections. It is particularly impressive for its detailed and rich descriptions that enable the reader to feel the full force of Hawa's experiences. Hoopoe Fiction, 20 Aug 2019. Pbk, 272 pages, ISBN: 978-9774169304. £10.99 / USD17.95 / €14.27.

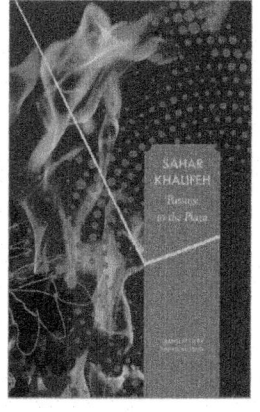

Passage to the Plaza by Sahar Khalifeh, translated by Sawad Hussain, is a second novel from *Banipal 63*'s list of "The 100 best Arabic Novels", originally published in 1990 as *Bab Al-Saha*. Set in the author's home town of Nablus, Palestine, the acclaimed novel confronts and lays bare the contradictory lives Palestinian women are forced to live, to go along with their traditional role while running families and being community leaders. Nuzha, a young woman ostracized and shamed, lives in the town's neighbourhood of Bab Al-Saha in a so-called house of ill-repute. But when the Intifada of 1987 starts, the house becomes a welcome sanctuary – for Hussam, an injured resistance fighter, Samar, a university researcher exploring the impact of the Intifada on women's lives, and Sitt Zakia, a pious midwife. Issues of freedom, love, respectability, nationhood, rights of women and Palestinian identity – both among the reluctant residents and the inhabitants of Bab Al-Saha at large – are vividly recounted through the eyes of its female protagonists. Seagull Books, 1 March 2020. Hbk, 224 pages, ISBN: 9780857427700. $24.50.

BOOKS IN BRIEF

Clouds over Alexandria by Ibrahim Abdel Meguid, translated by Kay Heikkinen. Longlisted for the 2014 IPAF, this novel completes the author's trilogy on Alexandria, begun with *No-one Sleeps in Alexandria* and *Birds of Amber*. In it he describes life in the famous city, beginning in an era of openness to the wider world and ending at a time of closure to outside influences. The events of this final novel take place in the 1970s, when the cosmopolitan spirit that has characterised the city throughout its history has disappeared. In place of the melting pot of ethnicities, religions and cultures comes intolerance and hatred, destroying Alexandria's secular traditions. Five idealistic students find themselves in trouble as their leftist activism makes them a target both of government surveillance and Islamist groups seeking to curtail the city's social life. Their participation in the explosive 'bread riots' is followed by the crushing experience of prison, and their young lives change forever. It is a story of love, aspiration for social change, disillusionment, and frustration that will resonate widely today. Hoopoe Fiction, April 2, 2019. Pbk, 304 pages, ISBN: 978-9774168673.

Guard of the Dead by George Yarak, translated by Raphael Cohen. This second novel of Lebanese author and journalist George Yarak was shortlisted for the 2016 International Prize for Arabic Fiction. It tells the gripping story of Aabir, a hospital undertaker who lives in constant dread and apprehension that his past dark history in the Lebanese Civil War will return to haunt him. He's occupied with stealing and selling gold teeth from the corpses in the morgue until one day he is kidnapped from the hospital. He then knows he hasn't escaped his past and the many crimes he witnessed. But what or who is still chasing him? Hoopoe Fiction, 19 May 2019. Pbk, 244 pages, ISBN: 978-9774169106, USD 12.96 Ebook: USD11.99

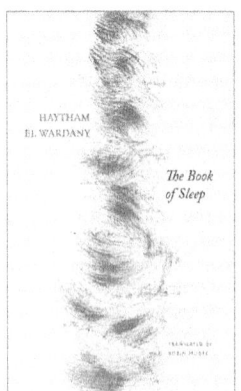

Book of Sleep by Haytham El-Wardany, translated by Robin Moger. "What is sleep? How can this most unproductive of human states be seen as having agency? What happens to the waking selves we understand ourselves to be?" Written in the spring of 2013, as the government of Egypt's President Mohammed Morsi was definitively unravelling. Drawing on forms of poetry, on philosophical reflection, political analysis, and storytelling, this genre-defying work examines the intricate connections of sleep with reality and dreams. "My concern was not to create a literary product in the conventional sense, but to try and use literature as a methodology for thinking," said El-Wardany. Seagull Books, 15 May 2020. Hbk, 168 pages. ISBN: 9780857427410. $21.50 / £16.99.

Ice by Sonallah Ibrahim, translated by Margaret Litvin. Set in Moscow in 1973, Dr. Shukri, an Egyptian historian, is undertaking a year of graduate studies in the "heart" of socialist utopia. He pinpoints the stagnation of Brezhnev-era Soviet life: ethnic tensions between republics, penniless Russian pensioners, drunks sharing a bottle of vodka, a Kirgiz roommate whose Russian girlfriend comes to live in his dormitory room, Arab embassy officials working the black market, liberated but insecure Russian women, Arab students debating the October 1973 Arab-Israeli War, and strong black Georgian tea. Based on Ibrahim's  time as a student at the All-Russian Institute of Cinematography in Moscow, 1971–1973, *Ice* is a fascinating and powerful addition to the growing number of the Egyptian author's works now available in translation. Seagull Books, November 2019. Hbk, 270 pages, ISBN: 978-0857426505. £14.99 / USD 20 / €18.36

Mama Hissa's Mice by Saud Alsanousi, translated by Sawad Hussain. This saga by the award-winning Kuwaiti author of *The Bamboo Stalk*, is set in a dystopic future Kuwait, and spans nearly half a century and four generations, plunging readers into both the country's recent history and a future apocalyptic scenario. Three friends, Katkout, Fahd, and Sadiq, battle courageously against increasingly rabid intolerance, sectarian violence and fundamentalism that has become like "a civil war that is only missing weapons", as the author has described it. They start a group, Fuada's Kids, to carry on fighting against the growing sectarianism, and live through an "environment on fire, directly impacted by what was going on in neighbouring countries". Fahd's grandmother, Mama Hissa, is a fount of fables and superstitions, and warns them not to make God angry, or the sky will fall. Echoing the author's own experience of censorship, Katkout, who is also an author, finds his novel has had four chapters removed from it by the censor. Alsanousi's latest novel is stark and powerful and speaks out for tolerance, friendship and justice. Amazon Crossing, January 2020. Pbk, 400 pages, ISBN 978-1542042178. £8.99

The Slave Yards by Najwa Bin Shatwan, translated by Nancy Roberts. Set in late nineteenth-century Benghazi, the novel tells the story of Atiqa, the daughter of a woman slave and her white master. Atiqa is happily married with two children, but when her cousin Ali unexpectedly enters her life, she learns the true identity of her parents, both long deceased, and slowly builds a friendship with Ali as they share stories of their past. She tells of growing up in the "slave yards", an encampment for Africans brought to Libya as slaves, and learns about her mother Tawida, who had a deep and enduring relationship with her master while enslaved to his wealthy merchant family.

Shortlisted for the 2017 International Prize for Arabic Fiction, it opens an important window on a dark chapter of Libyan history. "This beautifully written novel is a milestone because an Arab woman writer dared to investigate, describe, and expose two slaveries: that of slaves and that of women", wrote Fadia Faqir, author of *Willow Trees Don't Weep*. Najwa Bin Shatwan is a Libyan academic, author of several short story collections, plays, and three novels and was the 2018 Banipal Visiting Writer Fellow. In 2010 she was selected as one of Beirut39's thirty-nine best Arab authors under the age of forty. Syracuse University Press (Middle East Literature In Translation) April 2020. Pbk, 302 pages, ISBN: 978-0815611257. USD24.95 / £20.95

The Egyptian Assassin by Ezzedine C. Fishere, translated by Jonathan Wright. Protagonist Fakhreddin had been an idealistic young lawyer, seeking to fight corruption from his modest quarter of Cairo. A botched attempt on his life forced him to flee the country, propelling him on a wild journey that led to Afghanistan's jihadi training camps. Transformed into a trained killer, he never lost sight of his goal of revenge, but what had happened to his son, Omar, the only person who really mattered to him? Behind Fakhreddin's bold, nail-biting exploits are his broken family, his broken heart and his ultimate search for redemption rather than revenge – and a way home. Ezzedine C. Fishere is an acclaimed Egyptian writer, academic, and diplomat with a number of bestselling novels, including *Embrace on Brooklyn Bridge* (IPAF shortlisted 2012). AUC Press/Hoopoe Fiction. 15 September 2019. Pbk, 368 pages, ISBN: 9789774169311. $17.95 / £9.99 / LE250

A Shimmering Red Fish Swims with Me by Youssef Fadel, translated by Alexander E. Elinson. In 1980s Casablanca, Farah arrives from her small town life with big dreams of becoming a singer. She meets Outhman, who longs to leave the city and seek his fortune elsewhere. They fall in love, but trouble brews on the horizon. A bitter struggle is raging over construction of the monumental Hassan II Mosque, which will raze their entire neighbourhood and build over its ruins. The government insists it is a necessary sacrifice for the good of Morocco. Outhman and Farah are caught up in events beyond their control, stuck in a world that seems to work against their happiness. A narrative tour de force, power plays and petty jealousies, deceit and corruption, beautifully written (and translated) with a wealth of detailed, enjoyably descriptive prose. *A Shimmering Red Fish Swims with Me* is the author's tenth novel, and the final part in his modern Morocco series. AUC Press/Hoopoe Fiction, 5 November 2019. Pbk, 440 pages, ISBN: 978-9774169373. £11.99 / USD17.95 / €15

Thirteen Months of Sunrise by Rania Mamoun, translated by Elisabeth Jacquette. The author blends real and imagined tales of Khartoum life to create a rich, complex and moving portrait of contemporary Sudan. From painful encounters with loved ones to unexpected new friendships, Rania Mamoun illuminates the breadth of human experience and explores, with humour and compassion, the alienation, isolation and estrangement that is urban life. This is the author's only collection of short stories to date, with the title story published in *Banipal 30* (2007), and she has also published two novels. Comma Press, 9 May 2019. Pbk, 80 pages, ISBN: 9781910974391. £9.99.

TEEN & YOUNG ADULT FICTION

Ghady and Rawan by Fatima Sharafeddine and Samar Mahfouz Barraj, and translated by Sawad Hussain & M. Lynx Qualey. This latest title in the Emerging Voices from the Middle East series follows the close-knit friendship of two Lebanese teenagers, Ghady, who lives with his family in Belgium, and Rawan, who lives in Lebanon. Every summer they meet up in Beirut, and the rest of the year, keep in touch by email. In the emails, they relate the ups and downs of their daily lives in Brussels and Beirut – Ghady's feeling homesick and struggling with racism at school, and Rawan's changing relationship with her family. This story about Lebanese adolescents explores universal subjects pertinent to young people everywhere as well as how the love and support of a good friend can help resolve difficulties as well as sweeten life's triumphs and good times. University of Texas Press, Aug 2019. Pbk, 134 pages, ISBN: 978-1477318522. £19.05 / USD 16.95 / €11.85.

Trees for the Absentees by Ahlam Bsharat, translated by Ruth Ahmedzai Kemp & Sue Copeland. The Arabic original was runner-up for the 2013 Etisalat Award for Arabic Children's Literature, and is the author's second novel translated with Neem Tree Press. Young love, meddling relatives, heart-to-hearts with friends real and imagined, Philistia's world might seem like that of an ordinary university student, except that it's all happening in occupied Palestine – and when your father is in indefinite detention, nothing is straightforward. Philistia has a part-time job washing women's bodies at the ancient Ottoman hammam in Nablus, the West Bank – her late grandmother, who had been a midwife and washed corpses, had taught her the ritual ablutions and the secrets of the body: the secrets of life and death. Philistia embarks on a journey through her country's history – a magical journey, and one of loss and centuries of occupation, and as trees are uprooted around her, she searches for a place of refuge, a place where she can plant a memory for the ones she lost. Neem Tree Press, 26 September 2019. Pbk, 96 pages, ISBN: 978-1911107231. £8.99 / USD 12.30. eBook ISBN: 9781911107248

MEMOIR

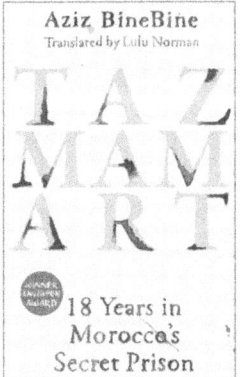

TAZMAMART, 18 Years in Morocco's Secret Prison by Aziz BineBine, Translated by Lulu Norman. Barnaby Rogerson writes: "A beautifully composed memoir that chronicles twenty years of death and degradation in a secret state prison, yet also reads as the spiritual pilgrimage of an ascetic ... a compassionate testimony of the loves and aspirations, childhood memories and adult ambitions of those buried at Tazmamart."

Morocco's infamous secret prison Tazmamart, still a powerful symbol of contemporary political oppression, was built in the Atlas Mountains in 1972 specifically for political prisoners and where young army officer Aziz BineBine was incarcerated for 18 years. His story is a detailed account of the practical and mental measures he took in order to survive, and an unfiltered depiction of the agony of prison life. Written with touching simplicity and tremendous tenderness, *Tazmamart* is a hellish journey through the abyss of despair. Haus Publishing, 20 April 2020. Hbk, 220 pages, ISBN: 978-1-912208-88-3. £14.99 / €17.13

NON-FICTION

The Thousand and One Nights and Twentieth-Century Fiction, Intertextual Readings by Richard van Leeuwen, University of Amsterdam. In this remarkable work, presently shortlisted for the 2020 Sheikh Zayed Book Award (SZBA) in the 'Arab Culture in Other Languages' category, the author analyses the important influence of classic *The Thousand and One Nights* on 20th-century prose from all over the world. Works of approximately forty authors are examined: those crucial to the development of the main currents in 20th-century fiction – modernism, magical realism and post-modernism. Six thematic sections discuss the authors/works, from a narratological perspective, supplemented by references to the cultural and literary context, and show how *The Thousand and One Nights* became deeply rooted in modern world literature. Published by Brill, Leiden, 2018; Series: Handbook of Oriental Studies. Section 1, The Near and Middle East, Volume 124. E-book: ISBN: 978-90-04-36269-7. Hbk: 842 pages. ISBN: 978-90-04-36253-6. £161 / €182 / USD210.

CONTRIBUTORS

Mosab Abu Toha is a young Palestinian poet and writer from Gaza. A graduate in English language, he taught English at Gaza's UNRWA schools 2016–2019, and is founder of the Edward Said Public Library, Gaza's first English-language library. Mosab is currently a visiting poet and scholar at Harvard University, with the Department of Comparative Literature.

Khalil Alrez is a Syrian novelist and translator, born in 1956. He has published one play and nine novels. His translations from Russian include *Selected Russian Short Stories* (2005) and *Selected Stories of Anton Chekhov* (two volumes, 2007).

Abdelouahab Aissaoui is an Algerian novelist, born in Djelfa, Algeria, in 1985. He graduated in Electromechanical Engineering from Zayan Ashour University in Djelfa and works as a maintenance engineer. In 2012, his first novel, *Jacob's Cinema*, won the novel category of the President of the Republic Prize. His second novel, *Mountain of Death* (2015), won the Assia Djebar Prize, regarded as Algeria's most important prize for the novel. His third novel *Circles and Doors* (2017) won the 2017 Kuwaiti Suad al-Sabah Novel Prize, and also in 2017, he won the Katara Novel Prize in the unpublished novel category, for *Testament of the Deeds of the Forgotten Ones*.

Mohamed Arbi was born in 1985 in Nabeul, Tunisia. Since 2014 he has published three collections of poetry. His first collection won the prize of the Tunis House of Poetry and in 2018 he won the Assilah forum foundation's Buland al-Haydari Prize for Young Poets.

Raphael Cohen is a professional translator and lexicographer who studied Arabic and Hebrew at Oxford and the University of Chicago. He is based in Cairo and is a *Banipal* contributing editor. He has translated novels by Mona Prince, Ahlam Mosteghanemi, Eslam Mosbah, George Yarak and Mohamed Salmawy.

Humphrey Davies is a literary translator with his translations of Elias Khoury's *Gate of the Sun* and *Yalo* winning the Saif Ghobash Banipal Translation Prize in 2006 and 2010 respectively. Other translations of works by Elias Khoury include *As Though She Were Sleeping* and *My Name is Adam*. Other works translated include Ahmad Faris Shidyaq's *Leg over Leg*, Alaa al-Aswany's *The Yacoubian Building*, plus works by Naguib Mahfouz, Gamal al-Ghitani and Bahaa Taha.

Jan Dost, born in 1965 in Kobani, is a Syrian Kurdish poet, writer and translator, with five novels in Kurdish, five in Arabic, and three poetry collections. He is a winner of the Galawej Award for Kurdish literature. He has translated into Arabic *Mem and Zin*, the famous Kurdish classic by Ahmad Khani, and other Kurdish and Persian works. He lives in Germany.

Jabbour Douaihy was born in Zgharta, Lebanon, in 1949. He holds a PhD in Comparative Literature, Sorbonne, and is Professor of French Literature at the University of Lebanon. To date, he has published eight novels, as well as short stories and children's books. His novels have been regularly shortlisted and longlisted for the IPAF prize, with *The Vagrant* also winning the Lebanese Hanna Wakim Prize and its French translation winning the 2013 Institut due Monde Arabe Prize.

Huda Fakhreddine teaches Arabic literature at the University of Pennsylvania. She is author of *Metapoesis in the Arabic Tradition* (Brill, 2015) and co-translator of *Lighthouse for the Drowning* (BOA, 2017) and *The Sky That Denied Me* (Univ. Texas Press, 2020). Her poetry translations have appeared in *Banipal, World Literature Today, Nimrod, ArabLit Quarterly, Asymptote,* and *Middle Eastern Literatures*. Forthcoming is *The Arabic Prose Poem: Poetic Theory and Practice* from Edinburgh Univ. Press.

Maher Jarrar is a professor at American University of Beirut, in the Civilization Sequence Program and the Department of Arabic. He has a PhD in Arabic and Islamic Studies, Tübingen University, 1989. He was Visiting Professor, Center for Middle Eastern Studies, Harvard University, 1996 and 2011, and a Fellow at the Wissenschaftskolleg, Berlin, in 2002-03. He has published numerous books and articles in the fields of Islamic studies, Arabic literature, and literary criticism.

Paula Haydar is Assistant Professor of Arabic in the Department of World Languages, Literatures, and Cultures at the University of Arkansas, USA. Her translations include works by Elias Khoury, Jabbour Douaihy, Rachid Al-Daif, Sahar Khalifeh, Adania Shibli and Jamal Naji.

Hawad is a Tuareg poet, born in 1950 in the Aïr region in what is today Niger, and from the mid-1980s published many literary works. These include books of poetry, combined literary forms similar to mythical epics, lyrical prose, and novels. Hawad deploys a method he calls *furigraphy* (a play on the word calligraphy) to create space in his poetry and to illuminate certain themes, while composing his poems aloud in Tamazight. He currently lives and publishes from Aix-en-Provence, France. His

CONTRIBUTORS

Testament nomade was translated into Arabic by Adonis.

William Maynard Hutchins has translated many contemporary Arab authors including Naguib Mahfouz. He was joint-winner of the 2013 Saif Ghobash Banipal Prize for *A Land Without Jasmine* by Wajdi al-Ahdal (Garnet, 2012) and won ALTA's 2015 National Translation Aaward for Ibrahim al-Koni's *New Waw*. His most recent work is al-Koni's *The Fetishists*.

Said Khatibi is an Algerian novelist, born in 1984. He studied in Algeria and France, graduating with a BA in French Literature from the University of Algiers and an MA in Cultural Studies from the Sorbonne. He has worked in journalism since 2006 and lives in Slovenia. His published works include novels, short stories and travel literature.

Muhammad Khudayyir was born in Basra, Iraq, in 1942 where he still lives. He worked in the teaching profession. He has published a novel, *Basrayatha* (1996, English edition 2008, trans. William M Hutchins), and several collections of short stories, with one translated into French *Le Royaume Noir* (2000). He was awarded the 2004 Owais Cultural Award for his contribution to literature

Alia Mamdouh is an Iraqi writer and novelist, born in 1944. She studied Psychology and graduated from Mustansiriyah University, Baghdad, in 1971. She edited the weekly Baghdad newspaper Al-Rasid. before leaving Baghdad in 1982. She has been writing fiction since 1973, first a short story collection. followed by eight novels, some translated into English, French, Italian and Spanish. Her best known novel is *Naphtalene* (1986), which is translated into nine languages.

Rosie Maxton has a BA from St. Andrews University, Scotland, in Arabic and Medieval History, and an MA in Arabic Literature from the University of Cambridge.

Suneela Mubayi gained her PhD in Arabic Literature at New York University, and currently teaches Arabic literature at Cambridge University. She translates literature between Arabic, English, and Urdu, and has published in *Banipal, Beirut39, Jadaliyya, Words Without Borders* and elsewhere.

Muhsin al-Musawi is a literary critic and Professor of Classical and Modern Arabic Literature, Comparative and Cultural Studies at Columbia University, USA. He has been an academic consultant for many academic institutions and taught for over two decades in the Arab world before going to Columbia University. He is editor of *Journal of Arabic Literature*, and has received the 2001 Owais Award for Literary Criticism and the 2018 Kuwait Prize for Studies in Arabic Language and Literature.

Stephanie Petit studied Linguistics at SOAS University of London. Since 2017, she has worked as a Digital Archivist in the Endangered Languages Archive, SOAS, where, among other things, she maintains digital collections of Modern South Arabian.

Saif al-Rahbi is a poet and prose writer, born in 1956 in Sroor, Oman. He was sent to school in Cairo when a young boy, and there began his lifelong passion for literature and poetry. He is the foundef and currently editor-in-chief of *Nizwa*, Oman's main quarterly cultural magazine, and has published many volumes of poetry, prose and essays.

Nancy Roberts has translated many novels by Arab authors, including Naguib Mahfouz, Salwa Bakr, Mohamed el-Bisatie, Ezzat el Kamhawi and Hala El-Badry, also Ghada Samman, Laila Aljohani, Ahlem Mosteghanemi, and Ibrahim Nasrallah. Her most recent literary translation is *The Slave Yards* by Najwa Bin Shatwan, Syracuse University Press, Spring 2020.

Chip Rossetti has translated several works of Arabic fiction, including *Beirut, Beirut* by Sonallah Ibrahim, *Utopia* by Ahmed Khaled Towfik, and the graphic novel *Metro* by Magdy El Shafee. He is Editorial Director of the Library of Arabic Literature.

Wadih Saadeh was born in Lebanon in 1948. He has published eight collections of poems and has one of selected poems, *A Secret Sky*, in English translation. In 1988 he emigrated to Australia, where he lives and works as a journalist. A volume of his collected works was published in 2018.

Fakhri Saleh was born in Jenin, on the West Bank, in 1957. He is a well-known writer and literary critic and has published many books on Palestinian literature, the Arabic novel, poetry, and literary criticism. He has translated into Arabic Terry Eagleton's *Criticism and Ideology* and Tzvetan Todorov's *Mikhail Bakhtin: The Dialogical Principle*. He studied English literature and philosophy at the University of Jordan, and has served as Vice President of the Arab Writers Union.

Barbara Haus Schwepcke is the founder of Gingko as well as the chair of its board of trustees.

CONTRIBUTORS

After receiving her doctorate from the London School of Economics and Political Science (LSE) she worked as a journalist (for ZDF German Television and the Süddeutsche Zeitung), as publisher of Prospect Magazine and as an editor for the Harvill Press. In 2003 she founded Haus Publishing.

Yehouda Shenhav-Shahrabani is an Arab Jew. He is a professor of sociology at Tel Aviv University and chief editor of the 'Maktoob' Series for translations from Arabic at the Jerusalem Vanleer Institute. He translated five novels of Elias Khoury into Hebrew: *White Masks*, *The Journey of Little Gandhi*, *Complex of Secrets*, *My Name is Adam* and *Stella Maris*.

Hannah Somerville is a London-based investigative journalist. She has a BA in Arabic and Spanish from the University of Leeds and an MA in Arabic Literature (SOAS, London).

Mbarek Sryfi is a Moroccan poet, and lecturer in Arabic language at the University of Pennsylvania, from where he gained a PhD in Arabic Literature and Islamic Studies. His MA is from the École Normale Supérieure, Rabat. He has been a visiting professor at Al-Akhawayn University, Ifrane, Morocco.

Paul Starkey is an award-winning translator and Emeritus Professor of Arabic, Durham University. He is Chair of the Banipal Trust for Arab Literature and a contributing editor of *Banipal*. Recent translations include *Praise for the Women of the Family* by Mahmoud Shukair (2016 IPAF shortlist), and *The Shell* by Mustafa Khalifa, for which he was won the 2017 Sheikh Hamad Award.

Jake Syersak is a poet, translator and editor. He has two poetry collections, *Mantic Compost* (Trembling Pillow Press, 2020) and *Yield Architecture* (Burnside Review Press, 2018). Forthcoming in 2020 are two full-length translations of Mohammad Khaïr-Eddine's works: the poetry collection *Proximal Morocco* and the hybrid novel *Agadir*, co-translated with Pierre Joris. He edits *Cloud Rodeo*, an online poetry journal, and co-edits Radioactive Cloud (a micropress).

Maia Tabet was born in Beirut, 14 July 1956. She has translated works by Elias Khoury, Iman Humaydan, Abbas Beydoun, Najwa Barakat and Alawiyya Subh (Lebanon), Khaled Khalifa (Syria), Ahmed Fagih (Libya), Habib Selmi (Tunisia), Lua'ay Hamza Abbas (Iraq) and Ali Muqri (Yemen). She is co-translator of Saudi writer Abdo Khal's *Throwing Sparks*, winner of the 2010 IPAF. Her work has appeared in *Banipal*, *Fikrun wa Fann*, *Portal 9* and the *Journal of Palestine Studies*.

Susannah Tarbush is a freelance journalist specialising in Middle Eastern cultural affairs. She writes the *Tanjara* blog, and is a consulting editor of *Banipal* and regular reviewer.

Sophia Vasalou is currently a senior lecturer in philosophical theology at Birmingham University. She is the author and translator of several books on theological ethics and philosophy. She studied Arabic in London and has a PhD in Islamic theology from the University of Cambridge. Her latest literary translation is the IPAF-shortlisted novel *The Old Woman and the River* by Ismail Fahd Ismail.

Aida Fahmawi Watad graduated from Haifa University in 2009. She is currently a senior lecturer in Arabic Language and Literature at Al-Qasemi Academy, Haifa, and researches modern Arabic literature. In 2017 she founded the "Akhtar min Hayat" (More Than One Life) readers' club, in which she hosted numerous Arab and Palestinian scholars and writers (in person and over Skype).

Abdo Wazen is a Lebanese poet, translator and author of many collections of poetry, translations, novels and critical essays. He has worked as a cultural journalist in Beirut since 1979 and is currently cultural editor of *Independent Arabia* online newspaper.

Jonathan Wright is an award-winning translator of fiction by Arab authors, including Mazen Maarouf, Amjad Nasser, Ahmed Saadawi, Hassan Blasim, Saud Alsanousi, Youssef Ziedan, Hamour Ziada and Khaled el-Khamissi.

Youssef Ziedan, born in 1958, is a well-known Egyptian novelist and scholar, specialising in Arabic and Islamic studies and author of more than sixty books, seven of them novels. His most famous novel, *Azazeel* (2008), won awards for its Arabic original and English translation, and is translated into 16 languages.

Raef Zreik, born in Eilaboun in the Galilee, is a prominent Palestinian lawyer and academic. He is Associate Professor in jurisprudence at Carmel Academic College, Haifa, academic co-director, Minerva Centre for the Humanities, Tel Aviv University and on the editorial board of the *Journal of Palestine Studies*. He has an LLM from Columbia University and a PhD from Harvard Law School.